A WOMAN
MUCH MISSED

ALSO BY VALERIO VARESI
IN ENGLISH TRANSLATION

River of Shadows

The Dark Valley

Gold, Frankincense and Dust

Valerio Varesi

A WOMAN
MUCH MISSED

Translated from the Italian by
Joseph Farrell

MACLEHOSE PRESS
QUERCUS · LONDON

First published in the Italian language as *L'affittacamere*
by Sperling & Kupfer in 2004

First published in Great Britain in 2015 by
MacLehose Press
An imprint of Quercus Publishing Ltd
Carmelite House
50 Victoria Embankment
London EC4Y 0DZ

An Hachette UK company

Co-funded by the
Creative Europe Programme
of the European Union

ISBN (TPB) 978 080575 345 9
ISBN (Ebook) 978 1 84866 687 0

2 4 6 8 10 9 7 5 3 1

Designed and typeset in Adobe Caslon by Patty Rennie
Printed and bound in Great Britain by Clays Ltd, St Ives plc

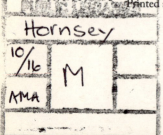

I thank Simona Mammano,
assistant police officer, for advice on procedural matters.

And Ilde Buratti, for her support and invaluable suggestions.

Author's Note

There are two different police forces in Italy: the CARABINIERI are a military unit belonging to the Ministry of Defence; the POLIZIA are a state police force belonging to the Ministry of the Interior.

The maresciallo (carabinieri) and Commissario Soneri (polizia) can only be coordinated by the questura, otherwise they report to different ministries. As to the different hierarchies, the maresciallo is a rank below the commissario.

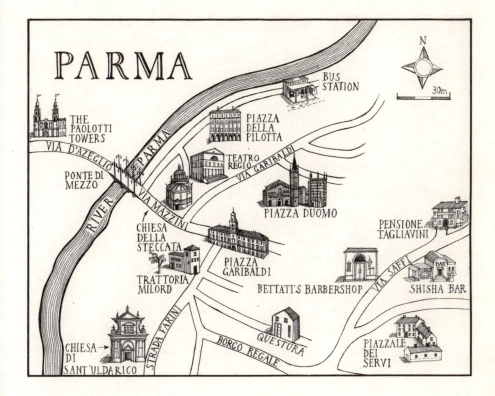

PARMA

THE PAOLOTTI TOWERS

VIA D'AZEGLIO

PONTE DI MEZZO

RIVER PARMA

VIA MAZZINI

CHIESA DELLA STECCATA

TRATTORIA MILORD

CHIESA DI SANT'ULDARICO

STRADA FARINI

PIAZZA GARIBALDI

BORGO REGALE

QUESTURA

PIAZZA DELLA PILOTTA

TEATRO REGIO

VIA GARIBALDI

PIAZZA DUOMO

BETTATI'S BARBERSHOP

BUS STATION

PENSIONE TAGLIAVINI

VIA SAFFI

SHISHA BAR

BAR

PIAZZALE DEI SERVI

N

30m

I

THE AFTERNOON WAS slipping idly by in an insidious silence. No word from the squad cars, nothing but yawns from the operations room and not a soul in the immigration office. As he walked along the deserted corridors, Commissario Soneri was already looking forward to the leisure of the festive period, during which he would be able to entertain thoughts he had kept at bay for weeks but which, now that he had dropped his guard, were surging cheerfully into his head. The pre-Christmas atmosphere made these moments to savour.

He heard a telephone ringing in his colleagues' office, and someone chattering away on the floor above in the premises occupied by the Drugs Squad, at this time of year even the pushers were taking time off. From his own office, he could look out onto the courtyard of the questura and see in the middle distance the wide gate which framed a section of Via Repubblica as though in a viewfinder, through which could be glimpsed big cars and ladies in fur coats caught up in the frantic round of seasonal acquisitions. Christmas to him meant memories of beechwood burning in the stove and the clink of spoons on plates of *anolini in brodo*, but he had no wish to abandon himself to melancholic recollections. To distract himself, he focused on the motionless fir trees lined up darkly in the mist and an elderly lady approaching under the shadow thrown by them. She was leaning on a walking stick, a little stooped, and was dressed in a dark green overcoat which reached to her ankles, carrying a large, floppy bag over her arm. He had a feeling he ought to know who she was. When she reached the centre of the yard, she stopped and looked around, but it was not clear whether she was there to observe the cloister, which she seemed never to have visited before, or was unsure which way to go. Soneri stared at that solitary figure, at her awkward, circumspect behaviour and laboured progress, and knew instinctively that something was troubling her.

A few moments later, his telephone rang. "There's a woman here who would like a word with you, sir," said the officer on the door.

"Did she say what she wanted?"

He heard the officer's mumbled words. "She says she has some worries about a friend of hers, another woman."

"What kind of worries?" the commissario said impatiently.

"She rang the doorbell, but no-one answered. The same when she telephoned."

"See that she talks to Juvara," he said brusquely.

It would be the usual story: some old soul dying alone in her own home. An elderly lady, a stroke, the sort of thing the newspapers headline, LONELY TRAGEDY. In addition to being annoyed, Soneri also felt mildly disappointed. The old lady had at first sight aroused his curiosity, but now that feeling had evaporated, leaving mere routine and banality. By the time he resumed his seat, the peaceful atmosphere of the afternoon seemed to him definitively disrupted. He decided he had better write up some reports which had lying on his desk for a couple of weeks, but he had scarcely begun when the old woman's voice penetrated from Juvara's office next door.

"I rang several times, I tell you, including last night."

The inspector's questions were muffled, but the woman's words pierced the wall. "No, no, look – it's out of the question. She never just goes away, and anyway she has a boarding house to look after. I don't know if you know it, Pensione Tagliavini. Her name is Giuditta Tagliavini. Everybody knows her. They all call her Ghitta for short."

The name brought back to him the memories that had been buzzing around in his head a few moments previously, when he was on the point of falling into a state of depression. That was the name he had been groping for. Who did not know Ghitta? Half the student body had passed though her furnished rooms, and many had gone on to become professors, doctors, lawyers or engineers. Not to mention the girls from the nursing college or the secretarial courses.

"Look, Ghitta always pops out a couple of times a day, but if she was going away she'd have let me know."

Soneri heard her voice alternate with Juvara's as she told her tale, and he found himself assailed by memories from thirty years ago when, standing in front of the Pensione Tagliavini, he was for the first time bowled over by the smile of a girl with a nurse's white uniform folded over her arm. That was the first chapter in a love story, full of the passion and candour of two twenty-year-olds. Much later, when they were married, he used to tell her that the credit for everything should go to the pensione, to the endless comings and goings which had aroused the attention of a young, over-zealous police officer.

"Please believe me, sir, Ghitta goes out on Thursdays, never on Sundays."

Ada, Soneri's wife, had died fifteen years earlier, leaving him to wonder what it would have been like for them to grow old together and bring up that son for whom she had died in childbirth. The baby boy had not lingered long either. He was already dying when he was delivered, and never uttered a sound. Soneri had vivid memories of his wife, but he could not recall anything about the baby. Sometimes he had the impression of something fluttering unseen around him, pleading to be loved for his own features, for the colour of his eyes and hair. His pain had no face to weep over.

"I'm not the only one who's rung the bell. Others have tried too, but there's no answer, only silence."

Silence, the same response he received time after time when in his dreams his unconscious urged him to seek out the face of his lost wife or child. He was accustomed to listening to it as the clearest, most eloquent, most pitiless, indeed the only voice possible.

Juvara must have been busy typing up the report because the old woman was dictating her address. Soneri made out only "Fernanda" and then "Via Saffi". The Pensione Tagliavini was in Via Saffi, even though it could not be seen from the street. There was only the name at the foot of the address board on one side of the front door. He remembered the ditty made up by some of the more boorish students, vengefully chanted under a window by a rejected suitor:

> *You want to screw a pretty whore?*
> *Then make your way to Ghitta's door.*

He jumped to his feet and went next door. Juvara and the old woman were both standing behind the desk and turned wordlessly as he appeared in the doorway. She had a pale, soft face that seemed somehow boiled, but he recognised her instantly. Fernanda Schianchi, the next-door neighbour who took in lodgers when Ghitta had no vacancies. The woman returned his look but she did not react save for an almost imperceptible wink, as though between former lovers. She picked up her bag, put it over her arm, took the walking stick she had propped against the desk and slowly walked out.

The commissario did not speak at once. He went to the window and watched the woman walk across the courtyard towards the main gate at the far side, where the rushing crowd would swallow her up. He worked out in his head the route she would take. Via Saffi was not far off, but why had she taken the trouble to come along in person rather than telephone? Did she know perfectly well who he was, or was she keen to make sure by looking him in the face? She had, after all, asked for him by name.

He picked up the telephone and called the front gate. "That old woman who has just gone out, did she ask for me by name?"

"Yes, sir. She told me she wanted to speak to Commissario Soneri, otherwise I wouldn't have bothered you."

He saw her black, slow shadow under an arch. She paused briefly beside the porter's lodge, then stepped out into the street. Only then did Soneri turn to Juvara with a questioning look.

"She was worried about her neighbour. There was no reply and she doesn't think she's gone out. Her name is—"

"Ghitta Tagliavini," Soneri said.

"You know her?"

The commissario gave a wave of his hand to say that, yes, he knew her well.

"Did she have anything else to report?"

"She's rung the bell and knocked on the door."

"Do you have any idea why she came over here in person?"

Juvara shrugged, unsure how he should reply.

"Doesn't it seem odd to you? She could have telephoned, couldn't she?"

"I had the impression . . ." The inspector stopped, searching for the right word.

The commissario was staring out the window again. He turned and gestured to Juvara with the hand holding his cigar, prompting him to go on.

"Well, the first thing she said to me was, 'You're not the commissario'."

Soneri turned, walked past Juvara's desk and out of the door without saying another word. The inspector watched him bound across the courtyard, passing under the archway and out through the gate.

As he made his way along the crowded street, the commissario was struck by the strange link between the thoughts that had been in his mind that afternoon and the reality he was faced with now. The past, the happy years he had spent with his wife, the Pensione Tagliavini, and then, out of the blue, with no apparent connection, the sight of the old woman in the courtyard, almost as though she had stepped out of his head. She had come looking for him, she had come to speak to him, and he was certain she had recognised him in spite of the countless men who must have passed through her life in the years when the pensione was fully operational.

He walked more quickly in an attempt to catch up with her, but the crowds prevented him from moving as fast as he would have liked. He went over in his mind the best way to Via Saffi, and wondered how far she could have gone by now with her shuffling, stooped gait. Remembering the way made him feel once more as though he was shipwrecked amid recollections that were as silent and isolated as flashes of summer lightning. As he turned from Via Repubblica towards Piazzale dei Servi, he looked along the pavements, but nowhere could he make out the figure of an old woman moving along slowly. He stared down the dark lanes which opened off both sides of the street, but he saw nothing. Arriving at the front door of the Pensione Tagliavini, he pressed the buzzer next to the name SCHIANCHI, but heard neither a voice nor the click of a switch being pressed. He rang again, and then gave up. He crossed to the other side of the street and took up a waiting position. A black mood settled on him like the mist which was thickening at the bottom of the street, pressing against the barriers of Via Saffi and wrapping itself round the steeples of the Battistero.

Half an hour later there was still no sign of Fernanda. He took out his mobile and called Juvara. "Did Signora Schianchi leave an address?"

"Thirty-five, Via Saffi," Juvara said.

The commissario cut off the call. Though he was irritated at the inspector, who, he said, did not ask enough questions and lacked the curiosity required in a man in his position, he knew that he, not Juvara, was to blame and was annoyed with himself. He had not focused properly, he had been careless. A commissario should know that every person has a story to tell. Perhaps ninety-nine out of a hundred are of no interest, and the problem was that it was impossible to tell which was the genuine article unless you listened to them all.

He rang the buzzer again, to no avail. He tried the other numbers on the board, until finally he heard a click and the door opened. He found himself in a hallway lined with bicycles. He felt stunned and confused, as though he were on a journey back through time. Nothing had changed in that hallway since the days when he and Ada had exchanged final moments of intimacy after their dates. More than anything else, he was aware of the slight smell of damp emanating from the dark walls and the earthy odours rising up from the cellars. He was brought abruptly back to himself by a woman in a tracksuit leaning over the upstairs bannister.

"I'm looking for Fernanda Schianchi," Soneri said.

"She away." came the reply, in laboured Italian.

The commissario climbed the stairs to the landing. Three doors led off it. He recognised the one that opened onto the Pensione Tagliavini. "Where did she go?" he asked.

"Not know," the woman said, now annoyed. "Yesterday she say she go," she added with a shrug. With her blue eyes and short blond hair, the woman must be Slav.

Soneri did not move. He put a cigar between his lips and stood there deep in thought, observing the door of the boarding house. It bore a brass nameplate on which PENSIONE TAGLIAVINI was carved in flowing italics. He heard the woman go back into her apartment without saying a word, followed by the sound of the bolt being pulled across behind her. Fernanda seemed to have vanished into thin air, as had Ghitta. As he moved towards Ghitta's door, he heard someone ring her bell downstairs. Just as he was going to investigate, the lights went off. He turned back to switch them on again, but tripped in the dark. As he found the switch, the buzzer went again. He rushed down, but lost time locating the button to open front the door. He got it open just in time to see a motorbike accelerating away into the mist gathering over Via Saffi.

He went back up to the landing. His weariness was dispelled by a sudden sense of urgency and by a suspicion which weighed so heavily on him as to become a certainty. He approached Ghitta's residence and tried to force his way in by shaking both handles on the double doors. One side vibrated, causing the lock to rattle, a sign that the door had only been pulled shut, not double locked. He took out his telephone card and put it into the gap between the doors at the level of the lock, a trick he had learned from a burglar many years previously. At the fifth attempt the lock sprang open.

He was greeted by the heat of a gas stove, inside which a blue flame was dancing. Not much had changed there either. He remembered clearly the long corridor where he now stood, with doors leading off on both sides, the wall-mounted telephone with the ledge underneath for writing messages, the directory and the piggy bank for payment. The hatstand was still there, as were the prints of old Parma and the dressing table with the mirror where you could check your appearance before going out. There reigned over all a kind of provisional peace, suggesting a momentary absence. Lamplight shone in through the windows and was reflected in the glass drops of the chandelier, sending out faint sparks of light. In the semi-darkness Soneri recognised aspects of the house he had visited dozens of times, waiting for the girl who would become his wife, but now he felt like a robber. He did not switch on the light, even though he was gripped by a tension which left him rigid. He moved along the corridor until his attention was attracted by the door to one of the bedrooms which had been left ajar.

That was the room where Ghitta slept, the only one that had always been locked. He pushed the door open with the back of his hand, wrapped a handkerchief round his fingers and switched on the light, but as he did so he realised he already knew what had taken place and that he was sure of what he would see. The light shone on a double bed onto which a drawer had been overturned. He knew what that meant. He stood staring at the jumble of cheap jewellery and souvenirs, postcards, photographs, holy pictures, old belts, fountain pens and one small, lined notebook with a wine-coloured cover. He turned back into the corridor to continue his search. Ghitta was in the kitchen, between the table and the sink. In the dim light he recognised the outline of her tiny body stretched out on the floor. She could still have been, in that darkness, the person he remembered, but the moment he switched on the neon lighting, with its mortuary glow, she became nothing more than just another corpse, already stiff and cold on the equally chill marble flooring. No matter how closely he observed her with the professional eye of the police officer, she still seemed to him an inviolate body, without bruises or wounds. A couple of coffee cups had been left on the draining board, and on the table he noticed two medicine bottles and some pills. He gently raised the old woman by one shoulder, and her whole body, light and almost desiccated, moved as one piece. There was no trace of blood. He made an effort to organise in his mind what he had seen so far, but found himself facing a mass of contradictions: the door pulled shut with only one turn of the lock; no sign of forced entry; the corpse left in such a way as to indicate a solitary death; the drawer turned upside down; the probability of theft, but two cups with some coffee still in them suggesting a friendly encounter.

He took out his mobile, dialled the number of the crime squad and asked them to contact Nanetti, head of Forensics. His colleague called back a few moments later. When the commissario gave him the address, Nanetti said, "Isn't that the Pensione Tagliavini?"

Everybody knew the place. Compared to those new hotels with banners flying, revolving doors and mock-Persian carpets, the ageing boarding house resembled an archaeological dig, and now Soneri was confronted with the task of excavating it, artefact by artefact. He left the kitchen and turned back towards the bedroom, but first he opened the doors of the other four rooms. Everything appeared neat and tidy, even if each room seemed somehow abandoned. In one there was a suitcase with trolley wheels, which, when he tried to lift it, he decided must be full. In Ghitta's room, he noticed that the chest which the overturned drawer belonged to had been pulled away from the wall. It was an ordinary, everyday piece of furniture with a layer of walnut veneer over soft wood – fir or poplar. Soneri peered in and discovered that the old woman had hammered in a nail to which she had attached a piece of cord of the sort used to bind salami. As he pulled on it, a little cloth bag, small enough to fit in the palm of his hand, emerged. He opened it and found inside Ghitta's meagre treasure: a few gold rings, pairs of earrings, a chain with a medal of Jesus, a bracelet, a watch and in a little box, a ring made of white gold and inlaid with lapis lazuli stones. It did not take much to deduce that these were the only objects of any value in the apartment. Even if there were others, the intruder had not bothered to look for them, since he had ignored the ones now in Soneri's hand.

A few minutes later, Nanetti arrived. They did not even exchange greetings. Soneri ushered him into the kitchen, where he had left the light on. Nanetti followed the same rigmarole that Soneri had many times previously observed, leaving the commissario to wonder at the rigorous discipline of the old-style police academies where the two men had undergone training.

"Looks like a natural death," Nanetti said, after a cursory examination. Other officers busied themselves around them, one of them taking photographs.

Chewing his cigar, which had gone out, Soneri stared hard at his colleague. "Looks like, but isn't."

Nanetti stood quite still for a moment, pondering that statement, then without uttering a word, put on his latex gloves. The two men crouched down face to face over the body, and only then did they become aware of a tiny slit in the old woman's dress between her breasts. They unbuttoned the top and pulled aside the vest, leaving her breasts exposed. Between the two drooping, shapeless breasts there was a cut no more than two centimetres in length, slightly open and violet at the edges. Only where the garment had come in contact with the torn flesh was there a faint trace of blood.

"A magnificently executed laparoscopy," Nanetti said.

"What do you mean, laparoscopy!" the commissario said. "They slaughtered her the way you slaughter a pig."

2

HIS COLLEAGUE'S CREAKING joints distracted Soneri as he bent over Ghitta's face, noting her staring eyes and her white hair left dishevelled from her final attempt to fight off her assailant. Her mouth was slightly open in an expression of astonishment. She must have known her killer so well that she was taken aback by what was happening to her.

"A real expert," Nanetti said as he got back to his feet. "He laid her out in that position to stop the flow of blood."

The commissario nodded, but he felt annoyed with himself for not having thought of that right away. Only then did he notice that Ghitta's hands were clenched in a fist a little below her waist, still gripping the pleats of her skirt. Her upper arms, pulled in alongside her chest, led him to surmise that she had hunched her shoulders in one last, futile gesture of self-defence. While the forensic squad scrutinised everything, Soneri moved fretfully from Ghitta's room to the kitchen, followed by the officers' hostile looks. He wandered into another room and stood there quite still, besieged by memories of Sunday afternoons spent there when he was Ada's boyfriend, half-dressed, agreeing plans for the future or making love in silence.

This apartment unnerved him because of the way it super-imposed a past filled with hopes onto a present reeking of death. He struggled to believe that the same theatre could stage two such different plays, but the many years that had passed had altered what at one time appeared immutable, and now his job had brought him back to one of the places of his youth. It was never a good idea to return to a place where you had once been happy.

The forensic squad went about their work steadily and meticulously. Eventually the commissario grew tired of watching them as they collected fingerprints, conducted a painstaking examination of each and every shelf and drawer and searched for biological traces. Aware of his own unfinished business, he wondered if he could leave. When the orderlies turned up to take away the body, he remembered Signora Schianchi. What had happened to her? Had she too been attacked before she got home? He realised that, somewhat oddly, he was more interested in Fernanda Schianchi's absence than the death of Ghitta, perhaps because he believed that clearing up the first case would lead to the solution of the second. Or was it merely that she had come looking for him, and he had brushed her off onto Juvara? He felt the first dawning of a wave of guilt. She had come to the questura specifically to find him. She wanted to speak to him in person. Was this only because she remembered him from the days when he used to frequent the pensione?

He went out onto the landing to make a call on his mobile, and as he was dialling the number he noticed that his hands were trembling. He gave Juvara the order to drop everything and instigate a search for Signora Schianchi.

"She must have someone – some relative, a son or a daughter. She'll have gone to see them." He cut the inspector off curtly, annoyed at his objections.

When he turned round, he found Nanetti standing next to him. He pointed to Fernanda's door. "Is there no-one in?"

"Another old lady lives there, but she's faded into the mist."

Nanetti twisted his moustache and gave a grunt to indicate that the whole thing was a real mess. "Do you think we need to break in?"

Soneri thought the question over silently. "I'm afraid we have no choice, but I think it's best to hold off a bit. Maybe she's simply gone to spend Christmas with some daughter. Juvara's on to the case."

"Yes, it's probably better to wait and inform the magistrate before we do anything. That way we'll keep our noses clean."

"Who's on duty?"

"Saltapico."

"It would be," the commissario said sarcastically.

"Are the others any better?" Nanetti said.

The thick walls of the house deadened the noise. All that could be heard was the forensic squad as they occasionally moved things around inside the apartment.

"There's something funny about the disappearance of this other woman," Nanetti said, leaning back against the banister on the landing. He broke off when Soneri's mobile rang. It was Juvara, whose tone was subdued. "Commissario, this woman doesn't have anyone. She was widowed twenty years ago and there are no children. She has a nephew, but he lives in Milan."

"Did you call him?"

"Yes, and his wife said they haven't seen her in years. They speak on the telephone every so often. Just yesterday the signora telephoned to wish them a Merry Christmas."

The commissario hung up abruptly, profoundly annoyed with himself. He had blundered. He should have received the old woman in person.

"Do you think the two women were on good terms?" Nanetti said. The commissario had no idea what he was getting at. He disliked the indirect approach employed by some of his colleagues, but he made an effort to control himself.

"What do you mean? They saw each other all the time. Fernanda even rented out some of her rooms occasionally."

"So you would think she'd have a key to let herself in."

Once again, Soneri felt an idiot. Why had that not occurred to him? In fact the thought had crossed his mind, but at that point he was still hopeful of finding Fernanda. Now he was less sure. Nanetti said nothing more and left Soneri to follow his own line of reasoning to its conclusion. It was highly probable that before coming to the questura Fernanda had seen what the commissario had subsequently discovered.

"Maybe you're right. If so, that's why it's becoming more and more important to get into Signora Schianchi's apartment," Soneri said.

"I'd wait for the magistrate. After all, there's no great rush. It looks to me like a straightforward case, like a game of chess." Nanetti left him with that thought, trusting his men to get on with their job. The commissario went back into the apartment, wondering if Fernanda had stumbled upon Ghitta's body stretched out on the kitchen floor. And if she had seen her, why had she not told Juvara?

Before he could come to any conclusion, the telephone in the hall began to ring. Soneri rushed to get there ahead of the other officers. He picked up the receiver and said "Hello!" in a firm voice.

From the other end of the line, all he could hear was a sigh followed a few moments later by a click as the line went dead. A short time went by and then the telephone began to ring once more. He turned back and repeated his greeting, this time in a tone of weary resignation. The only reply he received was the sound of the receiver being replaced so quickly as to make him think that the caller had had his finger poised to press the button. It could have been a wrong number the first time, but not the second. Whoever it was had expected to hear Ghitta's voice and had hung up. Now they would be aware that something had happened at Pensione Tagliavini, but then perhaps they would have known that anyway if the phone had simply rung out. He calculated how much time he had before the press informed the city about the old woman's death. Seven or eight hours, he thought – an interval in which, just possibly, someone would carry on behaving as normal. Perhaps they would even ring the doorbell and give him the chance to make their acquaintance.

He lit his cigar at the stove. Forensics had left, so he was able to take some liberties. He opened a cupboard and was tempted to make himself a coffee. From the kitchen doorway the whole length of the dormitory-style corridor was in view, and from where he was standing, Ghitta would have been able to keep an eye on everything and everybody. Nothing ever escaped her watchful gaze – who was coming, who was going, or who went to the toilet most often. Soneri could even recall some of the other residents. Selvatici, a law student, had the room facing the one occupied by his future wife. During the day, even on Sunday afternoons, he could be heard padding back and forth in his room, addressing an imaginary jury. In contrast, during the night he bustled about continually, seemingly as agitated as an animal in a cage. Soneri also remembered a girl called Robertelli, a flautist who studied at the conservatoire. And then there was Nelli, a student of engineering. He paid a reduced rent because he was good at fixing things around the house. His clearest memories were of the nursing students in their white outfits, each more beautiful than the next. It was no surprise that he ended up marrying one of them. In that long corridor with the landlady's room down at the far end, they seemed to parade in front of his eyes, along with the university students. In the late afternoon or evening, when Ghitta was not in the kitchen, she would take her place in the sitting room to the left of the entrance. It was tiny, not much bigger than a cupboard, and had just the one window, which looked onto Via Saffi, and from there Ghitta watched the world go by.

Soneri decided to take a seat in the same position. He looked out at the journalists on the other side of the street, at the bar now owned by a Pakistani, and at the comings and goings of a sort of foreign legion living in the houses once occupied by people who had prospered and moved on. A squad car was parked outside No. 35. A number of curious passers-by stopped to stare at the vehicle and ask the journalists what was going on. He was dismayed when he imagined the rumours already circulating around a city that was too small to keep secrets. In all probability he was wasting time sitting there since everybody already knew, and no-one was likely to come calling on that misty night. He held his cigar hidden in the palm of his hand and kept on peering out into the semi-darkness, concealed by those pieces of dull furniture, in a timeless, imprecise dimension between today and yesteryear.

He experienced a deep sense of solitude, which was hardly a new sensation for him. Investigations frequently induced this state of mind, but this time there was a new element. He felt as though he had been projected beyond his own comfort zone, like a piece of shrapnel hurtling through the air and growing cold at the place where it had happened to land. That pensione, his dead wife, the lost opportunities, the unachieved plans, the transformed district now inhabited by foreigners, the only people capable of finding comfort in those old houses – everything was reduced to that ethereal yet fiery substance that constitutes memory.

The telephone once again jolted him out of his reverie. He got up unhurriedly and walked the length of the corridor. He picked up the receiver but gave only an indistinct grunt.

"Ghitta," came an unusually deep, male voice at the other end of the line.

"Just a moment. Who shall I say?"

Moments went by as the caller seemed to hesitate. "Who is this?" the man said in a decidedly unfriendly, peremptory tone of voice.

"The signora is busy right now but—" Soneri said, and before the phone was slammed down, he heard a curse from the caller which seemed to be addressed to someone at the other end.

The commissario hung up, but a thought was taking shape in his mind without finding precise form. He returned to the sitting room, took out his mobile and called Juvara.

"I need . . . I'd like you make a bit of a scene, something to get rid of the journalists and all the people hanging about outside here."

"Alright, as long as you don't want me to make any sort of speech. I never know how to answer their questions."

"There'll be no need. Simply tell them that the inquiry is proceeding."

"So what am I supposed to do?"

"Get a car and come to number thirty-five Via Saffi. Bring an escort. When you arrive, I'll open the door and you come up with two officers. When you go back down, the journalists will throw hundreds of questions at you, so tell them that the apartment has been sealed off and that the inquiries will get underway again in the morning. They'll be in such a rush to write up the story that they'll lift the siege."

"And what if they leave someone behind to keep watch?"

"That's a risk we'll just have to take," the commissario said.

He sat back in the armchair. He always enjoyed looking out on the city on winter nights when everything was sunk in a deep sleep and when everyone who went by had a good reason for so doing. He took pleasure in imagining or working out what that could be.

Angela seemed to have a knack of detecting from a distance the moments when the commissario was floundering in a morass of jumbled thoughts, and of coming to his rescue just when he was sinking ever more deeply. Perhaps it was because she was jealous of that world to which he denied entry to everyone, or perhaps because their relationship was made up of bursts of fiery passion.

"What are you up to?" she said, before Soneri could even say hello.

"I'm keeping a lookout."

"You always had a talent for voyeurism," she said teasingly.

Soneri moved his mobile to his other hand so as to be able to smoke more easily. "If it were any other way, I couldn't do this job."

"Where are you?"

"Pensione Tagliavini. Does that mean anything to you?"

"That squalid little boarding house?"

"What's squalid about it? To me it brings back all kind of lovely memories."

"Sometimes you amaze me, commissario. How could you not know that the old lady hasn't been letting rooms to students for some time?"

He had indeed lost all contact with that part of the city. There was a gap due to the fifteen years he had spent with the police in Milan. The bar run by Pakistanis, the district full of foreigners and even the Pensione Tagliavini itself had all altered the appearance of that quarter without his having taken it in.

"It's been some time since I last had any reason to be interested in this area, ever since I went to Milan. If you just drive past it, you're not aware of the changes. So who did Ghitta let out her rooms to?"

"Guess! Do you know what a knocking shop is? A whorehouse? In other words, people go there to screw," Angela said in the face of his silence.

"They do that in five-star hotels too."

"I know, but that's boring. What do you say if I come along and join you there?"

"No, that's not possible." Soneri's swift reply barely concealed his apprehension.

"It's really flattering for a woman to suggest an evening of intimacy with her man, only to be refused because he's scared," Angela said.

"There are journalists downstairs. And anyway, Ada used to live here."

"You see, I was right. They let rooms by the hour," she said, clearly upset. She hung up without another word.

He did not call back, but breathed a sigh of relief and waited for Juvara to arrive. When he did finally turn up, he had followed the commissario's instructions to the letter. Soneri found him standing with two other officers on a landing illuminated by a naked bulb which gave off a light the colour of camomile tea.

"Saltapico has arranged the autopsy for tomorrow morning," Juvara said.

"He's not hanging about."

"What do you make of it all?" the inspector said as he came in.

"Nothing. I'm trying hard to understand what was going on in this house, what Ghitta was doing during the day. Somebody telephoned asking for her but slammed the phone down when they realised that something wasn't right. I got the impression it was a pre-arranged call, always made at a fixed time, on a certain day. Otherwise, why would they have hung up?"

"Nanetti says that whoever killed her was no amateur."

"Yes, he'd studied the perfect position to make sure there was no flow of blood. He left no trace and, even more importantly, got no stains on himself. This might indicate that it was someone who was well known in the house. It might even mean it was someone who'd been seen around here and couldn't risk compromising himself. Or maybe he was just a scrupulous killer."

"We'll find out tomorrow," Juvara said. "The police doctor will clarify how she met her death. She could have been stunned first, or else poisoned and then . . ."

"There's no knowing. Reality is always surprising," Soneri said, thinking to himself how much the old city had changed without his noticing. "Very good, then. Set up the scene the way I told you to."

From the window, he watched to make sure that everything went as planned. As the journalists crowded round Juvara, the commissario read the embarrassment on his face as he tried to push past them. The cars sped off, leaving the reporters to contemplate their empty notebooks. They would get the information they needed in a series of telephone calls to officials and police officers whom they had courted unobtrusively at various social events over the years.

The street emptied quickly, leaving only a few cyclists, a couple of cars and the last customers in the shisha bar. After a while, the shutters at the bar were pulled down, and everything settled to the normal calm of a foggy winter's night. Around eleven o'clock, Soneri rose to his feet and walked along the landing without switching on the lights. His eyes were now accustomed to that darkness broken only by shafts of light coming in through the windows. His thoughts returned to what Angela had been saying and to the way the pensione had been partially transformed into a shady hotel for couples with something to hide, when he was surprised by the telephone. He lifted the receiver, said nothing but listened intently.

An elderly woman's voice began to pronounce Ghitta's name, but then stuttered to a halt. Soneri then heard a groan, followed by laboured breathing, almost a rattle of the sort associated with asthma, which in turn gave way to a sibilant exhalation of breath. The commissario remained silent. He felt powerless and apprehensive, as though watching a madman teetering on a high ledge. It did not last long. The breathing seemed to fade away, before a weak, almost indistinguishable voice muttered, "I can't take it any more," and the line went dead. He stood there clutching the handset while the mirror further along the landing reflected back an indistinct image of him trembling. In front of that same mirror, as he said his goodbyes on Sundays, Ada would remind him in a whisper not to make any noise that Ghitta could hear and never to telephone after ten o'clock in the evening, this being an inflexible rule of the Pensione Tagliavini. Once again he found himself measuring time past, and once again he felt concern at the growing frequency of assaults by memories. He returned to the living room and resumed his watch over the street. By midnight he had finished his cigar, but even though it was no longer than a match he left it in his mouth. In the street below, a man dressed in a somewhat dandyish fashion passed by No. 35. Soneri was certain it was not for the first time that evening, there was something familiar about his leather shoes, which shone as though highly polished. In that street of sober colours made darker by the mist, they were the only things which glistened. The man wore a loose belt over a dark overcoat, left open to reveal a white shirt, a purple bow tie, tight-fitting trousers and was sporting a hat that was a little like a bowler. That eccentric elegance confirmed to Soneri that there was something out of place.

He got a better look at the man when he walked past for the third time. By that point, the way he passed and repassed the building could no longer be dismissed as mere random chance. The man stopped on the far side of the street and looked up several times at the living room window, causing the commissario to draw back behind the curtain for fear that the man might catch a glimpse of his shadow. He watched as he started pacing about once more, talking into his mobile. He seemed on a mission, executed with the scrupulousness of a vigilante paid to keep certain premises under observation, or to check that the Pensione Tagliavini was still enveloped in darkness. Half an hour later, Soneri heard a car draw up at the door. He opened the shutter fully and peeped out. A black Mercedes was idling in front of the main entrance, but none of the occupants got out. The car drove away again.

There was a level of activity around the house which Soneri could not fathom, and this set him to searching for something which could explain the various presences in those rooms, give a name to the phantoms which manifested themselves in telephone calls, and explain the shadowy figures glimpsed in the mist or half-concealed behind the windows of vehicles. Forensics had carried out their work too meticulously and had carried off nearly everything. All that had been left behind was the small wine-coloured notebook lying on the bed alongside Ghitta's scattered jewellery. He picked it up and retired to the living room once more, hoping to work out what it contained in the faint light coming from the street through the shutters, but no sooner had he sat down than he heard the click-clack of high heels on the street below. The sounds were firm, indicative of someone who was in command of the situation and who knew where she was going. A young woman with a large bag was making her way along Via Saffi, and the street echoed to the rhythmical beat of her tread. She crossed the street just before No. 35 and walked up to the front door.

The commissario drew back from the door of the apartment until he heard the key being inserted in the lock at the foot of the stairs and saw the light going on. The woman climbed the stairs quickly. Soneri closed the door before she appeared on the landing. He was unsure where she was going until he heard the sound of the heels moving towards the entrance to the pensione. He heard someone fumbling with keys and at that point, before the woman had time to put her key in the lock, he pulled open the door.

She gave a start and moved back half a step.

"Come in. Police," the commissario said calmly.

The woman was taken aback, but Soneri took her by the arm just above her elbow and drew her in.

"What's going on?" she said.

"That's the very question I'd like to put to you. What sort of time is this to be visiting friends?"

"I'm not here to visit anyone," she replied, visibly relieved. "I live here. Didn't you see that I have my own keys?"

"Once upon a time it was strictly forbidden to come back to the Pensione Tagliavini after midnight."

"How do you know?"

"Ah well," Soneri said, with a mildly pained expression. "Which is your room?" he said, resuming a professional tone.

The woman pointed to the door next to the room once occupied by Ada.

"The cupboards are all empty."

"I don't spend much time here. One night every so often when I'm working late. Where's Ghitta?" she said, craning her neck in an attempt to look over Soneri's shoulder.

"Are you related?"

"No, not really."

"What does that mean? A distant relative?"

"It means we come from the same village and everyone there is related in some way."

"Which village?"

"Rigoso."

It was one of the most southerly hamlets in the province, situated between Emilia and Liguria before the ridge over-looking that finger of Tuscany which resembles the handle of a frying pan. She had all the features of the mountain people from those parts: pale skin, clear eyes and squirrel-coloured hair with blond traces, like the chestnuts from the Apennines.

The woman pushed open the door of her room, but the commissario stopped her. "I should warn you that you won't find things the way you left them."

She switched on the light and one quick glance was sufficient for her to see the chaos typical of every house where the forensic squad had been at work. "At least they had the decency to leave the bed alone," she said.

"Inconveniences of this sort can be easily remedied," Soneri said.

The woman gave him a quizzical, searching look, as though some suspicion had been confirmed, but then she remembered she was dealing with a police officer. "Ghitta?" she said.

The commissario nodded.

"What happened?"

"Murdered."

Her head dropped. She did not speak.

"Were you expecting that?"

Still uttering no word, she stretched out her arms and all of a sudden seemed afraid. Soneri saw her body shake with short, rapid quivers.

"How could I ever have imagined . . ." were the only words she managed to speak before breaking off with a half incredulous, half puzzled expression.

". . . that they'd kill her?" the commissario finished the sentence for her.

The woman nodded and then seemed to notice with some annoyance the lamplight glaring in her face. She seemed shaken to the core. The commissario once again took her by the arm and led her into the living room, switching off the light in the corridor as he passed. They ended up sitting facing each other, like lovers, in that pensione where so many lovers had come and gone. Their expressions could only just be made out in the faint light from the street. Soneri continued to look out from time to time.

"Had she received threats?"

"I'm not sure, but the atmosphere in here had changed a great deal in recent years."

"Because couples were coming instead of students?"

"The clientele was certainly different, but that was because of Ghitta's condition. At her age, she could no longer provide three square meals a day. And anyway, today's students are all well off and prefer to rent flats. Couples come here for two or three hours and then go away. And they pay well. In spite of the fact that there was less effort involved, Ghitta was more and more stressed."

"Maybe because they brought along prostitutes and she was worried about her licence."

"I don't think so. From what she told me, she was dealing with couples who were lovers, or sometimes with upper-class escorts."

"Do you sleep here often?"

"No, only once a week. I work in a big store and when I do back-to-back shifts I don't go home."

"But today's Sunday."

"In the run-up to Christmas, we stay open on Sundays and they ask us to do overtime."

"You haven't told me your name."

"Elvira Cadoppi."

"Do you commute from Rigoso?"

"No, that would be too far. I live in Capoponte."

The tone of each response left something hanging in the air, and the commissario felt an undertow of ambiguity in the conversation. In the half light, he could not make out the woman's eyes or her expression. Being able only to imagine them, he returned to that quizzical look thrown at him some moments earlier, in which he had caught a gleam of suspicion.

"Did she ever tell you anything? About what made her anxious, I mean."

He had the impression that she reacted as though shocked or startled. "You see the time it is when I get here? We would only meet for half an hour at breakfast and then talk about home and the people who lived there, most of whom are unfortunately dead. The only ones left are all elderly.

In any case, I'm the only one who has a key. You can trust people from the same background as yourself more than others."

Soneri insisted on asking questions about the past, about Ghitta's life in a village which was perhaps nothing more than a lime pit of memories.

Elvira surprised him by saying, "She used to go there every week, even though she didn't have any good memories of the place."

"Was she visiting family?"

"There was no-one left."

"What made her memories so unpleasant?"

"It's not easy to explain to someone who doesn't know our ways."

The commissario waved the point away. "I was born in the country myself."

"Ghitta was called on to attend to twisted limbs, St Anthony's fire, fractures, aches in the joints or even women who'd missed a period or couldn't get pregnant."

"A faith healer," Soneri said, recalling the customs in the villages. "A *strolga*, we used to say in dialect, someone half way between a witch and an astrologer."

"That's right. Old people up there used to call her in quite often. They trusted her powers and most of the time they really did get better."

The commissario nodded. The essential thing was to believe in it, to accept it. He found himself floundering in total confusion, without a clue. He seemed to be adrift as he continued to chatter about a far-off town populated only by the elderly. He was about to ask about what had been going on in the pensione when Elvira got in first:

"In spite of everything, they never liked her." She spoke with a conviction which irritated the commissario, who wondered if her plan was to get away from the subject he most wanted to discuss.

"So why did she keep going there?" he said, trying to make the question sound casual.

"The fact is that the people in the village spoke badly about her as a person, but they also treated her with respect and even fear for what she could do. Healing illnesses is a skill handed down from one generation to the next with a secret formula which has to be whispered during the 'visits' so that other people don't hear."

"I know, I know," Soneri said, turning his face towards the street.

"Women who possess this skill are considered highly dangerous," Elvira said in a hushed tone which somehow spoke of vigils, snowy nights and candle-lit conversations on straw in damp stables while waiting for a calf to be born. "They believe these women possess the magic power to make men go mad and ruin whole families. And Ghitta . . ."

"And Ghitta what?"

She remained silent for a while. "A long time ago, Ghitta had an affair with a married man. Everybody in the village knew about it and at that point . . ."

"At that point, she fled to the city."

The woman nodded. "But she was not really on her own," she added.

"The man followed her?"

"No, I mean that she was pregnant."

"Where is her son now?"

"I don't know. We never spoke about him. I found out from people in the village that she put him in some institution for a while – because he wasn't right in the head, I mean. But I've no idea where he might be now."

Yet another transformation. The bright image of Ghitta

was clouding into one of an unhappy woman who had left so much wreckage in her wake. He began to think that all this was due to the disillusion brought on by the passing of time, that the fault lay in his having failed to see things clearly at the outset. Experience had taught him that any attempt to scrape under the surface will lead to the discovery of something rotten.

"And the other one? Her lover," Soneri said.

The woman looked up, but he could not decide if it was an attempt to look him in the eye or a gesture of impatience. "He left as well. His wife wouldn't have him in the house any more, and nearly all the property was in her name." She paused and then went on, "He and Ghitta went on seeing each other for a number of years, but then he disappeared."

"Do you think this might have anything to do with Ghitta's murder?"

He saw her shake her head in denial, but in the dim light it was easy to mistake the meaning of every gesture. The two of them were no more than voices and vague outlines to which bodies and faces could be arbitrarily assigned. At that hour everything appeared to have lost its geometric solidity, particularly the mist-covered city itself and the network of circular lanes at its heart, now deprived of all clear-cut dimensions. A sheet of falling water acted like a badly focused lens to distort distances and create deceptive perspectives. In such a cityscape, footsteps ring hollow and seem absorbed by a looming abyss to which every path leads, and men feel more and more alone.

It was past three in the morning. The commissario got to his feet with the certainty that the night would not bring him anything more helpful. "Get to bed," he said quietly to the woman, with the concern of a doctor.

He was gripped by deep anxiety as he went down the stairs, and when he came out onto the street, a sense of sadness brought a lump to his throat. He looked along the road. The thick fog raised a soft wall all around him. It was, as ever, the most faithful representation of his state of mind.

3

EVEN IN HIS dreams Soneri found himself stumbling through a mist so thick that he had lost his way. His mother used to say that dreams evaporate if the sleeper is woken up and are remembered only if he awakes of his own accord. He was coming round from the deep sleep he had fallen into at four o'clock in the morning when his mobile, sounding more like a barrel organ, began ringing out with "*La donna è mobile*".

"Your ears must be buzzing this morning," Nanetti said.

The autopsy! He had completely forgotten.

"Saltapico and the police doctor have been going on about you. Where can he be? What's he up to this time? He's never there when you need him."

"Whereas Saltapico's always there when you don't need him," Soneri retorted, not fully awake and not at his best.

"Forget it. It was a quick, straightforward job."

"Like Ghitta's death."

"More or less. She was laid out on the ground. Very probably the killer put his knees just below her shoulders, on her humerus, thus preventing her from using her arms, and then stabbed her in the heart."

Soneri tried to interrupt, but Nanetti went on: "He used a narrow blade sharpened to a point. The heart was ripped into a dozen pieces."

"It looked like a single stab wound," the commissario said.

"Yes, there's only one entry point, so in fact the knife was pushed in and pulled out once. When it was inside, the blade was twisted round and round so as to tear the old lady's heart to pieces."

"So you're saying that without extracting the knife, he managed to take the heart apart."

Nanetti grunted in agreement. "What do you make of it?"

"I'm amazed that Ghitta could arouse such hatred."

"That was my first reaction too. Who would have guessed? A landlady getting on in years. What was she caught up in? But then another idea crossed my mind." Nanetti paused, waiting for some sign of curiosity from the commissario, but Soneri had not yet got over his ill humour at being so rudely awakened, and was in any case following his own line of thought. Nanetti went on: "Perhaps the killer was in a hurry."

"Anybody responsible for an act of slaughter like that is moved either by fear or hatred," Soneri said.

"Fear doesn't tell us very much. You've got to understand fear of what," Nanetti objected.

"Just so. In my opinion, this killer was in the grips of the most dreadful of all fears, the fear of the unknown."

"Maybe he was a sadist, a madman."

"Do you know what Saltapico will be telling the journalists? We will not neglect any line of enquiry. Our investigation will cover the full three-hundred-and-sixty-degree spectrum."

"Which means that after we've been once round the track, we'll be back where we started."

Soon afterwards, by now in his office, Soneri did indeed have the sensation of being back at the starting line. From his window, he looked down at the courtyard of the questura, at the entrance gate at the far end, and the crowded street and fir trees in the cloister where Fernanda had first appeared as though springing up from his past. All that now remained of the world he had once inhabited had lost its sharpness and had faded into an unrecognisable dullness – with the corpse of Ghitta lying at its centre.

Where to begin? He then remembered the material collected by the forensic squad, but when he had it all brought up, meticulously tagged, he found nothing of any particular use, and thought to himself that such objects wrenched from their context, drained of meaning, stuck inside a nylon bag and then laid out in a row on a table, had no story to tell. On the other hand, the diary, which he remembered only now, still seemed as warm as when it had been in Ghitta's pocket, perhaps because it was so small, no bigger than a notebook carried in a handbag, and had a wine-dark cover evocative of passion and frenzy.

Ghitta's letters were childlike and uneven, which at first glace suggested that writing was not something that came to her naturally. The big handwriting made brevity a necessity, so all that was recorded were the times and names of those who came and went around the pensione. However, the woman gave her clients the most extravagant nicknames, taken from her dialect, and this rendered them unrecognisable. Soneri spent a quarter of an hour flicking through the pages, and came away with his head filled with a gallery of characters but with no clue as to who they were, like a list of code names in a spy story. Who was this Blackbag who had booked a room at 4 p.m. on a Wednesday? It was not even definitely a room. All that was written was the name with a time along-side. And Bolshoi? Who could he be? There followed a squad of odd characters: Fastlast, which seemed to mean "comes last", and therefore in a hurry, Half-light, Bombardier, Duce, Abbess, Rasp. Names spread over the pages and the days of the month, including Sundays, but nothing on Thursdays. He checked week by week and found confirmation. No appointment or booking on Thursdays. Fernanda had told him that that was the day when Ghitta went to Rigoso to do her round of visits.

He looked again at those baffling nicknames. One stood out because it turned up every so often but without a time listed against it, and the name itself could have been either a common family name or a feminine diminutive – Pitti.

The door was flung open just as Soneri was looking up from the paper on which he was making a list of all the characters, hoping to find the explanation of the riddle. It was Juvara, out of breath even though he had walked only the few metres from his office to the commissario's. "A friar has just arrived, a Franciscan from Sant'Uldarico," he said, enunciating his syllables.

"Did he come bearing Christmas greetings?" Soneri said, filling the extremely lengthy pause Juvara needed to get his breath back.

"No, but he left this," Juvara said, placing on Soneri's desk a bundle wrapped in paper, inside which a knife could be made out.

The commissario stared at the object without touching it, as though he was faced with some exotic insect and was working out how to pick it up. With the tips of two fingers, he pulled open the parcel to see more clearly what it contained. It was a knife, long and slender, double-edged and with a rough wooden handle. He stood gazing at it for some minutes, moving his head from one side to the other to get a picture of its outline rather than taking it in his hand and turning it round. Memory came to his aid. He recalled perfectly where he had seen this type of murderous blade before. It was the kind used by pork butchers to slaughter pigs, and this was the season. He raised a distracted glance to

Juvara's puzzled face, and there rose up before his eyes scenes from years ago of freezing winter days with the frost on the trees, the farmyard made ready for the sacrifice, and the beast, grubbing about outside its sty, unaware that it was savouring the last moments of joyful life and liberty.

Once anxious grandmothers had ushered the children away from scenes of the cruelty of death, everything then took place in a few harrowing seconds. The mysteries of life and death had to be concealed from small children, whether the bull mounting the cow or the slaughter of the pig, but Soneri had managed to peep through the shutters and had witnessed the hook being stuck into the beast's throat to hold it still, the second slaughterman inserting the knife into the innards, and the animal screaming. It was that desperate, piercing screech of rebellion which remained most strongly imprinted in his ears.

He was brought back to himself by a timid gesture from Juvara, to which he replied with a wave of apology.

"The friar said that someone had brought the knife personally to the church at dawn this morning, at around six o'clock," the inspector said.

"Someone actually came to the church with the knife?"

"He went to confession, and then begged Friar Fiorenzo's pardon before leaving, saying he would be leaving a package."

"Is the friar still here?"

"Yes. I asked him to wait because I thought you'd want a word with him, but I warn you that you won't get much out of him."

"Show him in," Soneri said.

Friar Fiorenzo, a living icon of the Franciscan faith, had an appropriately subdued look about him.

"Commissario, I know what you're after," he began, in a voice given its timbre by the pulpit and ecclesiastical chanting, "but you must be aware of the obligations that fall to a confessor."

"I know, I know, but I hope that since we are dealing with a case of murder . . ."

Friar Fiorenzo gave a deep sigh and moved the conversation onto a spiritual level. "Evil is always present among us."

The commissario realised that the friar was going to be a hard nut to crack. He felt uneasy, like a bull charging the torero's cape without ever making contact.

"Was it a man or a woman?"

Once again a deep sigh, but one that seemed this time to Soneri more impatient. "A woman."

"Did you see her face?"

"Even if I had, I wouldn't have been able to make much out in the dark. It was six o'clock in the morning. I'd only just opened the side door to the church and had taken my place in the confessional. We always get up very early. In the side nave, it was almost completely black. The only light came from the candles burning under the statue of Sant'Uldarico. I heard the door open and someone coming towards me. I realised it was a woman only when she began speaking."

"I fully understand that you can't tell me what she confessed, but are you able to give me a summary of the general sense?"

"She asked forgiveness for her sins. The prior expressed in everyone's name the joy we all felt for a person who appeared to be redeemed. God had touched her heart and now she was intent on living differently."

"When did she tell you about the knife?"

"After her confession. I gave her absolution and a blessing and told her to say some prayers. We then waited a little in silence and I heard her sigh. She even wept a little."

"And then what happened?"

"She whispered that I would find a package near the confessional, but said nothing about its contents. She asked me to wait a few minutes before going to collect it, so I understood she wanted me to leave her time to get away. There was no need for this request, because I never leave the confessional before nine o'clock, when another brother takes over. I wait there in the dark for others to come to make their confession, and I say prayers in the meantime."

"But in this case you did go out."

"I waited longer than was necessary, but I was afraid someone might trip over the package, so I went to find it. It was sealed with adhesive tape, but when I opened it I understood everything."

"You connected it with the confession you'd heard?"

"I'll leave you to draw your own conclusions."

Soneri stared at him with a mixture of admiration and disappointment. He really was stubborn, and it would be easy to be unnerved by him.

"Did you know Ghitta?"

"Very well. She came to us often because she said we were the only thing that remained the same in the midst of many changes. She was a bit lost, but that was in large part due to her boarding house, which was facing problems."

"What you say is true. Everything is different. So many foreigners, people from elsewhere. I imagine the churches are empty."

"If they are empty, that's no fault of the incomers, but of those who place the centre of their being outside themselves. Evil has no other explanation. Take Ghitta . . ."

Soneri detected a gleam of light and seized it. "You believe there was a conflict of interest involved?"

"Commissario, you know more than me about the motives

of criminality. The very fact that you put this question to me suggests you have something else in mind."

This was true. He was out to obtain as much information as possible from the friar, but he did not dare ask direct questions for fear of causing him to draw back.

"I have only one aim: to find the killer, male or female. If the woman who presented herself to you . . ."

The friar pursed his lips with the expression of a man deep in thought. "I am no policeman, but from what I know of souls I can confirm that she appeared to me sincere. And anyway," he added, with a touch of irony, "they all come to me to make their confessions."

Soneri smiled. "Did she accuse herself explicitly?"

"No, she spoke to me about responsibility, but in a wide sense."

Soneri had before him a way out of the impasse, but the friar seemed immovable in his justified reticence. Dealing with a hardened villain would have been more straightforward. He looked again at the knife. At least they had the weapon used in the crime.

"How many people come to make their confession at dawn?" he said.

"Very few. Most people come to pray. Some mornings I hear someone coming in, but they don't kneel down on the other side of the grille from me. I am aware of them moving about between the benches until the sound of creaking wood announces that they've knelt down to say a prayer. Or perhaps I hear a coin being dropped into the steel collection box containing money for the candles, and when I come out I notice an additional light beneath the statue of Sant'Uldarico. Like this morning." The friar paused, making the last phrase stand on its own as though it had nothing to do with the rest of what he had been saying.

But the commissario could not help asking, "Did someone light a candle this morning?"

"Two candles," Friar Fiorenzo said, raising the same number of fingers of his right hand. "Something which happens very rarely, so when I heard the second coin being dropped into the steel box I did something I never do. I pulled the little curtain over the confessional aside and peeped out."

"What did you see?" Soneri said, with some urgency.

"Unfortunately very little, on account of the dark. It looked like a man of average height, elegantly dressed. He had his back to me as he went out."

"How long had he been in the church?"

"If I counted accurately the number of times the door opened and closed, he was there quite a while. At the beginning, I paid no heed. There are one or two elderly people who come to pray early in the morning because they can't sleep at night. It was the coins which aroused my curiosity: two candles in the one morning."

"Do me a favour, Father. From now on, keep an eye open for people coming into the church."

The friar nodded, and bowed his head as though he had just been told off, but then, with a flowing gesture of his habit, he pulled back a sleeve to reveal a white, hairy wrist on which a steel watch shone out incongruously. He gave the slight bow of a humble page before turning to leave silently. Soneri and Juvara exchanged looks expressive of the sense of impotence they felt in the presence of the friar, and which they felt about the crime itself. Vexed by thoughts which led nowhere, the commissario rose abruptly to his feet and went out. He was a few hundred metres down the road when his mobile rang. As he stopped to reply, he realised that he was heading for Via Saffi.

"Did you find anything in that brothel?" Angela said, with brutal directness.

"It's not a brothel."

"It is, at least in a metaphorical sense."

"That may be so," the commissario agreed. He had arrived at 35 Via Saffi, and was staring at the building which housed the pensione. The only residents in the area seemed to be immigrants, mainly Arabs and Africans. From the window of the bar opposite, a Pakistani man in a flowing, *caffelatte*-coloured tunic kept him under observation. An elderly gentleman passing on his bicycle had the air of a survivor.

"There are only foreigners here now," Soneri said.

"The city has changed, commissario," Angela intoned, as though beginning a lecture. "It's too long since you were last involved with this district. Anyway, you always attach too much importance to memories."

"I rely on them, like everybody else. Otherwise, what's left?"

"I did hope that our present would have given you some consolation. Anyway, it's time you faced up to the fact that all those things you so jealously guard in your locker give off a nasty stench. They're as phoney as a piece of badly executed restoration work."

"You can't accept that I had another life before I met you. You should have got me when I was young."

"You could take that as a sign of love."

"Alright, but leave me on a long leash. I'm an anarchist and a stray, like the people who now inhabit this district. And so are you, by the way."

"We're made for one another." Angela gave a sardonic

laugh. "We spend our time sniffing out traces of ourselves in the hope of bumping into each other every now and then. But don't fool yourself about memories. They only sparkle because they're so far away. You know those oxen's yokes you see hanging on walls? They're admired now because they're freshly varnished and shiny, but before they became collectors' items they stank and were grimy with shit."

"Rather the shit than the aseptic sterility that's all around us. At least shit's a fertiliser."

"I just wanted to say that you should bear in mind that Ghitta may not have been entirely whiter than white."

"I have learned that no-one in this world is whiter than white, and that includes you and me. It's a question of timing. We perform different roles at different times."

"And your role at the moment is to play the sleuth, but it seems to me you could do with a lesson in the geography of the old city," Angela said.

"You can play the part of teacher this evening. It's embarrassing at my age to have to take private lessons, so it's better to do it under cover of dark, in the mist."

After he had hung up, he turned and noticed that the Pakistani was still watching him through the windows of the bar, so he pushed open the door and went in. There was the scent of incense from a few sticks which were burning slowly, spreading their aroma around. In the centre of the room, some men dressed like the barman were chatting in their own language.

"Did you know Ghitta?" Soneri asked the owner.

"The old lady who lived at number thirty-five?" the Pakistani said, examining Soneri's cigar with such admiration that the commissario, out of professional instinct, wondered if he had mistaken it for a joint.

"That's her."

"She let out rooms, but not to immigrants like us," he said, with some asperity.

"Did you see her yesterday?"

"Early in the morning when she went out to do her shopping. I didn't see her after that."

"She normally went out at dawn and then again in the afternoon?"

"Every day. She seemed to enjoy walking in the dark."

"You can see everything from here," Soneri said, imagining whole days spent seated at the window with the mist almost rubbing against it.

"I used to be a hotel porter in England," the man said, as if justifying himself.

"Did you notice any new faces yesterday afternoon? People you hadn't seen before?"

The man looked at him with his dark, shining eyes which almost gave the impression that a film of water was flowing over them. He turned towards the bar where his wife was standing, and the two of them spoke for a few moments in their own language. His voice had the tone of an order.

"We saw a man coming out around midday," he said. After a brief pause, he added with a malicious smile, "and he was on his own."

Soneri understood that he knew about the comings and goings of various couples. It was for that reason that a man on his own seemed out of place.

"Do you remember how he was dressed? Did you get a look at his face?"

"He was quite tall, dressed in a dark coat which reached below his knees and he had the collar turned up. He was wearing a hat and glasses."

"So you weren't able to see the outline of his face clearly?"

The man shook his head in denial, but gave the impression

of holding back when he was on the point of saying something more. The commissario knew how to wait, so after a few seconds he made a tiny gesture with his hand to break the silence, and congratulated himself on his mastery of sign language, a code which overrode all the languages in the world.

"I'm not sure if it's fair, and I'm not even sure if it's true," he stuttered.

"What?" Soneri said softly.

"I had the impression that he was in a rush, but don't ask me why. I wouldn't be able to give you an answer."

He understood perfectly. People often failed to grasp some deep purpose which was not immediately decipherable.

"Fat ... thin ... ?" the commissario asked, inviting the man to continue, but still speaking softly.

"Thin," the man said, running his eye over his own body which was decidedly slender, and a little bent.

"Do you know Fernanda Schianchi as well?"

"She lives at number thirty-five as well. She doesn't go out much because she can't walk very well. Aref, the Moroccan fruit-seller in Via Dalmazia, delivers her shopping to her at home."

"When did you last see her?"

"Yesterday afternoon. She went out about three o'clock. It's nearly Christmas, so I assumed she was going out to buy something."

Soneri digested this in silence until someone from inside the café, cutting the air with a wave of his arms, shouted, "Mohammed!" The man gave him a nod and turned away.

Outside, Soneri stopped for a smoke in Borgo delle Colonne, once the most "red" street in the city, but now a place where the recently refurbished mansions of millionaires, with their reinforced doorways, alternated with more dilapidated dwellings previously inhabited by working-class people, but now home to a noisy, multilingual community which spilled out onto colonnades now pressed into service as verandas.

"Has the police doctor established the time of death?" Soneri asked Juvara over his mobile.

He heard the inspector put his telephone down on the desk and start to type on his computer keyboard. "Some time between eleven and twelve. The time was confirmed by Nanetti's investigation of the coffee left in the cups and by other findings."

"The Pakistani owner of the bar on the other side of the street from number thirty-five saw a man coming out of Ghitta's around midday. There was no-one with him and he seemed to be in a hurry. He's the likely killer."

"We've found out quite a lot then?"

"We know he's a man who was wearing a coat and a hat. And you think that's a lot?"

Juvara, embarrassed by his undue optimism, made no reply.

"Has Saltapico made up his mind about issuing a search warrant for the Schianchi house?"

"The paperwork will be ready in the morning."

Soneri walked along the street, feeling the surprised and wary eyes of Arabs and Africans on him. They could smell the policeman in him, with the same unerring precision as had communists fifty years previously. The other common factor was the sense of being outsiders, but the newcomers felt no pride in that status. Once again Soneri was overwhelmed by that sense of the vanity of life which had accompanied him since he had embarked on this investigation. He was convinced that his loss of contact with that part of the city was not due to chance factors, but to an unconscious exclusion. The murder of Ghitta had compelled him to confront what he had suppressed, and the memories which now came flooding back were so disturbing because he was afraid of verifying their inconsistency.

In the mist, the Campanile del Duomo and the spires of the Battistero seemed to have been sliced off. Every so often a car, its arrival announced by the roar of its engine, or a bicycle free-wheeling silently towards the city centre, would emerge from the grey of the fog. Soneri found the remedy for his anxieties in a plate of *tortelli d'erbette*, and in Alceste's unashamed, open use of the dialect. The *Milord*, so firmly anchored in tradition, offered him reassurance against any wavering sense of identity.

Not even a bottle of Bonarda was sufficient to cheer him up, so he was still in a grim mood as he rose from the table and made for the door, giving Alceste a wave as he went. He had no wish to see anyone, much less face the daunting uproar at the questura and the thousand useless words his colleagues would throw at him, their good humour on show like a pennant at one of that endless round of meetings in the capo di gabinetto's office. He slipped into his office without looking right or left, but once on his own he found himself dispiritingly bereft of any inspiration as to how to breathe life into the inquiry. There was the corpse of an old woman, a knife mysteriously delivered to a friar confessor in a church at dawn, and a tall, thin man with no recorded distinguishing features seen coming out of Ghitta's house around noon, alone and in a hurry. All the rest was smoke and mirrors, starting with the house itself where in his youth Soneri had faced life with such enthusiasm, and continuing with those shadowy beings who had gone there on the night of the murder when many people, still unaware of what had occurred, would have dropped by for a regular visit or to renew old friendships.

"Juvara!" he shouted down the internal line. When the

inspector appeared, the commissario found himself noting his loosened belt. "Just think what you'll be like after the feast of the Epiphany, with all those sumptuous dinners lying ahead of you."

Juvara did not reply immediately and when he launched into some form of self-justification, Soneri cut him short by issuing an order: "I want you to start gathering information on Giuditta Tagliavini." But even as he spoke the words, he knew he would be doing the job himself. He was no good at delegating responsibility, as the head of the force was forever reminding him. Now they just let him get on with it, having slowly come round to the idea of having a foreign body linked to the police only by the obligatory practices of investigative procedure.

"Is Nanetti examining the knife?" he asked Juvara.

"Yes, he says it's not something you can just buy in the shops. It's very unusual."

"I know, "Soneri said. "It's used by a pig butcher, the so-called *corador*." He knew he had no proof that would stand up in court, but the first glance had been sufficient to convince him.

"The what?" Juvara said.

"The *corador*. He's a specialist pig butcher whose job it is to pierce the beast's heart when it's slaughtered. It's the dialect word for one of the two butchers. The other is the one who sticks the hook in under the throat," he said, leaving the inspector gawking with an air of infantile amazement. "Do you have the search warrant for the Schianchi house?"

Juvara went back to his office and returned with the headed form, indicating that it had been issued by the office of the Procura della Repubblica. Soneri gave it a distracted glance and decided it offered him the only way forward on an afternoon which was as grim and dark as his mood.

He set off to follow the same route he had seen Fernanda Schianchi take, and when he reached the centre of the cloister he stopped to look around, as the old woman had done. It was indeed very attractive, as he realised for the first time, having never before taken the time to look. He went through the main gate to Via Repubblica. From there he was less sure of the path the old woman would have taken, but he did not waste much time dwelling on it. Her disappearance merged with the wider mystery of the Ghitta affair. When he got to Via Saffi, the night was drawing in. On the landing, he ran into the Slav woman.

"Did you notice a man around here yesterday? Thin, tall, with a black overcoat. In the morning, I mean," he said.

The woman's eyes opened wide and she shook her head vigorously before saying, "Us always away. Not much home."

She did not manage to add anything else before her husband appeared behind her. He gave a backwards jerk of his head, an order issued by a master, and she scuttled into the house as obediently as a dog dispatched to its basket. Soneri felt an instinctive dislike of the man, and he introduced himself without so much as offering his hand. When the man discovered he was dealing with the police, he tried to put on a smile which he meant as deferential, but which only appeared hypocritical.

"We work, we always out," he said, anticipating the questions.

"I'm talking about yesterday, a Sunday."

The man was temporarily caught off guard but quickly recovered his air of brazen insouciance. "Sundays, go visit relatives." His tone revealed a man who feared the authorities, but was not above mocking them.

Soneri glowered at him, angling the tip of his cigar upwards with his teeth. He would not have hesitated to put pressure on him, but he believed his reticence could be taken as a silent clue, so he backed off without for a second taking his eyes off the man, who beat a flustered retreat. The commissario stood alone on the landing until the light went off, but before he could switch it back on, he heard the sound of Fernanda's buzzer. As he made his way silently down the stairs, the buzzer was pressed again, echoing in the empty space. When he reached the outside door, he thought he could hear someone speaking on the other side, out in the street. He pressed the button to open the door, as though Fernanda had replied, but no-one came in. He let a few seconds pass before he swung the door fully open, but all that came in from Via Saffi was a misty darkness. A car started up and was quickly lost in the thick clouds of fog.

Had some suspicion caused the person who had pressed the buzzer to make off, or had there been a warning signal from the Albanian? Or perhaps from the Pakistanis? Perhaps it was the same person who had come to Ghitta's door the previous night and, having heard the news of the murder, had come to talk to Fernanda.

He went back up the stairs and decided to go in without waiting for Nanetti. The forensic squad had given him a set of keys they had come across inside the pensione and one of them was most likely to be the key to the neighbour's apartment. He found the right one after a couple of attempts, but he had the impression the Slav was listening behind his door.

Schianchi's apartment had a very different feel from Ghitta's. Nothing was out of place, everything was neat and tidy as though the owner had just finished doing her house-work. The heaters were all switched off, and the electricity and gas had been turned off at the mains. There were all the signs of a planned departure, as though Fernanda, like many other people all over the city, had set off for her Christmas holidays. On the surface there was nothing strange. Fernanda had gone to the questura to report her friend missing, and then taken a train or taxi and gone on her way. Everything surrounding the death of Ghitta Tagliavini seemed normal. Only Ghitta's shredded heart betrayed the brutal deviation from what would otherwise have looked like a routine case of a natural death.

The furniture here was almost identical to the furniture in Ghitta's pensione – poorly designed but somehow pretentious. The dark wallpaper, the cloudy mirrors, the faded glaze on the majolica ornaments and the greying curtains all seemed to have aged at the same pace as Fernanda. He was walking around the apartment, trying to work out the sequences of her meticulously prepared departure, when he came across on a series of photographs lying on a desk in the bedroom, one of which showed Fernanda and Ghitta in the company of a gentleman fitted out in the ostentatious finery of a dandy. He took the photograph out of the frame. On the back was written: GHITTA, PITTI AND ME AT THE ASTRA CINEMA.

He had already found the name Pitti in Ghitta's notebook, but only now did he realise that he must have been the foppishly dressed figure he had spotted in Via Saffi on the evening after the murder. He could also have been the man Friar Fiorenzo had seen lighting two candles to Sant'Uldarico. Pitti, a name redolent of elegance, recalling the Palazzo Pitti in Florence, with its grand fashion parades. The agitation which overwhelmed him almost stopped him from hearing the ringing of the telephone in the hall on the other side of the wall, but the caller would not have been Pitti, because he was already aware of the old woman's death.

4

THE FORENSIC SQUAD found Soneri bent over the kitchen table rummaging through a pile of photographs, but they managed to get on with their own painstaking work without him saying a word or having to move from the table. When they left, he gave them a vague wave. It took the aria "*La donna è mobile*" from his mobile to distract him. For some time he had been fiddling with the Options window on the screen in an effort to find a simpler, more anonymous ringtone, but he doubted whether a more routine sound would attract his attention, so he left Verdi's aria where it was, doing nothing more than changing the image from time to time.

"Commissario, I'm ready to teach you a lesson you won't forget," Angela said, teasing him with the possible meanings of her words.

"Now?" he grumbled, in an expressionless voice.

"It's nearly nine o'clock. You must be really snowed under if you've even forgotten dinner."

"I'm looking at some photographs."

"You've got your wedding album out?"

By way of a reply, the commissario gave a deep sigh, which Angela took as a sign of some profound affliction.

"Commissario, what's happening to you? This investigation is poisoning you."

"It's stirring up all manner of memories, and making me wonder who I am."

"What a brilliant investigator," Angela said, trying to bring this line of thought to a close.

"What we do from a certain point in life onwards is just an attempt to fill the void opening before us. That's why we draw up plans, set targets and rush about trying to achieve them, but from time to time the idea that none of this matters returns to torment us. Relentlessly. Even murderers, with their manic need to assert themselves, seem to me slightly absurd. If only they knew . . ."

"What have you seen in those photographs?" Angela said, deducing that they were the cause of his malaise.

"Ada in the arms of another man."

"Retrospective jealousy?"

"Not in the slightest! It's just that I knew nothing about it. I don't care if she had other lovers, but I do care that she kept it hidden from me and that I've been under a misapprehension all this time. Can you understand that? Even the memory of what we once were to each other is crumbling. The memory of Ada and the memory of this city that I thought was still the way it used to be."

They were silent for a few moments and that silence conveyed to the commissario that he and Angela shared everything. It was in such moments that they felt closest, but soon their different temperaments quickly reasserted themselves.

"You're allowing yourself to sink too deeply into a state of melancholy," Angela said at last. "I don't like men with no character. It's always easier to let yourself go than to raise yourself up – and after all you like a challenge, don't you?"

Soneri sighed. "Everything about this inquiry draws me more deeply into my past, and I don't need to tell you that getting the better of time is impossible."

"So get on with finding the person who killed the old lady as quickly as possible, and that way you'll keep nostalgia at bay."

"No, I've got to proceed cautiously, little by little. It's the best way."

"Meet you outside the pensione?" Angela said.

The commissario looked out the window which gave on to Via Saffi. "Alright. I think there's enough mist about."

Shortly afterwards they were walking side by side, unrecognisable in the darkness of the narrow streets. The few people who passed by were all wrapped up in heavy coats covered with damp frost. Theirs was a journey very similar to awakening from sleep, a walk in a graveyard of memories.

"Do you know who the man in the photograph was?" Angela asked.

"No. Maybe another guest in the house."

They walked on to where the *Red Club* had once been, but the site was now occupied by a car park.

"You used to get the best Malvasia in the old city of Parma there," Soneri said, in the tones of someone recalling a dead friend.

"And their tripe? And what about your other favourite, the *busecca*?"

The streets were now enveloped with mist, with one doorway after another emerging from it, somehow reminding Soneri of loose eggs sticking out of the old grey newspaper that was used to wrap them. Further on, Tirelli's bicycle-repair shop, whose owner had once been an avid supporter of the cyclist Gianni Motta, had been converted to a Chinese takeaway. Students used to stand outside his door taunting him with their chant: "*Tirelli, Tirelli, stinky and smelly.*"

"Maren the baker has gone too," Angela said, putting her arm through his. "There's a mobile phone shop there instead."

Two eyes in the window gave off a subdued light in the middle of the garish colours surrounding them. Angela and Soneri walked more quickly as though motivated by an urgent need to observe the changes, she to point them out and he to absorb them.

"Don't tell me you never noticed before," she said.

"I haven't been down here for some time. I've avoided these places, perhaps because I was afraid of seeing what I see now," Soneri said, stopping in front of a rusted shutter. Above it was still possible to make out the words: PEPPINO'S TASTES BEST!

As they stood in front of the shop a breeze got up, sending the mist drifting among the houses. A little further ahead, music as full of vibrations as a muezzin's rhythmic call to prayer blared out from an Arab café. Soneri had the fleeting fantasy that the mist was dust from the desert, the narrow streets the lanes of a Kasbah, and they themselves lost tourists with no idea of the way home, two little Ulysses without an Ithaca. Fortunately the Duomo bell rang out from the darkness to give them reassurance.

"At least that's still there," the commissario said.

"Cities are like children. They change from one year to the next, so if you don't see them for a while, you don't recognise them any more. Some things do stay the same though," Angela said, starting to move off again.

They walked down the middle of Borgo Gazzola. Here and there, little red lights, similar to those placed over tombs in cemetery walls, cut into the mist, their flickering lights alerting men that ladies of the night, with their air of brazen indifference, awaited them behind closed doors. It brought back to his mind the "whore whirl", the licentious baptism of flesh that awaited all first-year students at the university.

"It's not for nothing that it's called the oldest profession in the world," Angela said, referring to the enduring nature of the street.

Now it was Soneri who was in a hurry. He wanted to familiarise himself once more with the local geography, get to the very heart of that quarter where he had once been happy and to which he had not wanted to return. So it was that he was glad to stumble across Bettati the barber's in Borgo del Naviglio, and to see that this shop at least was unchanged. The wide-meshed shutter permitted a glimpse of the same old iron door with the over-ornate handle, the yellowing sinks, the pedal-adjustable chairs and the padded seats. Perhaps he still had in his cupboard the high chair with the horse's head for children, and the calendar with nude dancers for adults.

"He's the only one left," Angela said, while the commissario entertained an image of Bettati trimming an imam's beard or tidying up the crow-black hair of a Chinese client.

Once again, Angela shook him out of his gloomy meditations. "Commissario, everything passes, remember?"

Soneri gave a wry smile. "You fall asleep a child and you wake up an adult. What happens in between is no more than a fleeting dream."

With one of his sudden impulses, he turned on his heel and said goodbye, blowing a kiss in her direction as he went.

He hurried down Via Saffi like a man fleeing from a danger which is imaginary and therefore all-pervasive. He slowed down only when he was opposite No. 35 to look into the shisha bar, now full to overflowing with men, some dressed in their kaftans. Through the misted-up window they were no more than shadows, a kaleidoscope of teeming, warm, living humanity. He continued on his way, returning to the calm of the streets where the mist had settled, giving the impression of not wishing to move.

In Piazzale dei Servi he decided to turn back towards the Pensione Tagliavini. He felt drawn to it by the same compulsion felt by many who had once frequented it and who continued to orbit around it at night-time.

Instinct had taken over from reason and after a few minutes he understood the urgency which had taken hold of him. With the shadows glimpsed behind the windows of the shisha bar still in front of his eyes, he spied another shadow as it crossed ahead of him in the darkness, a shadow in which he made out for a moment a sort of gleam, the faintest of reflections emerging timidly and briefly from the thick depths of the mist.

He walked more quickly to where the light was stronger, and there in the distance, hazy but recognisable, he saw him: Pitti. His sheer elegance put him in a class of his own, outside any normal category, as did that gleam which Soneri could now distinguish more clearly and strongly, like a pilot-light bursting into flame. He sped up as he passed in front of No. 35, where the mist seemed deeper and visibility more limited. The lamps along the street appeared to set the circle of surrounding vapour on fire, while scarcely illuminating the cobbled road and the walls of the houses. Believing the other man to be close at hand, he pushed forward like a rugby player, stumbling uncertainly towards the junction where the old slaughterhouse stood, but it was like plunging into a dark nothingness. Panting after his exertions, he heard a car speed off with a muffled roar. It was already some way down the road when its tail lights flashed, and by then it was too far off for him to be able to make out the number plate.

He drew up, cursing, and made his way back up Via Saffi, noting the Pakistani bar-owner pulling down the shutters with a clatter. It was one of the signals which announced nightfall. Behind the curtains of the low houses, Soneri imagined insomniac old men tossing in their beds, counting the passing hours as they vainly pursued sleep. He stopped once more in the centre of the street, lit his cigar and decided to go up to Ghitta's. The silence of the night, floating on the drifting mist, was making him feel unwell.

He took up his position behind the window overlooking Via Saffi. Now that the mist had settled, lifting only in fleeting bursts, his range was limited to perhaps twenty metres of the street below. He felt like a voyeur, as Angela often called him, but he saw nothing wrong with that, though he knew it was more than his job demanded. He enjoyed letting his imagination roam free, as he was attempting to do now with the few passers-by. Perhaps by creating a life around the pensione, he might be able to pick up the hint of a lead.

A piece of the wooden furniture in one of the bedrooms creaked. In that apparent immobility, life continued to leave its imprint on restless matter. The walnut or cherry-tree wood of the wardrobes and the ash of the headboards continued to live even after their death by axe or plane, responding to climate and season by unexpected contractions. Soneri got to his feet and walked along the corridor. The snapping sound had come from one of the rooms next to the kitchen. He opened the first door, revealing an iron bedstead and a varnished cupboard. The next room was Elvira Cadoppi's. Inside he saw a wooden chest of drawers, which must have been the source of the noise he had heard, before his eye fell on the suitcase he had noticed the previous evening. He remembered that the report drawn up by Forensics had listed its contents: articles of clothing, cosmetic brushes and a pair of winter shoes. The case was empty now, as were the drawers and the wardrobe.

He took up his position behind the window once more and again observed the motionless scene of the street, interrupted from time to time by some solitary cyclist, but after a few seconds he became aware of the click-clack of high heels even before he saw the figure of Elvira. When he was able to see her more clearly a few paces from the front door, he noted that she had with her another case similar to the one in the bedroom. He waited for her to climb the stairs, and just as she was putting the key in the lock, he switched on the lights.

The woman seemed more irritated than surprised. "You'd be better off taking a room here. You'd be more comfortable," she said, with forced irony.

"I don't have as many cases as you."

Elvira glanced down at the case she had in her hand and for an instant the commissario thought he could detect a hint of embarrassment. "We girls like to change often."

"You told me you stopped here only one evening a week."

"During the Christmas rush they need us to work a lot of extra hours."

"There's an empty suitcase through there. It was full yesterday."

Elvira picked up the tone of hostility in his voice, in spite of his half smile.

"I took my things to the laundry and I've got a change of clothing here," she explained, picking up her suitcase. Cutting the conversation short, she marched past the commissario and made her way to her room. This irked Soneri, who interpreted it an attempt to escape his questioning.

He stood in the doorway and noted that the two cases were identical. "You'll get mixed up," he said to her quietly and gently.

Elvira was caught off guard, but only for a moment. "I got them in the department store where I work. They were the last in the line, and they were more or less giving them away. They're designer goods, see?" She spoke with an urgency in which the commissario could discern an anxiety to get off the subject.

"I get it. A bargain. Do you know Pitti?"

Once again, the woman seemed to hesitate before replying. She gave a forced smile. "The man who goes around in the strange outfit?" she said, pretending she was struggling to call him to mind. "Ghitta knew him and told me that he dropped by from time to time. He looked to me like one of those homosexuals who love making a show of themselves in fashionable salons."

"Did he come here often?"

"I couldn't say. Ghitta didn't tell me everything. She mentioned him a couple of times, that's all I remember."

"Did she speak favourably or unfavourably about him?"

"She used to say he was very nice and knew a lot of people. Maybe he was useful to her."

"He comes down this way a lot," Soneri said, using this piece of information as bait.

Elvira gave him a hard stare as though waiting for some move from him. She was like a boxer squaring up to her opponent, but the commissario had run out of moves and stood there in silence, returning her gaze.

"If that's all you want to know, I'll be off to bed then," the woman said, with a glint of triumph in her eyes. She took two steps back and closed the door, but not before Soneri had another look at the two identical cases leaning against the wall.

His ill humour returned and compelled him to go outside. He lit a cigar and began walking in widening circles around the district. He heard the Duomo bell strike every quarter of an hour and he seemed to be at the same distance from it every time. He stopped where Via Corso Corsi joins Via Saffi, and thought he heard a far-off creak. He listened to the noise as it drew closer until he caught sight of a hunch-backed man wrapped up in layers of overcoats pushing a supermarket trolley overflowing with odds and ends. The creaking sound came from the trolley's unoiled wheels, but at that moment it seemed like a warning, like the bell rung by city guards collecting corpses during an outbreak of plague. Ahead of him, Soneri saw an individual ground down by the trials of life, but behind the long beard and almost white hair he recognised a familiar face. The man must have had the same impression, because there was a flicker in his clear eyes.

"Ciao, Fadiga," Soneri said.

The man looked up, and through the matted hair the commissario thought he made out a smile. He saw him give several nods of the head, causing his white mane to shake.

"The policeman," he said before setting off again with his jingling trolley.

Soneri let him go on a few steps, and as he was about to call out to him he saw Fadiga give him a signal. He followed him to Piazzale dei Servi, where some cars were parked beneath the trees. He kept his distance until the creaking stopped and out of the dark he heard Fadiga summon him in a whisper. His outline was visible behind a boxwood hedge. Soneri lit a match which revealed a cardboard shelter protected by the bulk of a huge magnolia.

"Is this your home?"

"When it's not raining. Otherwise I go to the refuge and hope to get a place there. I usually end up spending the night awake in the underpass."

"Rain or no rain, a bed would be better."

"And where am I to find one? With all these immigrants

around, there's nothing doing in the refuge, or in the soup kitchen run by the friars. Nobody wants to know about tramps like us. If you're not careful, you'll end up with a knife in your back. And then there are those Italians who set fire to you just for fun."

"You're safe here?"

"You can't be safe anywhere, but at least here, in all this mist, nobody can see you. But then again . . ." he said, bringing his index fingers together as he spoke, to mimic their face-to-face conversation.

"What are you afraid of?"

"They bumped off Ghitta, didn't they?"

The commissario lit his cigar and in the match light he noticed Fadiga's anxious expression. "Who do you think's going to see us?" he said.

"When they get to know you've been speaking to a policeman, they dump on you the blame for things you didn't do."

He was right. Soneri could think of more than one occasion when a rumour had resulted in violence, even though the whispers had proved unfounded.

"They used a knife, didn't they?" Fadiga said, sounding as though he already knew the answer.

The commissario nodded in the dark. "She'd fallen into bad company," he said. He wanted to put that as a question, but it came out as a statement.

This time it was Fadiga who nodded. "This whole district is bad company."

"Who was using Ghitta's as a place to screw?" Soneri said abruptly.

"I couldn't give you any names, but there were certain faces I recognised from the newspapers. I live on newspapers. I've got a trolley full of them. They're good for wrapping round my knees when I'm cold, as well as for a mattress or pillow. Newspapers are the uniform of tramps like me."

"Which are your favourite ones?"

"Any I can find. I get them from recycling bins – magazines, newsprint, anything at all, but the dailies are the best. The paper they use is the best for what I need."

"And that's how you saw the faces of some people who frequented Ghitta's place?"

"Yes. I don't just use newspapers to pad out what I'm wearing. I also have a look at them, even if they're out of date. I've plenty of time on my hands."

"But you don't remember the people you picked out?"

"I'm not interested in the names, only the faces, and I don't like most of them. The world is a dangerous place, as someone who works as a policeman must know. The fact that they might put a knife in your back is the least of it. Look at what's happened to me and to many more like me."

"You could get out of this life. Get back into society, I mean."

Fadiga shook his head. "This life is a pitiless race, and I had the misfortune to get a puncture. I tried to catch up with the leading group, but they were going too fast for me."

In the dim light, Fadiga seemed to the commissario to diminish in size as he huddled in his overcoat. Once, when Soneri was a student, he had been one of the best laboratory assistants in the Department of Physics, but his wife left him and psychological collapse was followed by professional disintegration. Eventually, he chose to live on the margins of society in scornful solitude.

The commissario carried on smoking, concealing his cigar in his cupped hand in the manner of peasants working with hay or soldiers at the front. He was unconsciously affected by Fadiga's fear of being noticed.

"How was Ghitta recently?"

"Like the area she lived in – much changed," Fadiga said, resting his hand on the handle of his trolley.

"More reclusive?"

"She walked up and down here, looking straight ahead, like everybody else. Nobody recognises themselves any longer in this quarter. The world is worse than it was. That goes for immigrants as well, because T.V. led them to believe that even dogs eat well here, and instead they've discovered it was all a fraud, and so they go around in a rage." Fadiga gave a deep sigh, and tiny drops appeared on the beard around his mouth.

"I don't even recognise the apartment in Borgo Dalmazia where I was born and brought up. They've modernised it, redone the toilets and transformed the shops into a garage. My once-upon-a-time wife is still inside, fucking another man. I go past the house only at night, when everyone's fast asleep, and with the help of wine I live in the dream of an eternal present. Anyway, what else can I think about? For someone like me, it would absurd to think of the future, and it's too painful to look back."

"Do you know Pitti?"

"Oh, that young damsel! He looks at you with contempt, but it's better to stink than spend your life as a lackey."

"Whose lackey?"

"Powerful people – members of parliament, industrialists, lawyers. Here too I only know their faces. Several of them used to frequent Ghitta's establishment."

Footsteps could be heard approaching along Via Saffi and Fadiga fell silent, listening until the regular rhythms moved off and faded into the dark gardens of the buildings.

"What kind of work does he do?"

"I told you. He licks arses, and maybe other things as well.

What kind of police officer are you if you aren't well versed in these things?"

"I've been away for many years. And I'm not very keen on remembering either."

He saw Fadiga nod vigorously and shiver in the shadows, so much so that the wheels of the trolley began to squeak.

"Exactly, but you used to go to Ghitta's as well, so you must know how things were," Fadiga said, taking a sip from a bottle of supermarket wine to ward off both the cold and unhappy thoughts. When he removed the bottle from his lips, Soneri saw a wasted mouth with several gaps among the teeth. It was clear he wanted to end it all and found relief only in alcohol. As he swallowed it down, he added: "She was no saint."

Soneri remembered Angela's unflattering reference to Ghitta, and wondered about memory's power to soften and falsify reality. Was it really only a dream, and was the human mind a skilled cosmetician with expertise in the game of light and shadow? His mood darkened as he felt many certainties dissolve in a rapid haemorrhage of thoughts.

"Alright, she was no saint," Soneri repeated to himself. "But that's no reason to rip her heart to shreds."

Fadiga seemed moved by this revelation, perhaps thinking for a moment that this could be his end too. "They must have really had it in for her," he muttered.

"But who could have had it in for her?" the commissario said.

"I don't know," Fadiga said, shaking his head. "What can we know about people who come from far away, or people in houses with iron bars on their windows and gates as tall as cypresses? Ghitta dealt with the rich and powerful, and she was a mere landlady. The powerful respect only their own, and make use of the rest of us. And once we've served our purpose, or start to ask awkward questions . . . Steer clear of the rich. That's the one lesson I remember well from my days as a communist."

The mention of times past caused a fresh upsurge of bitterness in Soneri. He watched Fadiga as he laid out the cardboard on which he would spend the night.

"She could have closed down and retired. I don't understand why she was so stubborn in carrying on as a madam," the commissario said.

"Some people just won't give up. They struggle on against all the odds, and won't admit it's useless to stand against changing times. The best you can do is keep abreast of the new conditions of life. You become a bit-player, and resign yourself to performing newer and newer roles as dictated by time, the most dictatorial of all directors. Ghitta did her best to keep up. That was her life, but there's not a student today who would go near a place run by a landlady, and not only because they've all got money now. They lack humility. And anyway, there's nobody left here now. The houses are empty."

The commissario drew on his cigar which was almost out and pondered the survivor's fate as lived by Fadiga. "When you see the photograph in a newspaper of someone who used to go to Ghitta's, put it to one side. I'll come round one of these evenings to look you up."

"It'd be better if we weren't seen together. I could end up like Ghitta. It's not that I care all that much, but I've always been scared of knives. I'll leave the pictures under the cardboard boxes. It'll look as though they just happened to be there."

5

WITH A VEIL of mist enveloping both, there was little difference between dawn and dusk, and this reinforced Soneri's impression of not having been to bed. He was waiting in the deserted Via Farini for Friar Fiorenzo to open the side door of the church, but when he entered he found a few elderly ladies already seated in the pews and other shadowy little figures scurrying about. He positioned himself in the dark corner furthest from the altar and settled down to wait. His enquiries consisted of more periods of waiting than action, which was why his colleagues called him "the Chinese policeman", although no-one had actually said it to his face.

Even in the faint light, he could make out almost the entire nave with its rows of seats and benches. The comings and goings of the old ladies were astonishingly well synchronised. All that could be heard was the opening and closing of the door of the confessional and the groan of the wood each time one of the ladies sat up or knelt down.

When he spotted him, he was as elegantly eccentric as ever, moving with suppleness and precision, barely brushing against the seats and benches as he passed. The commissario ducked behind a pillar. Looking rapidly around the church with a wariness which betrayed his apprehension, Pitti sat down and continued peering nervously about him. He took off the bowler hat he had been wearing to reveal an almost bald head covered with a little lifeless fuzz. He was halfway down the nave in the rows facing the entrance, and seemed poised either to get up and leave, or to run up to someone. Chewing on his unlit cigar in the semi-darkness, Soneri kept him under scrutiny.

Pitti twisted his hat in his hands and looked around in evident disquiet. He tapped his foot against the bench in front a couple of times, attracting disapproving glares from the old ladies. After a bit he got up, went over to the statue of Sant'Uldarico, put a couple of coins in the box and lit a candle. The commissario followed his every move, taking note of his trembling hands as he held the wick over the flame of a lighted candle. When he looked along the benches again, he noticed a middle-aged man in a dark leather jacket in a pew in the centre of the nave. Pitti remained motionless in front of the statue, in the pose of a man lost in prayer. He then walked down the aisle, edged along the bench in front of the man with the leather jacket and disappeared into the gloom of a side chapel to the left of the high altar. The commissario's eyes moved rapidly from one to the other. He could no longer see Pitti, but he knew he had to be somewhere in the dark recesses of the chapel. After making an awkward genuflection in front of the altar, the man in the leather jacket also headed in that direction. Now that he too was lost to the shadows, everything in the church was calm and settled: the old ladies coughing quietly from time to time, Friar Fiorenzo saying his prayers in the confessional and the statues of the saints turning their ecstatic gazes heavenwards. Soneri considered advancing into the darkness to catch the two men off guard, but that would have meant crossing a part of the nave where the flickering bulbs softened the darkness into a hazy light.

Some time after Pitti and the man had vanished into the

chapel, Soneri noticed a reproduction of it on a floor plan of the church affixed to the pillar opposite him. He read that the chapel was dedicated to Sant'Egidio, and under the notice, for the convenience of tourists, there were headphones with a recording of the history of the church. Fifty centesimi were all it took to light up the treasures on the walls of the nave and dome.

The effect was like a camera flash. The light exploded from hidden corners, shining out to magnify space and banish darkness. The old ladies' heads suddenly shot up as though brusquely awakened from sleep while the man in the leather jacket made an immediate dash for the exit. The light had caught him and Pitti standing face-to-face, but only for the one instant before he fled, instinctively sticking something into his pocket, perhaps something he had received only a moment before, something of importance to him and something he wanted to be sure not to lose.

Pitti headed less hurriedly for the door, retracing the steps he had taken only a few minutes ago. When he came out into the misty dawn, Soneri was waiting for him, half hidden in the doorway of a block of flats. He moved alongside him, causing Pitti initially to feign surprise and then to turn towards him with the haughty look of a *grande dame*. The commissario kept his eyes firmly on him until he saw the arrogance give way to vague bewilderment.

"Well, what?" was all Pitti, feeling himself cornered, managed to say.

Soneri did not make any immediate reply, but continued staring at him. "It's up to you to make the first move, Pitti," he said after a short pause, stressing the nickname.

Pitti seemed to have recovered some composure, but at close quarters his aristocratic attire seemed even more ridiculous.

"You stop a man in the street for no good reason and then you claim he's the one who's got to justify himself?" Pitti spoke with a voice which Soneri had expected to be shrill but which was instead deep bass.

"You know perfectly well who I am and why I've stopped you, otherwise you wouldn't have run off yesterday evening. What did you give that man?"

"Some money."

"Why?"

Pitti started laughing. "I gave him some money and that's all there is to it. What's it to you?"

"At five o'clock in the morning in an unlit side chapel in a church?"

Pitti drew back half a step, and it was clear he was afraid. "He'd been travelling all night and arrived in the city early in the morning. He told me he was having difficulties. What else do you want to know about my private life?"

The commissario made a gesture of indifference, inviting him not to pursue that line. "You're an unlucky man. You've chosen the very church Ghitta used to attend." He paused long enough to allow him to evaluate Pitti's nervousness. "And you were a friend of Ghitta's, were you not?" he said in a lowered voice and a more friendly tone.

Pitti drew a deep breath and nodded. "You think I know something about it?" he asked in a pained voice. He seemed afraid and his hands were shaking as they had done in the church shortly before while he was lighting the candle, but Soneri's persuasive tone seemed to be causing his distrust to fade, at least in part.

"You know a lot about Ghitta. You were the person she most confided in."

Pitti dropped his gaze with a speed which was the equivalent of an admission. "That's true. She did confide in me, but not everything. There was always a dark side to her, where I, as a matter of delicacy, had no wish to intrude."

"For instance?"

"There was a kind of near-witchcraft she practiced. I was never convinced by it, and I could never understand why so many people came to her."

"In the villages in the Apennines, certain traditions have lingered on. The people are all growing old."

Pitti looked the commissario in the eye again, but then quickly turned away. "That wasn't the only place she practised. Here in the city as well, and we're not talking about poor wretches but professional people, doctors even."

Soneri fiddled with his cigar for a moment or two, finding it hard to light it in the damp air. After the first puff, he gestured to Pitti to carry on, but it seemed he was still lost in thought.

"You think that's connected with what's happened?"

"I've no idea. It's more likely the abortions had some connection."

"I was told the opposite – that she did her best to help women who were having problems getting pregnant."

"That's true too. Ghitta could do all sorts of things. She was a diabolical woman," he added with a sarcastic smile.

Pitti talked and talked and Soneri saw the image of Ghitta he had fondly entertained for many years dissolve before his eyes. At the same time, a suspicion grew inside him – one which had nothing to do with the inquiry but which he found it hard to suppress.

"Who did she perform abortions on?" he said, with a trace of anxiety in his voice.

"In the early stages, on the girls in the house, but then there were married women as well, who couldn't let anyone know, their husbands above all."

Suspicion took root even more firmly in Soneri's mind, and one memory in particular set off a parallel, personal enquiry. Could the haemorrhage which killed Ada have been associated with the after-effects of a botched abortion? He had always rejected that hypothesis, but could recite by heart the medical report which implied that the cause of death might be linked to some unspecified "prior lesion". The photograph of Ada in the arms of another man came back to mind, and he found himself trembling on the brink of a void which was gaping open around him. He felt himself choking. He removed the cigar from his mouth and furiously spat out the smoke.

"Nobody ever really got to know Ghitta, and maybe that's why they killed her. She was hard to fathom. The most likely thing is that someone was afraid of her independence."

A car horn blared out in the mist and shortly afterwards Soneri heard the creak of Fadiga's trolley as it was trundled along the pavement. He was conscious that too many suspicions were distracting him and causing him to ask too many questions on an impulse, anything to fill up that silence which was swamping his thoughts.

"Who was that man you gave the money to?"

Pitti had not expected him to return to that subject and looked at him in surprise. It was only then that the commissario noticed that Pitti had skilfully guided him onto the subject of Ghitta's life in order to avoid difficult questions.

"A friend, I told you. I assure you he's got nothing to do with Ghitta's death. You'll know . . ." His voice trailed away for a moment. "I have many friends."

Soneri understood everything from the tone of voice. Pitti's sexual tendencies were easy to deduce, but perhaps that was not the real reason for the embarrassment from which he sought to extricate himself. "Are you always so grateful?"

"Are you always so crass?" Pitti said, in a thin voice.

A tense silence fell between them. After a few seconds, the commissario said, "Did Ghitta get into any bother over those abortions?"

"How would I know? It's more than likely. She was an expert, but after all she was a backstreet practitioner."

A doubt flashed into Soneri's mind with the speed of a bullet. Supposing it were all true? What if the germ of a hypothesis planted by the doctor after Ada's death really was the correct explanation of a wholly unexpected end? He lost his focus and all interest in Pitti, who was now observing him with deep incredulity. All of a sudden the commissario found he had no more questions to put to him. His mind struggled with images of the dark blood of foetuses ripped out by crude, improvised instruments, amid screams of pain. Slowly, overwhelmingly, he was assailed by that sense of the vanity of things which he had felt when faced with the photograph of his wife with another man, a vanity born from the wreckage of inner certainties he could no longer reconstruct.

He noticed that Pitti was studying him with an inquisitive expression and struggled to pull himself free of the grip of these violent emotions. He looked for way out of a conversation he could no longer endure.

"Where can I reach you?" He spoke in a tone that was meant to be friendly but which came out as an odd mixture of threat and supplication.

"I see you walk about a lot. So do I, so there'll be plenty of opportunities."

"Don't force me to play the policeman. I could have you followed, or I could have you brought in as a person who could help with our inquiry. That way everybody would know."

Pitti was alarmed. "There's no need. You can telephone me any time. Look in the directory under the name Gina

Montali, my mother. She lives in Borgo Marodolo. My name is Giancarlo Gualerzi. My mother always knows where I am and she can get a message to me. Please don't tell her you're from the police."

He turned to leave, but Soneri held him by the arm to check him. On Pitti's face there appeared a half excited, half timorous expression.

"So now I know who Pitti is, but who are Fastlast, Bolshoi and Rasp?"

"They too belong to Ghitta's dark side. She was a half moon – half in light, half in shadow."

"Somebody must know."

"Obviously you didn't know the woman very well," Pitti said, unintentionally twisting the blade in Soneri's wound. "She counted so many important people among her acquaintances, and they trusted her precisely because of her discretion. Only she knew who was concealed behind those code names she invented for each of her clients."

He gave every impression of being sincere. An ashen light wrapped itself around them as the street began to come to life. Some workmen in a lorry with a crane were busy putting up bunting and Christmas lights over the road.

When Soneri got back to the questura later in the day, he found Juvara waiting for him. The more time passed, the more unwilling he was to give up his meanderings around the city and take his seat in the offices of his division, even if his colleagues all left him plenty of freedom. He was the only one permitted to work on his own and turn up only sporadically at meetings. The organisational side of things was attended to by Juvara, who occasionally reproached him, but only hesitatingly, for his absences.

"What are you moaning about?" Soneri had said to him one day. "You can't wait to see me off, can you? Are you really not interested in getting ahead?"

The inspector had stared at him in amazement, and Soneri had realised at that moment what a decent man he was. On this occasion, however, Juvara's face was darker than usual. He began by showing him the record of the examination of the knife conducted by the forensic squad.

"Nanetti confirms that there are traces of the old woman's blood on it."

"Never doubted it," Soneri said, dismissing the report as a mere detail. "What else?"

"The questore tore a strip off me."

Through clenched teeth, the commissario uttered a "shit!" without Juvara hearing. He knew that the inspector bore the brunt of blame for faults which were not his, and that the real target was Soneri himself.

"What for?"

"There was a smash-and-grab yesterday and the thieves got away. The officers on duty said communication between us and the motorised division left a lot to be desired, and so a trade union official went to see the questore."

"Don't worry. He was getting at you for failings of mine. Did Capuozzo make much of a fuss?"

Juvara shrugged with a gesture which half implied assent. "Anyway, he's got it in for you too. He left word that he wants to see you this morning."

Soneri's irritation began to reach boiling point, so he decided it would be as well to reduce the heat by facing the questore without delay. Capuozzo's personal assistant's hypocritical smile caused his mood to darken further, and when he sat down opposite his superior, it continued to unsettle him, almost as much as the back of the old chair which jabbed him between the shoulders – like the barrel of a gun.

"Good to see you, Soneri. So how are we getting on with investigations on the landlady?"

He relaxed a bit at the question. It meant either that Capuozzo had got over his ill temper or that he too had been using Ghitta's for his assignations.

"Going to take time. It's not shaping up well."

"But you're on the job, working hard," the questore said acidly. It was not easy to make out whether that meant that he was getting nowhere, or that he was always absent, or perhaps both.

Soneri hesitated, unsure whether to reply in the same ironic tone or to ignore it. He chose the latter. "I'm doing my best, signor questore."

He instantly recognised the unconscious provocation in that "signor questore". Capuozzo went into a rage if he was not addressed as dottore. The words had slipped out, and now Capuozzo was making an obvious effort to remain calm, though he still looked like a man on the point of exploding.

"In all honesty Soneri, I see no sign of any great progress in this enquiry. I get annoyed when I read in the papers that we're groping about in the dark. They're on the telephone every two or three hours, and I don't know what to say. And you're never there. Now they're making up a story that there's some organised crime gang behind it all. I'm the one who's responsible for public security. It's my head that's on the block if it all goes wrong." He leaned over towards the commissario, stabbing his index finger three times against his chest with a theatrical flourish.

At this point, Soneri saw a solution flash before his eyes and without thinking he grabbed at it. "I'll drop the investigation. You can hand it over to one of our colleagues."

An embarrassed silence fell between the two men. For

Soneri this was not just another case. It was not merely an inquiry into Ghitta's death. The more he delved into it, the more he realised it was an investigation into himself. What was coming up as it developed was anything but pleasing.

"Really," he said with complete sincerity, "I don't feel like going on with it."

Capuozzo put his pen down beside a pile of papers. He clasped his hands, cracked his knuckles and leant forward once more, only this time he appeared preoccupied or deeply concerned. "Enough of this sort of talk. No more nonsense. I spoke that way to goad you on, but I realise . . . when all's said and done, it's only been a few days."

Soneri found the questore's regret flattering, even if he had no illusions about it. The feeling lasted no more than a moment, because immediately afterwards he understood Capuozzo's reasoning when the questore said: "They're all off on leave. Who could I give the case to? We can't exactly suspend investigations for a fortnight, can we?"

Soneri was one of the very few left in the office during the annual Christmas exodus, and his chief was only interested in ticking boxes. That was all there was to it. Taking advantage of the telephone ringing, the commissario rose to his feet. The questore waved him goodbye and he went out, floating on his own uselessness like fat on boiling water.

Juvara made an effort to stop him in the corridor, but even before he had a chance to open his mouth, Soneri cut him off with a brusque gesture. The commissario needed fresh air. He could not stand the stale atmosphere of the questura, an unmistakeable mixture of sweat, cheap perfume, cleaning products, smoke, dirt and half-full wastepaper baskets. He walked in the direction of Via Saffi, pursued by the stench. He had walked as far as Bettati's barbershop before he had managed to shake it off.

"Your hair obviously doesn't grow very quickly. It must be a good ten years since I last trimmed it for you."

"Unfortunately, it's longer than that," the commissario said.

Hardly anything had changed, apart from a few modern chairs among the padded seats where the bottoms of half the city had perched.

"The damp weather makes people want to hold on to their hair," Soneri said, looking round the empty room.

"The people who come to me don't have much hair to start with. The rest make their own arrangements. Anyway, I'm not going to be here much longer. Another couple of years until my pension matures and then I'll close down."

"I've not got much left now . . ."

"You think there's much left on me?" Bettati said, running his hand through his remaining locks, while at the same time looking in the mirror at his face and that of the commissario behind him. "The only ones of the old guard who held out were Ghitta and me. We don't see much of you nowadays. Is it true that the Schianchi woman has disappeared?"

The commissario nodded before sitting down in the barber's chair. For a moment, he had the illusion of being immersed in a scene from his youth, at a time when politics were regularly debated in Bettati's shop. It was a moment of concentrated pleasure he wished would last.

"Did you use to see much of Ghitta?"

"Not a lot recently. She always seemed to be carrying the world on her shoulders. The only thing that never changed was the Thursday trip to Rigoso – because of her son, among other things."

"Is he badly disturbed?"

"He's not quite right, but he's able to live on his own. She bought him a house in an area where he's practically the only resident. That way he doesn't disturb the neighbours."

"Is there nobody to look after him?"

"There must be somebody. There's a guy who comes to town from time to time – somebody from the village, judging by the clothes he wears."

"Any idea who he is?"

"None at all," the barber said, shaking his head. "I do know he brings her stuff from the villagers, fees for the treatment, mainly salame and home-made products. Ghitta takes her payment in kind, although don't ask me what she does with all that food now that she doesn't take in students."

"She has a different kind of client."

"I know, but they don't stop to eat all that often. They use their time in other ways."

"Do you know who used to hang about the pensione?"

"I hear rumours about important people, some of whom used to go there to study in their university days, but who go there now to get a leg over."

"Anyone you know?"

"No, there were so many of them. A bunch of long-haired weirdoes who never set foot in here. You were one of the few who ever got his hair cut."

"Well, I'm one of the better preserved of them," the commissario congratulated himself as he patted into place his mane of hair, now turning white at the temples.

Bettati took a look at his reflection in the mirror, and Soneri returned his gaze. The barber was getting on in years. As he raised his scissors and comb, his back had a definite stoop.

"You were the most moderate of a gang who would gladly let the world burn. Next to them, you were nearly a Fascist."

"Never a Fascist!"

"They used to say that about anyone who was different from them. They used to fill this shop with words and words and words. All that talk about the revolution, but when I looked at their hands they were delicate and lily white."

"They never did achieve the revolution."

"The problem is that the real proletariat didn't either. Say what you like but those kids were no proles."

From the mist which hung over the streets nearby there rang out isolated hammer blows which could be heard during the pauses in the conversation.

"Do you hear that?" Bettati said. "They're building a monument to the 1922 barricades. It's being worked on by two stonemasons from Crotone who haven't the least idea of what they're taking on. What's even worse is that the architect who drew up the plans, a young fellow whose speech is laced with English words, has no idea either. I spoke to him and he was convinced that it was something to do with clashes between workers and bosses. I explained to him that the bosses were represented by Balbo's Fascists and he was astonished that there were Fascists around as early as 1922."

"I don't recognise this district anymore," Soneri said. "What happened to all the people who used to live here?"

"A lot of them are dead, because the poor die young. The others have got rich and have built second homes outside the city. They don't come back anymore for fear it'd bring back memories of the days when they had patches on their arses. They hate anything to do with their past, because now they see themselves as respectable folk who vote for the right. They look down on the poor for the same reason. It reminds them of what they used to be."

"You mean the poor bastards who occupy the houses where they used to live?"

"Yes, because the new occupants aren't just poor – they're different. They're foreigners. They keep to themselves. They're not interested in changing the system. All they want to do is colonise the spaces that have been left empty, they want nothing to do with us. In all these years, not one of them has ever been inside my shop."

A sort of anguish, an unsettling feeling, seized hold of Soneri, bringing with it the sense of oppression he had experienced shortly before in the questura. Although he normally felt at home in it, the mist was now helping to imprison him. As Bettati's open razor ran down the back of his neck, he thought of the pork butcher's knife driven into Ghitta's heart and of the investigation which was keeping him locked in a cage of painful memories. By the time the barber removed the towel and shook it out, it was already completely dark outside. Bettati kept staring at Soneri's reflection in the mirror, as did the commissario himself. He seemed old and tired, and the longer he looked, the more the gap widened between what he was now and the image of himself he kept in his memory.

"Do you know the only one who has remained true to his principles?" the barber asked.

Soneri remained silent, inviting Bettati to go on.

"Fadiga. He made his own revolution, all by himself, by setting himself free of a world he no longer cared for."

"If nothing else, he's the only one who's not out for himself, but he has paid a heavy price for his choice of life."

Bettati nodded in agreement and the two stood silently under the neon light. The more he waited, the more Soneri felt his throat tighten with anxiety. He made to pull out his wallet, but Bettati stretched out his hand to stop him.

"No money. Nowadays I'm not in it for myself either. I stay open to talk to the old survivors, people like myself, or acquaintances who come back to visit. I only do it to keep myself alive a bit longer, and soon, as I said, I'm definitely going to shut down."

Soneri shook his hand and went out into the chill air.

Behind him, he heard the shutters of the barbershop slam down, and the noise gave him the shivers. A few seconds later, the mobile in his duffel coat pocket began to ring.

"Friar Fiorenzo was on the phone just now, sounding very agitated," Juvara said. "He says some guy called while he was doing catechism lessons, and insisted on meeting him right away. He's sure it's something to do with the death of the Tagliavini woman."

"Did he meet this man?"

"He couldn't get away from the children, but the man was in a rush and was quite threatening."

"So he's afraid?"

"I think so. He was also supposed to pretend that the caller was coming to make his confession. A set-up, in other words."

Soneri thought it over for a moment, pondering how many things seemed to gravitate around the church where Ghitta used to go to Mass.

"What happened?"

"Friar Fiorenzo was having none of it. The man hung up without making a definite appointment."

"Did the voice remind him of anyone?"

"No, there was nothing special about the tone of voice, but the friar did say he had the accent of someone from the mountain regions."

"Every day there's a new complication," Soneri said, thinking of that twisted mass of clues he could not untangle. "What about Fernanda? Any developments?"

"We've heard from her relatives in Milan, but they know nothing about her. Some of our colleagues went round to the house and confirmed that there has been no trace of the old girl."

"Ask Friar Fiorenzo to let us know immediately if the man calls back."

He was now walking down Via Saffi. As he passed No. 35 he glanced into the shisha bar, which was packed with customers. It was the only place which seemed to throb with life, joyful and disorderly, and to emit some enthusiasm for the future. Bettati's admiration for Fadiga had reminded Soneri of their agreement. When he reached Piazzale dei Servi, he waited for a car to turn into a courtyard through a heavy iron gate before slipping into the murky gloom of the hedges where Fadiga slept. He rummaged through the mound of cardboard, paper and meagre belongings. Fadiga had been as good as his word. Soneri found some pages torn from a newspaper and tucked under a cellophane-covered cushion. He stuck them in his pocket without looking at them and made off before he could be observed.

Angela was waiting for him in front of the Duomo. "Ready for lesson two?"

"I got too much from lesson one. I'm withdrawing from the course."

"Don't overestimate your intelligence. You've still got a lot to learn."

"Don't I know it! I was on the verge of abandoning the investigation, but the others are all on leave, so Capuozzo forced me to stay on. Do you think I'll be more motivated now?"

"You were about to commit an act of gross stupidity, commissario. No question about it. You're none too popular with your superiors because you're a kind of anarchist policeman, but if you throw in the towel you're only playing their game. Do you want to end up in charge of the passport office?"

"This is no ordinary investigation. I've had enough of probing into a past which is also my own. Did you know that Ghitta was carrying out abortions on the girls lodging with her? Did you know that on the official medical report on Ada's death it was stated that the death might have been caused by a prior lesion? All the rest is down to Ghitta, to the ideas that were in the air and to this unrecognisable district of the city. I'm not paid to wallow in my past. All I have to do is find out who killed the old woman."

Angela looked at him with a mixture of understanding and severity before her expression darkened. "I can't occupy your attention in the here and now – that's the real problem."

Soneri was too weighed down by his own depression to do anything to lighten Angela's mood, but he had no wish to appear a complete egoist by simply ignoring it, so he stretched out his hand and squeezed hers. It was enough. Emotional displays were not part of their repertoire.

They held on to each other as they began to walk towards San Giovanni Evangelista and the narrow streets of a city which had changed under the skin, where time and its larvae were burrowing into the old, flaccid body, causing it to decompose. They quickened their step, walking arm in arm now, clinging more and more tightly to each other as they recalled a whole catalogue of places associated with episodes in their own relationship, chattering freely with the candour of young people remembering a childhood from which they had only recently emerged. Their conversation was soon tinged with a sense of the cruelty of time passing, taking their dreams with it. The pain that this emotion induced led them to take refuge in adolescent acts. Still holding hands, they started to run, in part out of the illusion of being still young, in part to escape from the spectres that were gathering around them. As they ran, they came together in an embrace, stumbling over each other's feet as they did so. When they leaned against a wall to get their breath back, they were in a highly emotional state. Soneri heard Angela sniffling a bit in the chill, but he himself was overwhelmed by a mixture of emotions – sadness and happiness, nostalgia and anxiety for the future, a realisation of the naivety of their childish behaviour, a sense of the ridiculous, of the longevity of memory and of the impermanence of the present which coloured it, continually enhancing it.

Soneri took Angela by the hand once again. "Let's go," he whispered to her and they headed in silence for the *Milord*. They asked Alceste for a table in a corner.

"We shouldn't do this anymore," she said, still excited. "We shouldn't let ourselves get carried away by our emotions."

Soneri made no reply. He knew it was impossible as long as he was tied up with this investigation. "It would be as well to suspend the lessons," was all he said a few moments later.

"That was no lesson, more like an excercise in mindfulness."

"Time to order the antidote," Soneri said, turning to the menu.

He saw that tripe had been added in pencil at the bottom, ideal for dipping chunks of bread into. He ordered a bottle of Bonarda. He had never understood drinkers so well before, especially those who needed at least two glasses before facing the world and fooling themselves they were dominating it.

Angela had no need of alcohol to recover. Her warlike spirit was sufficient. Tears for her were only a brief retreat while she prepared for a fresh offensive. She gave Alceste, who had never really taken to her, the usual order of grilled vegetables and tap water.

"Do you want me to decant the whole bottle?" Alceste asked Soneri, indicating the Bonarda.

"I'll be happy to offer you a glass or two."

"You'll get cirrhosis of the liver."

"Either that or depression. I've no idea which is preferable. Remember what they used to say at university? Depression takes more prisoners than repression."

Soneri poured himself half a glass, sniffed the wine at length and took a couple of sips. "Didn't I tell you we needed an antidote?" he said, taking out the newspaper cuttings Fadiga had left for him.

He spread them out on the table under Angela's uncomprehending gaze. She quickly read out the headlines until Soneri stopped her. "The articles don't matter. It's the pictures that count."

"Old acquaintances?" Angela said.

"These are the people who used to go to Ghitta's to get laid."

She did not reply at once, staring instead at the newsprint faces of Franco Pecorari, Chair of the Council Planning Committee, and Renato Avanzini, C.E.O. of a construction firm. "Well, Pecorari was always well known for frequenting brothels. He used to preach free love, but only so he could enjoy it as often as possible. I'm surprised about Avanzini, always going on about his wife and family and always attending Mass at the Duomo."

"They're the worst kind of hypocrite," Soneri said.

She gave him an inquisitive look. "And now that you've found out about these peccadilloes, what do you make of it? There's a lot of it going on."

"Unfortunately, I'm not making anything of it. But suppose someone had tried their hand at blackmail, maybe even Ghitta herself."

Angela looked sceptical. "Why would she want to risk cutting off a source of revenue? After all, there was no great effort involved for her. All she had to do was prepare a couple of rooms, take care that the various couples never ran into each other, change the linen afterwards and occasionally make a meal with the excellent local produce of her mountain village. That's all there was to it."

The commissario took out a cigar, cut off the tip and stuck it in his mouth without lighting it, purely for the pleasure of rolling it about between his teeth and tongue. "It was Fadiga who put these cuttings aside for me. He says he often sees photographs of the men who used to go to the pensione in the papers. These are the first that he found."

"And they won't be the last."

Soneri bent over his plate of tripe and began to dip his bread into it. "If only I knew where Fernanda was," he muttered to himself, now convinced that he was responsible for having got himself into the hole he was in. If only he had been willing to meet her, if only they had recognised each other and broken the ice which had formed over the years due to their different roles in life, perhaps she would have provided some valuable clues for understanding what lay behind Ghitta's death. Had she not come to see him and no-one else? He would have been spared all this rummaging about in his memory. Everything was down to that initial error.

"You can't change what's happened, so you're just wasting time going over it. If you were a writer, you could score out a page and rewrite it, but in life there's no going back," Angela said, lifting a stick of celery to her mouth, but with little appetite.

"All I want to do is work out precisely what took place. I'm trying to give meaning to things, and I proceed by making one attempt after another. I only deal with what is plausible."

"But at times you're playing with risky hypotheses, as in

the case of Ada. In your line of work, you should know how to control excesses of imagination."

"I have proof that she had a relationship with another man before me. There's nothing to prove that she had an abortion, but I'm sure of it."

Angela threw her hands in the air and let them fall to her sides, as though facing the inevitable. "And supposing that's true? What would it change?"

"For so many years I've clung to an image of her that turns out to be far removed from the reality."

"Nothing can wipe out the happiness you enjoyed."

"No, Angela. It's just that we're made of nothingness, of illusions, appearances. Investigations do little more than reconstruct the mechanics of the facts, and that does not amount to much. Finding out who stuck the knife into Ghitta's heart, the nature of the wound, its depth and the kind of haemorrhage, that's no more than scraping the surface of a fact. But the killer's motive, the dance of phantoms which produced the rage – these are matters which can never be fully understood. At best you can make an intuitive guess, but it's a desperate business. The whole truth can never be grasped – our understanding of reality can only be partial."

Angela put down her fork, and sat lost in thought. Soneri's speech had upset her, perhaps because she was thinking along the same lines herself. He had spoken with such merciless clarity. In spite of the bitterness with which he had expressed himself, she liked her commissario all the more for these outbursts, which showed him to be more sensitive and more vulnerable than he would like to admit.

"One of these days I have to go to Rigoso. I want to understand the relationship Ghitta had with the people in the village," Soneri said.

"Will there be a hotel there? I'd love one of those old-fashioned country bedrooms with mismatched furniture and two chairs to hang your clothes over. Here, everybody goes to bed with everybody else, so couldn't we just . . ." Angela burst our laughing.

6

HE LEFT HOME very early, at an hour when the morning
frost made the hedgerows glisten, and when the swaying
Christmas lights sent waves of golden brightness through the
mist. The questura was almost deserted at that time, a situation he preferred. As he walked along the corridor, still heavy
with the smell of cleaning products, he heard his office telephone ringing. He leapt into the darkened room, bumping
into a chair and knocking over piles of papers. He was out
of breath as he replied to a strong, firm voice on the other
end – a voice more used to the pulpit. "It's Friar Fiorenzo, and
there's someone here who would like to speak to you."

"I'm on my way," he said simply. He knew who was waiting
for him.

He strode towards the piazza and as he crossed it the
clock on the campanile in the Palazzo del Governatore struck
seven. He entered the church by the side door, where the
friar was waiting for him. Soneri exchanged understanding
glances with him before looking along the benches at an
elderly, somewhat corpulent, man, his leathery skin tanned by
exposure to the sun in the fields.

"How long has he been here?" he said quietly.

"More than an hour. He arrived with a shift-worker who
comes to the city every morning."

"Did you manage to hear his confession this time?"

"I've taken care of his conscience. The rest is up to you."

Soneri picked his way along the rows of seats and only when he was beside him did the man turn abruptly, the way deaf people do. He smiled, revealing gaps among his long teeth, and held out a hand the colour of chestnut wood and resembling a tangle of roots.

"My name is Ettore Chiastra, a friend of Ghitta's." His introduction was awkward, accompanied by a slight bow. Looking doubtfully at the elderly ladies who were moving silently about the naves of the church, he added, "I've been looking for you for two days."

"I thought it was Friar Fiorenzo you were after," Soneri said.

"Well, the things I have to say to him are of a different order from those I have to tell you."

"I'm interested in everything to do with Ghitta."

The old man gave a smile. "I doubt it. We're talking about very private matters."

"When there's a crime involved, it makes no difference."

"I don't know if they've told you about me and Ghitta."

Soneri nodded. "There was some link-up," he said, joining his index fingers together, "and you were a married man."

For a few moments Chiastra, with the air of a man trying to ward off a blow, remained silent. "So you know. Ghitta lived the life she did. I was part of it, in other words."

"Is that remorse? Is that why you were looking for Friar Fiorenzo?"

"There's a bit of remorse, yes, but there's also the fact that my life has been knocked off course. You'll know that . . ."

Once again Soneri nodded in agreement. "After the scandal broke, when did you get back together?"

"We never really lost touch. We carried on writing to each

other during the period we were forced to stay apart."

"And more recently?"

"Now I give her a hand looking after her business in Rigoso."

"Does she have property there as well?"

The old man raised a hand as though the matter was completely obvious. "A great deal. Half the village is hers."

"And where did she get all that money?"

"Where do you think? She didn't need much to live on and what she earned she squirrelled away. And then there was that other factor."

"What other factor?"

"Resentment. She never reconciled herself to the fact that the village had put her on the street. She couldn't cope with being seen as someone who stole other women's husbands. As a whore, in other words."

"Did she suppose she could restore her reputation?"

"I don't know. But not one of them has ever changed their opinion of her. Maybe that's why she started buying up the whole village. You can hate the rich, but it's not so easy to despise them."

"Houses?"

"Many houses. She even bought a building with a bar, a boarding house and a doctor's surgery. She went as far as renting offices to the town council. She was out for revenge for the way she had been treated. She once said, 'They can say anything they like, but at the end of the day, it's me they all come to'."

"She didn't look like someone who had a head for business."

"You're wrong there. She could sniff out business opportunities like a hunting dog going after a hare. She was on top of everything that was going on. You know that she went from house to house curing illnesses?"

"Yes, she was the medicine woman," Soneri said, with a touch of irony.

Chiastra looked at him with a serious, worried expression. "You can believe what you want, but she cured everybody, otherwise they wouldn't have been so afraid of her."

"I know. She threatened them, even as she healed them."

"She knew what to say. She was articulate, and she had a tongue that could cut glass."

"The same as the people in your town. What did they say when the two of you began to lord it over them?"

"Nothing much, the same as before, but the difference was that this time we had the upper hand." He paused for a moment before adding, "And anyway, money always makes everything more acceptable."

Soneri took out a cigar but as he was about to light it, the reproachful glance of an elderly woman in a black veil brought him back to himself and reminded him he was in a church.

"Feel better now?" the commissario asked, gesturing towards the confessional. "You've offloaded all your regrets?"

"It was high time for me to face facts and put things right. I don't care much for my life now, but Ghitta was once young and pretty. She was lively and carefree, but I was a married man. To be frank, she had more to lose than me."

"And then there's the question of the boy."

The old man was obviously taken aback for a moment, and slumped against his pew. "That was the worst mishap of all. If only he had been the same as the others."

"Who's looking after him now?"

"He was in an institution for a long time, until Ghitta bought him a house that was out of the way. The social workers bring him food, but he lives like a savage. I try to go and visit him every so often, but he drives me away. He believes he's Mussolini's son, and delivers speeches to the few people who pass by."

A couple of tourists paid the fifty centesimi to illuminate the church and Soneri's eyes were immediately drawn to the chapel of Sant'Egidio. The sudden, unexpected burst of light changed the atmosphere and broke the intimacy of the conversation. After his momentary discomfort, Chiastra's expression was once again calm and controlled. The commissario decided it was time to change the subject.

"Ghitta used various nicknames for the people who came to her pensione. She wrote them down in a notebook I found in her bedroom, but I've no idea who they refer to," Soneri said, handing the list to Chiastra.

After laboriously putting on a pair of glasses, the man looked it over. "I've heard her use those names," he said, returning the list with no apparent sign of emotion, "but I don't know who these people were. Ghitta didn't have complete confidence in anyone, not even me." He seemed proud of this fact, and paused again before asking, "Are you sure there aren't some names missing?" He pointed to the list with his calloused hand.

Soneri looked again at the sheet of paper and reflected. "Could be. Do you remember any others?"

"Chiastra took back the list. "There's certainly one that's not here."

"Who?"

"Somebody known as Rosso, the Red. I don't know who he is. I once heard Ghitta speak on the telephone to someone or other and call him by that name. I remember she seemed very uneasy."

Soneri thought it over. "Are you saying she was afraid?"

"Perhaps. I'm not sure. She was agitated, let's say. In all the years I'd known her I'd never seen her in such a state."

"How long ago did all this happen?"

"Not long. Two months, perhaps. The cows had just come down from the mountains."

A pew behind them creaked, and Soneri turned to see an old woman moving away, muttering to herself because she had been disturbed by their whispering.

"Was she in that state even later?"

Chiastra stared at him and shook his head. "It's obvious you didn't know Ghitta. A real iron lady. After a quarter of an hour she'd forget everything." He spoke admiringly.

Was that why the murderer had been so cool? Ghitta was unafraid of any impending danger and was sure of her ability to control everyone around her. A whole world rotated around her – old students who had made their fortune, a village she had taken over, a circle of furtive, high-placed couples who relied on her discretion, not to mention girls and married women coping with unwanted pregnancies. Maybe the man who had killed her had nothing to do with these circles. But then there was that knife used in the slaughter of pigs.

"Do you know Elvira Cadoppi?"

Chiastra did not reply directly. "She has a room at the pensione."

"I gather she was the only permanent resident, because the rest . . ." Soneri said.

The man made a circular motion with his hand in the air. "Ghitta got both the Cadoppis out of trouble, even if they hate her for it. They were up to their necks in debt, and they couldn't pay their mortgage because their shop ran into difficulties. Ghitta paid everything off and took their house. That's normal, isn't it? She only took the walls, you might say. She let them live in it for a nominal rent, but she made Elvira come to the city to help her. She even found her a job as a sales assistant."

"It was all so easy for her."

"Ghitta knew a lot of people. And some of the guests of the pensione went on to become very influential"

"What kind of help did Elvira give her?"

"Cleaning up, various errands."

"She told me she never stopped working."

"Don't believe her. She used to give herself airs and graces, making out that she did whatever she wanted, but she was under Ghitta's thumb. She knew Ghitta could throw her and her family out the house at Rigoso, or could get her dismissed from her job."

"Doesn't she live in Capoponte?"

"I think her man lives there. It's not her house at all." Chiastra gave a snigger. "There's so much nonsense being talked."

"Who is her man?"

"Who could say? She's had so many I've lost count. Anyway, I don't know the younger generation."

All of a sudden an organ struck up and Soneri saw a priest cross the transept in front of the statue of Sant'Uldarico. The old women got to their feet and Soneri realised for the first time just how many of them there were. "Are you going to visit Ghitta in the mortuary?" he asked Chiastra.

Chiastra gave a nod before turning away, stumbling as he walked and making the sign of the cross before the high altar.

Soneri left the church without seeing Friar Fiorenzo. Now that the lights were off, the city seemed to him as dull as a ballerina without her sequins. He walked smartly in the direction of Via Saffi, and stopped at No. 35. The shisha bar was already open, with the usual uproar spilling out onto the street. He went in, but the stale smell of tobacco, the aromas and incense make him feel an outsider. Cartons of cigarettes and lighters were on sale at a table, while in a corner a thin man was cutting hair and shaving his fellow countrymen, who were seated in a row waiting, as though in a surgery. Mohammed was leaning on the bar, smoking quietly, heedless of the crush around him. Everyone seemed to know what to do and where to go, independently of him, so did no more than mark in a notebook what each one had taken. His wife attended to everything else.

Soneri showed him the photographs of Pecorari and Avanzini. Mohammed looked at them intently, but only for a few seconds. "Many times," he said, pointing to the door of the pensione. "Even twice a day."

"Who did they go with?"

Mohammed gave a malicious smile. "How should I know? The couples never arrived together. One first, then the other later. Sometimes they would come along, ring the buzzer, talk over the intercom, turn away and come back ten minutes later."

"What happened in the meantime?"

"Sometimes another person would turn up. Or else nothing happened."

"A woman, perhaps?"

"No. As I was saying, often no-one would come at all."

The commissario lit his cigar and thought this over. He was being given so many contradictory signals and could not decipher any of them. Mohammed's voice brought him back to himself. "The couples who want to keep out of sight are very careful. Don't forget that I used to work in a hotel. In hotels, people like to book separate rooms as though they don't know each other and arrive at different times, understand? Maybe they'd told the old woman to keep them apart. Maybe some of her clients preferred the others who used her premises not to know about them."

"What about the ones who came on their own?"

Mohammed gave a smile with his ebony eyes and shrugged. "It didn't happen very often. Elvira and that other guy, the one in the strange clothes." As he spoke, he made little effeminate movements. "They did come and go by themselves."

"Did you see them a lot?"

Mohammed nodded. "The last time was yesterday evening. Elvira also used to go to collect rents for Ghitta."

Soneri said nothing until a bearded Pakistani, speaking halting Italian, stuck a tray of lighters under his nose. Mohammed brushed him off with a peremptory wave. "You didn't know Ghitta was so rich, did you? She didn't seem to be," he said with a malicious smile.

The commissario was no longer concerned with that but with what he remembered of the district and of how different that memory was from the reality now opening out before him. For him it was a process of continuous, painful discovery, and he realised that behind the pain there lay a defeat. For a moment he had the impression of having lost his centre, the fixed point to which he had always been anchored. He tried to chase away that anguished sensation and succeeded only with an effort. Mohammed continued talking, but his voice seemed to him like a part of a discourse that had no sense.

"Ghitta really did have a lot of money. Around here alone she had something like ten apartments, or so Aref tells me. She helped women when . . . these are things nobody else does and that's why they cost so much. But the older women were afraid of her. They called her a witch and she threatened to lay a curse on them. Elvira treated them very badly. She was tough, that one."

"What about the man?" Soneri said, alluding to Pitti. "Did he do the same job?"

"No, he's not tough at all. He carried messages."

"What kind of messages?"

"Once he came here and told us that some person with money wanted to buy the bar. He was very insistent, and even went so far as to offer me three times what I had paid. But what would I do with all these people? Where would they go?"

Mohammed looked around and his glance invited Soneri to observe the number of people inside the bar.

"Did you understand why he was so keen on the purchase?"

"No. I'd never have paid so much for a place like this, but obviously he had his reasons."

By the time Soneri left the bar half the morning had gone. As he walked he called Juvara. He needed a report on Ghitta's estate. "I'm telling you she was stinking rich."

"It looked like she was on the verge of starvation."

"It's people like that who always hide the biggest surprises."

It was not Ghitta's estate that upset Soneri. The rooms in the pensione lined up in the order he had seen them on the day of the murder came back to mind, and in that image, making brief appearances, he once more found Ada. These images were no more than flashes, but they brought such great pain as to induce him to entrust to the inspector the task of tracing some of the student nurses who had been lodgers in the Pensione Tagliavini. He deluded himself that he would be able to stand back from the aspects of the investigation he found too painful.

In the meantime he reached Via Dalmazia, and picked out Aref behind a barrier of cardboard boxes. He spent ten minutes trying to get from him at least one of the addresses of the old women Mohammed had mentioned, but it was impossible to pin him down or penetrate his faltering, bizarre Italian. Finally, reluctantly, the commissario pulled rank and produced his identity card. Aref seemed terrified and dived behind his counter as though afraid of being assaulted.

"I only want one name and one address," Soneri said, trying to calm the man with the offer of a cigar.

Aref appeared reassured, though his worried, wary expression hardly changed.

"One name: Teresa," he finally said. "She live Via Corso Corsi, number fifteen, second floor. I bring her shopping."

The commissario made a vague sign of thanks and set off, now sinking into one of his ill-humoured moods. There was a pale sun overhead and the Trebbiano-tinted light indicated to Soneri that it must be near midday. In a short while the sky would cloud over, trapping the dullness among the houses.

He stood with his finger on the bell for some time before the door was opened. He read on the intercom the name TERESA RODOLFI, with a two in Roman numerals followed by the letter P.

The woman was stooped and appeared to be in pain. When Soneri explained the reason for his visit, the little warmth in her expression evaporated.

"Don't be afraid. She's dead."

"I know, but when anyone dies that way it's as if they'd left an order for a vendetta to be carried out against someone, and I've had enough of that sort of thing."

The woman sat down and appeared deeply troubled.

"Were you so afraid of her?"

"She was not like other women. There must have been a devil inside her. If you only knew how she would look at you while she was uttering those incomprehensible words."

"You mean while she was performing her rites?" Soneri suggested, recalling the faith healers he had known in country villages.

"Exactly. While she was muttering away, she would look up and you could see a demon in her eyes."

"What did she treat you for?"

"I had St Anthony's fire, and no doctor was able to get rid of it for me, so I went to Ghitta. She was known to everybody around here."

"And did she heal you?"

"In one week. From that point on I began to be afraid of her."

"Because she threatened you? Or because you were afraid of her powers?"

"She never openly threatened me. She was too clever for that. She would tell you about things that would make you afraid, or else talk about specific cases. By the end, I found I was dependent on her and her practices even after my problem with St Anthony's fire had been cleared up. That was the only way I could feel alright. When you are old and on your own you need to be reassured and she had that power, but at the same time she made it clear that just as she had freed you of your fears, she could as easily toss you back into an inferno of torments. That's why no-one had the courage to take her on."

"Why did you sell your house to her?"

"Do you imagine she didn't have her price?" The woman spoke with real feeling. "Oh yes, she made you pay alright. In the early stages, she would mark everything down as though they were small debts at a corner shop, but it gradually started to add up and she began to say it was time . . . But by then you were done for. Where could I ever have got all that money? Then she would say not to worry, that she would find a solution, but all the time the debt was rising. Then she started saying that if the money wasn't found, all the pain she had driven away would come back at once, and that anyone who didn't come up with the money would suffer the torments of hell. Can you imagine? So I decided to sell, but the man who did the valuation put a low price on it as a favour to her. She knew everyone. The result was I had to sell at a knockdown price, and she was the one who bought it. I went from being owner to tenant, and month after month that rabid bitch Elvira would come round . . ."

By now she was almost spitting her words, and Soneri was taken aback by how a little scratching, no more effort than hens do in the dirt, was sufficient to uncover the dung beetles. It was his job to claw away at the surface and come up with new theories, however provisional or incomplete they might prove to be.

"And she had you by the neck when it came to the rent too?"

"No, I can't say her demands were exorbitant. She special-ised in keeping people dangling, not choking them. She didn't charge me over the odds, but she had a way of making you aware that at any moment she could raise the price or throw you out altogether."

"Was she like that with other people as well?"

"Of course! In some cases, she would stoop to outright blackmail."

"Who did she blackmail?"

"I couldn't exactly say, but I do know the victims included some important women she had carried out abortions for. She didn't threaten them as such, but she would drop hints, let various things be understood, suggest that she knew such-and-such a person in the city. The result was they would do her favours, offer her little gifts. They kept her sweet and her every wish became a command."

"She used Elvira as her enforcer in these cases?"

"I don't think so. I don't know. I believe these were matters she attended to herself. I do know that in the past she used the girls in her establishment as nurses, and they all kept their mouths shut because Ghitta knew their little secrets. Some of them had abortions thanks to her."

Soneri's concentration wandered as he pursued spectres from his own past. Who knows what Ada might have done that was unknown to him? He had tried to fight off his anxiety, but now it was embedded in his being and snapped at him everywhere he turned in this investigation that he so longed to be relieved of.

When he recovered himself, he could see that Teresa was studying him. He rose smartly to his feet. "Well, now you're free of all these ghosts from the past and you can relax," he said, taking his leave.

He, on the other hand, was now surrounded by them. His mood was so low that he felt the need of a lunch at the *Milord*. Alceste's joviality, so typical of Parma, and the scents and tastes of the restaurant, would, he was sure, have the same effect on him as Ghitta's practices had on the old ladies. Everyone relied on their own superstitious rites, and his were Bonarda wine, *tortelli di erbetta* and a few slices of *culatello*. As he was taking his place he had a call from Juvara who had found a former nursing student who had boarded at the Pensione Tagliavini. She was from the mountains, like Ghitta, but from a village lower down the valley than Rigoso. Soneri was about to tell him to go and interview her, but how could he explain to him all he wanted him to find out? Once more, personal issues mingled with the investigation. Once more there were tasks he could not delegate.

Perhaps in view of that, he sank a bottle of Gutturnio, lingering over it and delaying getting to his feet. He sought that slight tipsiness advocated by Socrates as a lubricant of dialogue, but once he had left the *Milord* and was out on the dull and misty streets, he felt fearfully sober and cowed. He would have to listen once more to things about Ada he had never known, and another layer of inner certainty would be torn away.

He entered a neat and tidy house which reminded him of a dentist's waiting room. One glance at Marta Bernazzoli was sufficient to make him realise that he was dealing with a woman who never set aside her role as a nurse, not even outside the hospital. She was straitlaced and gaunt, and her very words seemed to cut with the precision of a scalpel.

Soneri sat down on a low sofa with chrome arms, and he pictured the woman in front of him standing in a long green gown with a mask over her face. He immediately understood that she lived on her own, and his thoughts raced to the abortions carried out by Ghitta. Her expression was half curious, half inquisitive.

"Have you formed any theories?" she said.

He shook his head. "Not so far. But I've seen various hypotheses dissolve in front of my eyes."

"That's a start. It might help clarify certain things," she said, as she took a seat facing him. There was a touch of irony in her voice.

"How long were you a lodger with Ghitta?"

"Four years."

"The nursing course only lasts three years."

"I stayed on a bit after the diploma. I needed time to fix things up, find somewhere to live."

"Of course, you're from outside the city."

The woman smiled, but it didn't reach her eyes. "I come from a place not too far from Rigoso."

She sounded somewhat piqued, and Soneri read in her

tone that rancour towards the world which lonely people sometimes feel.

"How did you get on with Ghitta?"

"We were young and she held us in check. She was like a mother to us."

"Did she get you out of trouble if anything went wrong?"

"If it was necessary. I know what you're getting at, and I suppose that's what we have to expect from a police officer," she said bitterly, almost contemptuously.

"It's my job. I have to scrape about in the mud, but I didn't spread the mud in the first place."

"Quite so," Marta replied severely, as though she were dealing with a clinical report. "Ghitta carried out abortions. That freedom was not granted to women at that time. Now it can even be done in a hospital."

"But she carried on afterwards, when an abortion could be obtained legally."

"Some women required absolute discretion. This is a small city, and Ghitta had an excellent reputation. I mean, there were never any accidents."

Each time she answered a question, Marta would peer at him with a cold look which did not conceal a certain impatience. Soneri could not work out if the look was meant to signal the end of the conversation, or had another purpose.

"She didn't teach you anything, did she? You're in obstetrics now."

Marta's expression hardened. "Do you think she didn't know what I was studying? There were girls who got into bother and she got them out of it. As she did with all the other women. Obviously she asked for something in return, especially from those who were training to be nurses."

The commissario felt his heart skip a beat, and his hands tremble. "Were there many?"

"I couldn't tell you about all of them. There were rumours flying about. Ghitta would say: 'Come and I'll teach you the business,' and they had to run. She didn't know the first thing about medicine. She relied on instinct."

"How long did she carry on?"

"How should I know? From the day I left I had no wish to hear any more about her, but I believe she went on as long as she could." Marta's words sounded more and more acerbic, as though shards of broken glass were cutting into her resentment.

"I can see you don't have happy memories of those days," Soneri said.

"And why should I? Ghitta was not what she seemed. She was a woman who . . ." She stopped there, but what she wanted to say was entirely clear.

"She seems to have made a good impression on many others who passed through the Pensione Tagliavini," Soneri said tentatively.

Marta's face grew dark, and a bitter, desolate smile gave a glimpse of what she was feeling inside herself.

"When you think back to your youth, you're always indulgent," she said with a forced laugh. "Unconsciously we falsify our recollections, and things that were nasty become pleasing. It's a consoling need, and it allows us to believe that a part of our life was lived to the full, while today . . . every one of us feels the compulsion to dream up a realm of gold so as to ward off the idea that we suffered without really living. That's especially the case for people like me, who now. . ." Her voice trailed off and the commissario thought she was on the verge of tears, but a moment later he saw her expression harden once more. He focused on the sense of what she had been saying and once again something seemed to snap inside him.

However regretfully, he shared Marta's judgments and so

summoned up the courage to ask her what he had worked out a short time previously. "So you too had to make use of Ghitta's services?"

The woman glared at him, perhaps trying in vain to recover that mask of coldness and semi-contempt with which she had first greeted him, but after a moment she seemed to accept that there was no escape. Without saying a word, her expression turned serious and almost imperceptibly she nodded several times

"That's why you hate Ghitta and those years with her?"

"Yes, but that's not the only reason."

The commissario felt a worrying compassion for her, and was even darkly attracted by her pain, to which, like so many of his age, he attributed the value of testimony. For that reason, he forged ahead with a line of questioning which had little to do with the investigation, but the fact of detecting in others an experience similar to his own helped to calm the surge of feelings whirling in his head.

"What else happened to you in those years?"

"You know perfectly well. You're a police officer, aren't you?"

"Can we wind back a bit? I'm not all that old."

"You surely remember the Dallacasa case."

"Yes, but I wasn't in the police force then. It happened twenty-five years ago."

"We're not so young any more. Mario was my man," she said, speaking as though she were choking.

"Did the crime take place before or after . . . ?"

"The abortion?" Marta burst out, no longer holding back, seeking to cope with her own emotions by recovering her steely reserve. "He was killed three months later. We were both students, and we agreed that we wouldn't be able to look after the baby. Mario was deeply involved in politics. He was an extra-parliamentary activist, as they were called then. If only I'd known . . . I lost my partner and my son in the one act. For me everything ended then and there."

"I seem to remember that the murder ended up being filed away without anyone being charged."

"The police couldn't have cared less about the case. Many of your colleagues wanted Mario dead. Have you any idea how often he was beaten up by the riot squad?"

"There were many investigations into the neo-Fascists, but nothing came of them."

"Even if they had gone after them, there was a cover-up at the highest levels. Nearly all policemen are right-wingers, but in spite of that, there was something strange about Mario's story. Can I tell you something one of your people told me in the strictest confidence? He said, 'You lot on the left kill one another. You don't even respect your comrades.' In the final analysis, they didn't want to stick their nose into internal feuds. They were quite happy there was one fewer activist to worry about."

"Do you have any ideas of your own?"

"I think the policeman was probably right. It wasn't easy to catch Mario out. He knew each and every one of the neo-Fascists. He was clever and they could never have trapped him in an ambush. And then there was the evidence of one person, the last man who saw him alive. He said he had seen him get into a car, apparently quite willingly. After that there was nothing more until they found the body."

"Were there political disputes with his comrades?"

"There were lively discussions, even quarrels from time to time, but Mario didn't talk to me much about his group. He kept his mouth shut on that front. He would disappear for weeks at on end, and wouldn't tell me what he had been doing. As he left he would say he was going to meet friends in different parts of Italy for conferences, meetings, seminars, but I never got to know what they were discussing."

Soneri looked around the room and again got the impression of immaculate but ascetic and soulless cleanliness. It looked like a den furnished with geometric rationality but with no trace of anything of sentimental value, perhaps to keep at bay the ceaseless assault of regret. He got to his feet, as did Marta. She walked along the hallway beside him in silent embarrassment. When they got to the front door, the commissario paused a moment with his hand on the door knob. "Did you know a student nurse called Ada Loreti?"

Marta stared at him intensely for a few moments, giving him the impression that her blue-grey eyes were peering into his soul. She nodded without saying a word.

"She was one of those that Ghitta . . . ?" Marta kept her eyes glued to the floor, only gradually raising them towards the walls, avoiding Soneri as though she were afraid of him. Then suddenly, she said, "I couldn't be sure. She was two years behind me. She had a different circle of friends."

"Try to remember. Don't be afraid of telling the truth."

"Forget it, commissario. Don't pay any heed to malicious gossip. I've only ever heard rumours. Resign yourself to the idea that the truth is beyond our reach. We've got to make do with what we see with our own eyes. It's just a matter of having trust in them."

She seemed immoveable and once again her eyes had the scornful glint they had had when she opened the door to him. He turned brusquely away and went down the stairs more ill at ease with himself than ever.

When he found himself on the street, he realised the afternoon had gone and that the light on one of the shortest days of the year was fading over the roofs of the houses on Via Saffi.

Juvara was slow to reply and was breathing heavily when he picked up the receiver. "Were you down in the cellar or sitting on Capuozzo's knee?" Soneri said.

"He's away on leave. His deputy's in charge now."

"Another one down! So there's only you and me, and that arsehole Chillemi."

"What can I do for you?"

"If there's anyone still around, could you get them to pull out the folders on the Dallacasa case?"

"I'll have them left on your desk."

In Piazzale dei Servi the sky was growing darker as night approached. He thought of Fadiga's refuge and went along to search inside it. Among the cardboard boxes, he found some new newspaper cuttings with a couple of photographs, one of a well-known lawyer, Aristide Zanni, and the other of the Chair of the Council Trade Committee, Romolo Gatti.

He hardly had time to study their innocent faces when his mobile rang. Angela wanted to meet him in front of the Battistero.

"This city's a bordello," were her opening words when they met.

Soneri was forced to agree. They made their way to the centre, with her insisting on taking his arm even if he disliked that way of walking. A crowd of people desperate to make last-minute purchases were crowded in front of the shop windows in Via Repubblica, like moths around a lamp. Angela tried to kiss him just as a police patrol was making its way slowly along the street.

"Do you want to ruin my reputation? That lot," he said,

pointing to the officers, "are capable of blabbing that Commissario Soneri has been seen in public smothering some woman in kisses while the murder inquiry is getting nowhere."

"Alright, let's go up to my office," Angela said.

When they were inside, Soneri had another attack of anxiety. "Is this your first time?" she teased him.

The commissario made no reply. The thought of Ada tormented him. The woman he had known was so different from the woman he was discovering, and each time he thought about it, he felt wounded and embittered.

He tried to forget, taking refuge somewhat childishly in Angela's arms, and she continued to give him comfort even afterwards. She sat down at her desk, making Soneri look like a nervous client in search of reassurance.

"Even when you speak about your wife you're still thinking like a police officer. You examine only the clues which favour prosecution, without taking all the other things into account. Ada needs a good lawyer. Isn't it odd that I'm the one called upon to defend her? Don't you agree?"

This was true. Angela had always been retrospectively jealous.

"It seems to me that I've lived part of my life in a coma, dreaming of a world which never existed," Soneri said, thinking aloud.

"If that made you happy, don't stop. What does it matter if it turns out not to be true? Haven't you always said that the inquiries you've been called on to conduct never uncover the salient facts, with all the inextricable tangle of motives, emotions and feelings that lie behind them."

"Yes, of course I have. At best I manage to describe the facts, but that's all I'm asked to do."

"Even two people who live together never really know each other. There's always one part of a person which remains in the shadows, some unspoken word which is jealously guarded. It happens with you and me," she said, looking at him with serious, good-humoured severity. She seemed more than ever the lawyer giving advice.

So as not to spoil the atmosphere, they ordered two pizzas which they ate at her desk in the office. Sitting there, they could hear the chaotic din, with its forced jollity and undertones of desperation, coming from the street below where crowds of people were rushing about doing their Christmas shopping. Little by little the hubbub subsided, and they could hear the shutters being closed as the city prepared to change character.

When he left Angela, Soneri walked across the Mercato della Ghiaia, past the arches of the Palazzo della Pilotta and out onto the wide, open space of Piazzale della Pace where he was struck by the rose-coloured outline of the Battistero, with the mist swirling about it. He walked slowly round it, while a solitary priest, bobbing up and down on the cobblestones, cycled diagonally across Piazza del Duomo. It was then that he saw Pitti. Dressed in a tailored, anthracite-coloured over-coat with tight-fitting trousers, a bowler hat on his head, he was the perfect image of a film star from the Thirties. Helped by the mist, Soneri was able to follow him from a distance without being seen. Pitti went down Borgo del Correggio before turning into Via Petrarca. Halfway down the street, he stopped at a doorway and disappeared inside.

There were many offices in the building. Among the brass nameplates the commissario noticed the Avanzini company. A photograph of the owner had been among the newspaper cuttings picked out for him by Fadiga. Evidently he was often to be seen at the Pensione Tagliavini, and this aroused Soneri's curiosity. He decided to light a cigar and hang about. He did not have to wait long. A quarter of an hour later Pitti made his reappearance, setting off in the opposite direction from where he had come. His footsteps echoed in the night.

Acting on instinct, Soneri decided not to arrest him on the spot. He preferred to let him move about freely, playing him like a fish on a hook, deluded into believing it could escape. He enjoyed trailing him. It filled the night with mysteries. It was always a pleasing sensation to see his hypotheses come to fruition, especially when, as sometimes happened, one developed into a lead, a clue. They returned to the austere solitude of Piazza del Duomo, before turning into Borgo Pipa and coming out on the new offshoot of Piazzale San Francesco, opposite the old prisons. He found himself once more in the district where the *Arditi del Popolo* had been active against the Fascists, and where he had spent much of his time as a student, but which now seemed foreign to him. Had he really lived in a dream-filled coma? He hardly had time to glance at Bettati's shopfront before Pitti led him into Borgo del Parmigianino, where he stopped in front of an elegant palace that had recently been renovated. Pitti rang the bell and went in, leaving Soneri waiting outside. Everything unfolded as previously, except that on this occasion Soneri did not recognise anyone on the mosaic of nameplates and buzzers on the intercom board. A quarter of an hour later, with the regularity of a busy delivery man, Pitti reappeared and plunged again into the labyrinth of streets. He was guided by memory, like a spider moving thread by thread over his web. Now he was moving towards the Duomo, but went round the back, swerving in the direction of San Giovanni Evangelista and turning into the rows of streets between Via Repubblica and the old city centre. He made his next stop in Vicolo al Leon d'Oro where he went into another doorway. Here again Soneri recognised no familiar names. The building was entirely occupied by offices, many with only internal numbers.

He waited and waited, smoking his cigar but shielding

it in his cupped hand to prevent the glow giving him away. At last Pitti came back down and set off into the network of streets in the old town, in the general direction of the Duomo. Soneri followed him, listening to the uniform, cadenced fall of his footsteps in the misty night until he came out opposite the dark, imposing bulk of the apses of the Duomo and the illuminated façade of the episcopal palace. They again traipsed along Borgo del Correggio, but this time Pitti was headed for Via Saffi. In the darkness, the creaking of Fadiga's trolley made itself heard as he made his way along the pavement like an unseen collector of bodies in time of plague.

Pitti advanced through the mist until it was pierced by the light from the window of the shisha bar, still crowded with drinkers. He slowed down in front of No. 35, then came to a sudden halt, leaving Soneri scarcely enough time to jump behind a van to prevent Pitti turning and seeing him. When he looked out, the commissario saw Pitti ringing the door bell. Was he looking for Elvira?

He waited at least a minute for an answer which did not come, so he chose to continue on his way, heading off in the direction of the barrier at the end of the avenues. Soneri pursued him. At the corner, an ageing prostitute pulled back her raincoat to reveal two enormous breasts supported by a scaffolding of lace.

Hunter and hunted trailed over a carpet of leaves which had fallen from the chestnut trees, until Pitti turned into Borgo del Naviglio and walked down Borgo Gazzola where the Arditi put up their resistance against the Fascist thugs and the lookout boy, Gazzola, was gunned down. They came out again in front of the old gaol, then turned a corner into Borgo Delle Colonne and were back again in Via Saffi. Pitti rang the doorbell at No. 35 again, this time with greater assurance, as though certain of finding someone to answer, and indeed there was a click of the lock and in he went. Soneri did not move. He would rather have gone over to the shisha bar, but the shutters were half lowered already and some customers were leaving the premises, stooping as they went out. Mohammed pulled the shutters right down with a bang, as he had done on the occasion when Soneri spent the whole night at the window of the pensione observing the street, waiting for something to happen, for someone to telephone and not hang up when they heard his voice. Now that its one place of business was shut, the street was asleep. There were only a few cars on the road, braving a mist which grew thicker as it eddied towards the city centre. He could still hear the creaking of Fadiga's trolley as he trundled about somewhere among the houses. The mist had grown so dense that the few passers-by almost bumped blindly into one another, pulling up at the last moment. Soneri made out the roundish profile of a person coming towards him, moving slowly, swaying from side to side as though burdened by some weight. As the veil of mist shrouding her parted briefly, he recognised her as Dirce, the old prostitute of the district, long ago adopted and tolerated even by the most jealous of the wives who lived nearby. Over time she had managed to accumulate a fortune which was rapidly dispersed when she, whose trade was sex, fell deeply in love at the age of fifty with a much younger man who deserted her after squandering all her savings. The commissario gazed at her scowling face and brazen air, suggesting a woman who has nothing to lose but whose expression retains a hint of bewilderment. When she passed him, her enormous back stooped as she walked, he still felt those eyes of hers, with the arrogance of total unconcern, burning into him, and he was overcome by a sort of embarrassment as though he had been touched by the warm hand of a stranger.

Pitti remained in the pensione quite a while. Time passed, measured by the ringing of the bells of the Duomo. Life had slowed down even more until it seemed to be passing imperceptibly. He imagined Fadiga walking past the house where once he had been happy and thinking of his wife two storeys up, now sleeping with another man, or Dirce recalling all the street corners from where she had led beardless youths and grown men into temptation. These were the last representatives of a world which had gone and which had taken with it their role and identity. The bell rang out at two o'clock. In the stillness of the night, Soneri heard a car come screeching to a halt. It was the same black Mercedes he had seen that time he had kept the pensione under observation. An elegantly dressed man got out without switching off the ignition, rang the door bell and got back into the car. A few seconds later, Pitti appeared with one of the wheeled suitcases he had seen in Elvira's room. He jumped into the passenger seat and sped off. Soneri threw away his cigar, which had died slowly in the damp air, and turned towards home, overwhelmed by a bitter melancholy of spirit.

7

HE WAS SURE he had dreamed that he was sleeping in Ada's room in the Pensione Tagliavini. It was odd that a desire that belonged firmly in the past should surface after so long, but he struggled in vain to recall any clips from the nocturnal film that had haunted his sleep. As he walked towards the questura, a black mood descended on him once more, transforming itself into a general irritation with everything and everyone he met. He wished the mist would envelop him and render him invisible.

One quick look in Soneri's direction was enough for Juvara to decide it would be unwise to address him, so he kept his head down over his keyboard. Soneri found the files on the Dallacasa case on his desk and immersed himself in them without so much as a glance at the rest of the post. The murder had been committed some twenty years ago and the body found in a field one week after the disappearance, with a nine-calibre bullet in its skull. There were also signs of a blow to the neck, making the death look like an execution. Mario Dallacasa was described as a leading light of the extreme left, even if in the years before his murder his commitment seemed to have wavered and he had been away from Parma for weeks on end without leaving an address with his family. There was one photograph among the pages of the report.

He seemed to have been a man of healthy, robust appearance who could have been an outdoors type, judging from the bushy beard covering a large part of his face. He came from the Apennines. On the accompanying index card, Soneri read that he was born in Tizzano Val Parma. It occurred to him that this was not far from Rigoso.

When Nanetti strode in, Soneri had largely got over his ill humour. "I didn't knock because I'd was sure you'd be out," Nanetti said.

He had a folder under his arm which he laid on the desk, glancing at the pages of the file as he did so. "A major breakthrough?"

"It's material which is new to me," Soneri said. "I'm looking into by a crime committed some years ago."

"It's always necessary to go back in time to understand what's happening today," Nanetti said with a chuckle. "And you're a great one for the long game."

That phrase made him reflect for a few moments before he remembered the routine of their encounters. He turned round, opened a filing cabinet and pulled out a bottle of port, lifting it up to the neon light to check the level of wine left.

"I'd have been worried if you'd forgotten that," Nanetti said.

"People either forget or delude themselves. There are no other possibilities," Soneri replied, only half serious

"Your port inspires healthy delusions," Nanetti said, taking a sip and smacking his lips. "I regret to have to say that the analysis made by my team does not open up similarly promising perspectives."

"So yet again I'm going to have to get by without your assistance," the commissario said, feigning disappointment

"The tests tell us nothing, so you've got a hard nut to crack. I mean, you're dealing with a real professional."

"Not an opportunist criminal?"

"I don't believe so. There are no fingerprints, no cigarette stubs, the prints left by the soles of the shoes are indistinguishable from hundreds of others and there are no biological traces. We're still trying to find some on the rim of the cup he drank his coffee from, but he seems to have cleaned it well before he left."

"He could have been in counter-espionage."

"Even clever killers nearly always leave something, but not this time."

They poured themselves another glass of port and the beginnings of a euphoric mood came over the commissario, although the grey light filtering in through the curtains did little to encourage good cheer. Soneri's eyes fell on the folder open in front of him. According to the report of the political branch, Dallacasa was completely *au fait* with the rules of the armed struggle and the underground movement. A foreign manual on the principal techniques adopted by spies and infiltrators had been taken from his apartment, something which perhaps the killer . . . On the other hand, there were strong suspicions that Dallacasa might have been a supporter of, or have had contacts with, actual terrorist groups. Several extra-parliamentary activists had established such contacts without actually turning terrorist themselves. And then there was that strange telephone call which, according to Chiastra, had put Ghitta in a state of fear and alarm – the call from the person she had called "Rosso".

But were these only bold hypotheses which owed something to the wine, or could there indeed be some connection with this old murder case? It could be anything.

"A professional, a real professional," Nanetti said with a touch of admiration in his voice. As a professional himself, he tended to see crimes from a technical perspective, without any concern for ethical questions. Considerations like screams, anguish or horror meant nothing to him. All that mattered were ballistics, the angle of entry of a blade, the calibre of a bullet, the chemical composition of a poison or the geometry of a blunt instrument. It wasn't that he was bereft of feelings, but simply that he momentarily stripped himself of all trace of them to put himself in a position where he could reason as a scientist. However, his remark on the professionalism of the killer brought back to Soneri the idea that the murderer might have acquired specific training in some sector, and had a secret skill concealed under other appearances.

Nanetti got up, his hips swaying as he moved, to leave. He always gave the impression of a large locomotive with over-sized track rods. Meanwhile the commissario lit a cigar and turned back to the pages of the Dallacasa folder. He read the statements of the people who had seen him get into the car on the evening of his disappearance. It had taken place in Via Montanara, the most southerly district of the city, on the road out to the hills. Everything seemed to point to the countryside where flocks of starlings would congregate when the grapes were ripening, but the bald statement and the arid, legalistic prose of the pages in the folder gave nothing more than a straightforward description of the facts.

It occurred to him that the best way forward was to go and see Bettati in his shop. He found him with a newspaper spread open in front of him, sitting in one of the chairs in the reclining position he preferred for his clients. "I've never had such a loyal customer," Bettati said when he recognised Soneri in the mirror in front of him.

"Hair grows quickly for youngsters like me."

"Have you seen this?" he said, holding up the newspaper. "Some right-wingers have come out against the monument to the Barricades."

"What did you expect? It's still a sore spot for Mussolini's grandchildren."

Bettati spun round and looked at him quizzically.

"Do you remember Mario Dallacasa?" the commissario said.

Bettati nodded gravely, as though the question reawakened an unpleasant memory. "There was a man who really did believe in revolution."

"No half measures with him?"

"He'd have walked through a brick wall to bring it on."

"Any idea who might have killed him?"

"It was a funny business. I don't believe the Fascists had anything to do with it. They said at the time there was some woman, or women, involved. He had a lot of female admirers."

"I've met his ex-girlfriend. She's never got over it. She's a broken woman even now."

"The nurse? She disappeared from circulation. She never goes out except for work. And to think that she was once extremely militant."

"Did Dallacasa have any contact with the terrorist movement?"

Soneri's question was blurted out and Bettati looked at him with a sort of distrust. "I heard rumours to that effect, but if there was any truth in it, the contact must have been with groups outside the city. The communist party was in total control here."

"The officers in charge of the investigations at the time believed his own side was responsible for his murder."

"Not those in his own group," Bettati said firmly. "I knew nearly all of them and they wouldn't have been up to it. They were good at using the megaphone and the cyclostyle, but pistols weren't part of their repertoire."

"Did you know any of those who did use guns?"

"You only got to know of those ones at a later date. When the police picked them up, you were amazed that so and so, who you thought was an ordinary activist ... there were whispers about others, but nothing more. Who can say how many people there are who keep their past buried away, and who now maybe live a quiet, respectable life? As you know better than me, the armed struggle was organised in little cells of a maximum of four people, meaning that no-one knew the name of more than three others."

From time to time, the noise from the yard where the construction of the monument to the Barricades was under way intruded on their conversation. Whenever a particularly loud bang rang out, Bettati threw a glance in the direction it came from.

"Supposing it really was one of his own side who murdered him, why would they have done it?" Soneri said.

"He liked being seen in public. He was also a born leader, somebody who could take others along with him. He never seemed to me the type who could adapt to the solitary life or to staying out of sight, as you have to do if you go underground. You can't make yourself noticed, and he wanted to stand out. If they'd put him on the stage of the Teatro Regio, he'd have been delighted."

"Yes, but from there to actually killing him ..."

"He thought building up the movement was the way forward. Maybe he tried to persuade them they'd got it all wrong. Maybe as a fellow traveller he was starting to get in the way too much. It's more likely they simply didn't trust him any more and thought he stank. Who can say?"

"You mean because the police had him in their sights?"

"He pushed himself forward too much. He'd become one of the points of reference for younger activists, and so the police kept an eye on him. If he really did have dealings with the people who had gone underground, he risked compromising them. That lot were pitiless. Their organisation mattered infinitely more to them more than any individual, and they wouldn't have stopped at any anything to preserve it."

Soneri smoothed his moustache and lit another cigar. "Maybe you're right. Did you come across anyone known as 'Rosso'?"

Bettati thought it over, but could not come up with anything useful.

"It seems he was one of the very few who could put the wind up Ghitta," Soneri explained.

"He must've had some balls."

"That's what everyone says about her. An iron lady. The thing is that to all appearances she was quite the opposite."

"People are like mist. All you see is the grey and then, quite suddenly . . . but by then it's usually too late."

Soneri thought of himself. He was in such turmoil because he had trusted appearances too much. As he was pondering these matters, his mobile struck up once more with its excruciating Verdi.

"Commissario, you were right all along. Ghitta was extremely wealthy. I'd never have believed it," Juvara said.

"We were just talking about appearances," Soneri said.

The inspector did not understand and for a while made no reply. To get over his awkwardness he began reading a list of possessions that could have belonged to landed aristocracy. Ghitta had apartments in the city, almost all in the zone between the Duomo and Via Saffi. In addition, there were some thirty houses and cottages in the country between Rigoso and Monchio, government bonds, two farmsteads, chestnut woods and shares in the municipal gas company. She even owned the parish house in Corniglio where the priest lived, meaning that the diocese had to pay her rent.

"So she could have evicted the parish priest and all the saints," Soneri mumbled as he listened to Juvara's report.

"And I haven't got to the one hundred thousand euros put away in a pension fund for her son."

Ghitta had spared a thought for her unfortunate son, semi-abandoned in the mountains, addressing illusory rallies of Fascist troops. She lived in complete security, and there was not a chink in her meticulous planning. Everything had been prepared down to the last detail, except for one thing. Soneri's thoughts went back to the man known as Rosso, to that disturbing phone call a few weeks before the murder.

Bettati put down his paper. "You didn't expect her to have squirrelled away quite so much, did you?"

Soneri shook his head, wondering how she had managed it.

"Ghitta saved everything. She wore the same clothes year after year, she emptied out the wardrobes of people who'd died and she sold off furniture thrown out by wealthy folk. She lived to accumulate. She'd have killed a flea to strip off its skin."

Bettati took off his white jacket and threw it over one of the chairs by the wall. He walked towards the door, followed by Soneri. At the doorway, they said goodbye to each other with a gentle pat on the arm. A silent melancholy had come over both men.

As he walked along the street, Soneri took out his mobile to call Juvara. "Draw me up a list of all the tenants in Ghitta's properties. Try to find out who they are, how much rent they pay and how long they've been there."

Investigations which did not entail moving a single step but only surfing the web were Juvara's speciality. "No problem," the inspector said. All I have to do is to check the databank."

"Alright, but waste no time. I'm in a hurry."

"It's lunch time now," the inspector objected timidly.

"Look, you're always searching for something to kick-start your diet."

Nevertheless, Soneri stopped off at a new place near the old San Francesco prison, but walked straight out again the moment he saw the phoney, pretentious décor, the obsequious demeanour of the young owners who wanted to pass themselves off as sommeliers, and the exaggerated flashiness of ordinary dishes which had been given improbable foreign names to impress customers. He felt the need to call into an old-style food store, where he looked fondly at the woman behind the counter, with her overall tied under her ample, matronly breasts, and at that face of hers, as shiny as a ripe apple.

He arrived at the questura with an unfinished piece of his *panino al prosciutto*, to find Juvara bent over his keyboard with a multi-bulb lamp on his desk.

"I thought you might like this. It's nearly Christmas," the inspector said when he met Soneri's puzzled gaze. The commissario was genuinely moved and offered a grateful smile. He always found it hard to express feelings, which seemed to him to be of their nature beyond speech. All the words which came to him were ponderous and inadequate. He went over to Juvara, put his hand on his shoulder, shook it a bit and murmured *grazie*, trusting that his tone of voice would communicate his feelings. "Go and get yourself something to eat," he said.

The inspector shrugged his shoulders and pressed a button on his mouse. The printer began to rumble and some pages emerged. Halfway down the list Soneri noticed the name of Teresa Rodolfi. There were also many students. Ghitta might not have been running a boarding house any longer, but she kept in touch with student life through the apartments she rented out.

"Friar Fiorenzo was on the phone. Ghitta's funeral is this afternoon."

Soneri had forgotten that Saltapico had issued clearance for the funeral to go ahead. "What time?"

"Three o'clock."

He looked at his watch. Half an hour to go. In the last couple of days, the mortuary had been sending impatient messages. The refrigerated vaults were almost all in use and the magistrate had finally given way. Soneri had no objection. Her wizened body had no more information to impart, and so for Ghitta too the time had come to take leave of this world after playing her final part.

He arrived at the church shortly before the beginning of the ceremony. Friar Fiorenzo was already in his vestments.

"Who asked you to say this Mass?" the commissario asked.

"Him," the friar replied, pointing to Chiastra who was standing near the coffin. "I would have done it in any case. Ghitta attended this church regularly. She found comfort and understanding here. She was the victim of great cruelty. If she sinned grievously, she did it partly to defend herself."

Soneri moved aside to survey the semi-deserted nave. Elvira arrived and the sound of her heels rang out before she muffled it by shuffling her feet along the ground. She was followed by Mohammed, who took a seat at the back. Finally, silently, Pitti turned up, dressed from head to toe in black, bowler hat in his hand and his remaining hairs arranged on his skull in a way that made it resemble a peeled onion. There was no-one else. Ghitta was saying her farewells in near solitude.

Friar Fiorenzo did not detain her long. He blessed the coffin and gave her the viaticum of eternal rest, then, since there was not even a sacristan to see to the more humble duties, went to open the doors himself. Two of the undertaker's employees filed in, and the brighter light allowed Soneri to note that the casket was made of cheap, light wood. There was one single bouquet on which Chiastra had written only the modest words, "From your son and those who loved you." Ghitta had contrived to economise even in death, while her partner had remained in the background even now that he was on his own.

They lifted the coffin and only then did Fadiga and Dirce make their appearance, both dressed in bulky, padded clothing. Standing apart, they watched Ghitta from a distance as she moved off, and perhaps in that desolate funeral service they foresaw their own fate. When they closed the hearse, Chiastra became aware that it would not be possible to follow it on foot. He looked around in dismay, but Elvira, Pitti and Mohammed had already gone and there was no-one else there. He went over to the undertaker and knocked on the window to ask for a lift. There was some animated conversation and he seemed to be pleading. Soneri approached and said, "Come on. I'll take you."

The old man clutched at Soneri's arm with his strong, calloused hands. It was as if his life had been saved.

Theirs was the only car following the hearse. In a corner outside the church, they saw Bettati, who had not gone in because he detested priests. He raised his hand in salute as the hearse passed by. Chiastra sat completely still, his hat on his knees, his face ashen and his hands clutched together as though in prayer. At the graveside everything was businesslike. A gravedigger was standing by, like a great vulture in the mist. Friar Fiorenzo mumbled the final prayers and the coffin was lowered into the grave. Soneri watched it dance on the cords as though it was empty, and it was at that point that

Chiastra burst into tearless sobs, a sort of prolonged lament of sheer despair. The commissario took hold of him and dragged him away while the first thuds of earth on the wood could be heard. When they reached the graveyard avenue, Soneri looked back and saw that only the gravedigger remained, working with his spade.

"Did you see how no-one came?" Chiastra said as they drove away. "And those few who did come were there out of a sense of duty."

"You should never expect gratitude."

"Nobody knew as many people as she did."

"Where can I drop you off?"

Chiastra stretched out his arms. "Where can I go now? I'll catch the last bus for Rigoso. That's the only place I have."

When they got to the bus station, Soneri parked his Alfa. The old man put his hat back on and opened the door to get out.

"Do you know if Ghitta made a will?" the commissario asked.

Chiastra stopped halfway out of the car, and it was clear from the expression on his face that it was only at that moment that the question of the inheritance had occurred to him. "I don't suppose so. Ghitta's thoughts were all about living. Death never crossed her mind. She had an iron constitution."

"With all that she owned, she must have occasionally thought about who to leave it to."

"Maybe," the old man said, but he sounded doubtful. "All she wanted was to be respected, and the only way to do that was to accumulate cash. As you can see, it didn't work."

They had nothing more to say to each other. The car door slammed shut and Chiastra walked with exhausted dignity towards the ticket office.

Soneri called Juvara. "Ring round all the lawyers in the city to find out if Ghitta left a will," he said. He pulled his car over to the side of the road, because he wanted to stretch his legs a bit. The fading afternoon light made the Christmas lights stand out all the more, while the mad scramble of the noisy crowds around the shops showed no sign of letting up and made him think the city was under siege. The familiar Verdian aria rang out in a pocket of his duffel coat, rescuing him from an incipient depression.

"Commissario, I tried to call you back," Juvara said.

"There's an appalling racket here, and with so many mobiles going off at once you don't know whose it is."

"But yours is unmistakeable."

"I know. I must get the ringtone changed."

"I've found the will."

"Where was it deposited?"

"With a lawyer called Zurlini."

"What does it say?"

"She's left everything to Fernanda Schianchi."

Soneri was struck dumb, stunned. His first thoughts were for Chiastra, who had not been able to count on gratitude any more than anyone else. He then wondered what had bound Ghitta to Fernanda to the point where she had chosen her as the heir to her fortune.

"What's the date on the will?"

"Two months ago."

Soneri stood stock still on the pavement, as though he was lost, but it was his thoughts that were in a tangle. He heard the inspector bawling more and more loudly, "Hello! Hello!" until he hung up. The commissario simply could not understand, and when he failed to grasp something his first reaction was anger, followed by depression. He walked under the dark arcades of Borgo delle Colonne, passing groups of North Africans with wary expressions leaning against the wall, then shops decked out in all the colours of Africa, and hearing unfamiliar tongues with unfamiliar diphthongs. In Via Saffi, he dropped into Mohammed's bar and took the one free seat. The place was filled with men returning from work, eating Pakistani food. Half a dozen tables had been drawn up to form one long bench where several children were gathered facing a bearded man who was teaching them the Koran and the language of their parents. At the far end, a trading stall had been set up where people were bargaining in loud voices, and not far from them a group was standing in front of a television set tuned to a foreign-language channel. Mohammed seemed entirely at his ease in the general hubbub, attending to the various groups one by one, serving someone at the bar and then dealing with an order from a table.

"There's a lot of homesickness for our own country," he said, implying that he too was a sufferer. "In the evening, many of them gather here to listen to their own language. It's like being at home for a couple of hours."

Soneri nodded and looked outside. The window was all steamed up, but he could see the doorway to No. 35.

"Any developments?" Mohammed said.

The commissario took the cigar from his mouth and shook his head.

"The tenants who lived next to the Pensione Tagliavini have moved out."

"When?"

"This morning, before daybreak. A van came and they loaded up everything in less than an hour. They didn't even say goodbye to us, although we knew them. The wife must have left earlier, because I only saw the husband."

"You've no idea where they went?"

"No. It was a very sudden move. My wife was upset because she was fond of that woman. You know how it is with people in a foreign country."

"They must have found a better house."

The man shook his head. "Perhaps. Anyway, it's better this way. Ghitta was murdered in that house. They must have decided it wasn't a good idea to stay any longer."

"You think they were afraid?"

Mohammed's eyes lit up. "I have my own opinion, but I don't know what you'd make of it."

"Opinions can be valuable," the commissario encouraged him. "The thing is to take them for what they are."

"There was something not clear, or maybe not clean, in that house. The woman next door once told my wife that she often heard yelling coming from it. She couldn't make out what it was all about, but they weren't calm people, and I'm not talking about the couples who met there. From what she understood, they were arguing about money and payments. And when there's money involved . . ."

"Did she hear Ghitta shouting as well?"

"No. It was men's voices, angry men."

"Quite often?"

"Five or six times, I think, but the lady wasn't always there because she was out doing things in rich people's houses. It was Ghitta who got her these jobs."

"You don't know anything else?"

"No. These are things this lady told my wife in confidence, and I wouldn't like to think that their departure . . ."

"Who is the owner of the apartment?"

"A man who builds lots of houses, that's all I know. This is a dead area where no-one goes out at night and people keep their doors locked. It's only foreigners like us who keep our shops open, and we have to be on the lookout. That's another reason why we upset them."

"Have you received threats?"

"No, or at least not so far, but that man in the strange clothes came back once to ask if we'd changed our mind. You get the impression that he's very interested. He raised the first offer, and for me they were crazy figures. You policemen have got it in for us as well. As soon as it's closing time, you arrive to threaten fines and closures if anyone makes a sound, although you people are not as bad as in other cities."

Mohammed went back to his work, leaving Soneri assailed by doubts. The customers at the tables were calling out impatiently for Mohammed, the children were chanting verses and voices were being raised at the trading stall. The commissario walked out into the mist, away from that world bubbling with vitality. His route took him up Via Saffi towards Piazzale dei Servi, in the direction of Fadiga's refuge. He now knew where to put his hands, and once again he felt a page from a newspaper wrapped in cellophane. He picked it up, stuck it in his pocket and headed for Via Repubblica and the last-minute shoppers. In front of the window of a perfumery, he took out the cutting and saw the photograph of the deputy mayor Roberto Lusetti, someone else he remembered from the "hot years" of the protest movement, another one who had marched in demonstrations and then, as the years slipped past, had been attracted to political life and had gone over, somersault by somersault, to the side of his erstwhile enemies.

The clatter of shutters rang out amid the roar of the late buses, and a light breeze caused the mist in Piazza Garibaldi, now empty of people, to billow about. He took out his mobile and called Juvara. "Could you check up on something for me?

The hesitation at the other end told him that the inspector

was on the point of going home, but before he could raise an objection, Soneri said: "I'd like to know who owns the flat at number thirty-five Via Saffi, the one between where Ghitta and Fernanda lived."

He was aware of Juvara's lack of enthusiasm for the task, but judging by the sound of air expelled from the padded seats which were standard issue in the questura, he had sat down again. "I hope it's been registered and that all I have to do is check with the data bank at the housing office. Stay on the line," he said, as though he were a telephone operator.

The commissario heard him typing rapidly. "We're in luck," the inspector said after a brief interval. "The flat is owned by a company, La Maison s.r.l."

"Can you go back onto the data bank and tell me what's behind that company name?"

Juvara said nothing, perhaps regretting his gift of the lamp, but went to work dutifully on the keyboard. "There's one director called Renato Avanzini, and his partner is called Amintore Cornetti."

"Where's their office?"

"Fourteen Borgo Fellini."

The commissario gave a mumbled *grazie*, but he had already switched off. He was deep in thought and failed to notice that Angela was now walking at his side. When he moved, he almost bumped into her.

"That's the first time I've ever felt like a guardrail," she complained. "Everyone has this idea that policemen are as adept as cats at picking up signals."

"I was thinking."

"If somebody mugged you, you'd walk away with no idea that you had a dagger between your shoulder blades."

Soneri gestured to her to drop it. She took his arm. "Are you still thinking about your wife and that other man?"

He had not been thinking of that, but her words made him remember putting the photograph in his pocket. He could feel it there, rigid inside the cellophane, every time he groped inside his duffel coat. He had stared at it several times, perhaps hoping to get used to the truth it revealed.

"I've just discovered that Avanzini is the owner of the flat next to the Pensione Tagliavini."

"So? You mean he could have been dropping in to do his screwing there rather than at Ghitta's?"

"No, in all probability we're dealing with something much more complex and disturbing. I believe they've created a kind of no-man's-land there where nobody could live any longer. There are only offices and immigrants. Everything's much easier when there's no-one around to stick their nose in."

"Very true. In this city they sell drugs by the kilo."

"That's a matter for the Drugs Squad. Did you know that Ghitta left everything to Fernanda?"

"What about her man? He stayed close to her all his life, and then ..."

"Women are like that ... they play the victim for years, but then they stab you in the back."

He felt her warm breath in his ear. "You're a shit," she said, with no trace of humour.

"I don't understand why it was Fernanda."

"Maybe she's only a cover to conceal the real heir," Angela said when they had sat down in the bistro where she went in her breaks from work.

The same idea had occurred to Soneri. But who was Fernanda standing in for?

"Diet this evening," Angela said, and he did not feel like contradicting her.

"You get better food at the clinic for dyspeptics," Soneri said after they had eaten, his appetite still intact.

"Your mind's elsewhere," Angela said resentfully. "You're only pretending to think about the investigation, but in fact you're focused on Ada."

"Unfortunately, there's not a world of difference between the two."

Angela held out her hand. "Let me see the photographs. You're carting it about with you as though it were a holy relic."

Reluctantly Soneri took out the photograph of his wife embracing another man.

"Do you recognise him?" Angela said.

Soneri shook his head.

"You know what I think? If this whole affair really is gnawing away at your insides, make it your business to find out who he is. You'll see it was a girlhood crush which your wife hid from you because she thought nothing of it."

Soneri was on the point of giving a reply from the heart, but caught himself in time. He did not want to confess that he was afraid, like a gambler who fears showing his cards. He said nothing, unable to engage in small talk. Angela looked at him for a few moments, then lost patience and announced that she was going to bed. "I've always despised those women who wag their tails imploring their man to pay them attention," she said as she left.

Soneri followed her as far as the exit, and stood in the piazza watching her walk off without even saying goodbye. He was fond of her, but had no idea how to abandon himself to his emotions. The very thought seemed to terrify him.

As he too walked away, all other thoughts faded from his mind, leaving only the one obsession – to find out who the man in the photograph was. Angela's advice spun round in his head like a refrain. He headed in the direction of Via Saffi, considering breaking into Fernanda's house and looking once more at those black-and-white snaps, slices of a lost life, but in Borgo del Correggio he saw Pitti and changed his mind. He decided to tail him. On this occasion, Pitti was dressed in an overcoat tied tightly round the waist and stretching below his knees, dark pinstriped trousers and well-polished black shoes. He had the usual bowler on his head and was carrying a walking stick.

Pitti turned into Via Petrarca and once more entered the building which contained the headquarters of the Avanzini Company. The commissario waited in the same place as the previous evening. The script was the same as before, except that now Soneri was beginning to detect some pattern in the trajectory which Pitti traced out, probably every night. When he came back down, he walked towards Via della Repubblica but did not stick to the quiet lanes near the main thorough-fare. Instead he crossed into the narrow streets on the far side and came out at Borgo Reale, entering a bar where the light was a pale bluish colour, allowing the profile of couples at the tables to be made out through the windows. Back on the pavement, his next call was Borgo Felino, where he stopped at no. 14, rang the bell and went up. Soneri let a few minutes pass before going over to the doorway. Beside the fourth button from the bottom, he read La Maison s.r.l.

A few slivers of Parmesan cheese in a bag which Alceste had made up for him were all he had left, and as he waited in the cold he took them out of the wrapping. The waiting went on for over an hour, leading Soneri to conclude that this was not a routine visit. Then he remembered the photo-graphs, and gave up the sentry duty. He made his way back to Via Saffi and crossed Piazzale dei Servi, where he heard the squeaking wheels of Fadiga's trolley. At that time of night the district took on a spectral appearance, with water drip-ping from gutters and the dark windows staring blindly out onto the street. He had the impression that everything was waiting for something to happen, but with no idea what it could be. Nor could he do anything but wait, like a hunter in a shooting stand.

He fished Fernanda's keys out of his pocket and went into the house. The shutters of the shisha bar on the other side of the street had already been pulled down and it was in darkness. He climbed the staircase noiselessly and opened the door. It was cold inside and he kept his duffel coat buttoned up as he sat down in the living room, staring at the envelope into which the old woman had stuffed the photographs at random. He spread them out on the table like the pieces of a jigsaw puzzle, and began searching for the face of Ada's mysterious boyfriend. There were so many photographs, mainly of young men with long hair and a hunger for life in their eyes. When he picked himself out in one group photograph, he was surprised that someone had frozen a moment of his youth and that he had found it by chance in an envelope which had been set aside by an elderly woman who had come looking for him in vain.

He continued patiently wiping the dust off the snaps with a handkerchief, pausing from time to time over some images which brought back a flash of memory. There passed before him fleeting images of a lost world populated only by the young, with all the carefree junketing of student life, the cheap clothes mended at home or else passed down from older brothers and sisters.

In one small photograph he found a group including Ada and, at the far right, Marta Bernazzoli. In yet another there was Ada again, this time near a bonfire in the country, holding a pan filled with roasted meat. He turned the photograph over and read RIGOSO, OCTOBER '74. They all seemed happy. He studied the faces closely and it was then that he again noted the mysterious friend. He had failed to recognise him in profile, with his long hair. Something now began to gnaw at him. He picked up the envelope again and began putting back the pictures, thinking all the while of that last snap taken at Rigoso. Why had they gone there of all places for their party? Was Ghitta involved?

On the outside of the envelope he noticed the name of a man whom he remembered as small, elegant, plump man, who went around with a large camera topped by a gigantic flashbulb bigger than his head. Trombi was known simply as "the photographer", and for many years his pictures featured in the local paper for which he did some work. His archive in Via Angelo Mazza was the best resource for the recent history of the city.

A noise on the stairs made him jump. He felt a sense of guilt over wasting time on an enquiry which he knew was purely personal and perhaps even futile, but had he not told Angela that could not find much of a gap between the investigation into the death of Ghitta and the other one he was conducting into the death of Ada? Had he not been on the point of throwing in his hand for exactly that reason? Meanwhile the sound on the stairs took on a familiar ring as he recognised Elvira's high heels. He clearly heard her arriving at the pensione, the clink of her keys followed by the clatter of the door being shut.

He was unsure what to do. Was it better to wait, as he had been doing up till now, or take action and confront that woman who had been lying about everything? In his indecision, he followed his instinct and stood listening to Elvira's movements next door. He made out her voice, with intervals of silence, and assumed she was on the telephone. Shortly afterwards there was another voice, but it must have been the radio or television because the voice fell silent and music started up.

Soneri began to feel uneasy. He went over to the window and stood staring out at the night which seemed to be suspended on a cushion of mist, it too waiting for a gust of wind to clear it away. He was thinking that Via Saffi was like the dry bed of a river, when he saw a man walking slowly in the middle of the road. As he came closer, Soneri recognised the figure of Pitti. When he was level with the shisha bar, he stopped on the pavement outside No. 35. A few moments later, the commissario heard the door bell ring inside the pensione with the same sound it had made all these years previously. A sense of déjà vu overtook him as he waited to hear the click of the lock being opened downstairs. Nothing happened, but then he remembered Mohammed telling him that sometimes they would ring and go away only to come back and ring again. Perhaps this was a device for guaranteeing that the coast was clear.

He could imagine Pitti making his nightly round of houses in the district, crossing Borgo Gazzola and greeting the prostitutes on his way into and out of Via Saffi. A few minutes went by until Soneri again heard the ring of the bell, accompanied this time by the click of the lock. He heard the outside door open slowly, the hinges creak, Pitti's footfall on the steps as he came closer, the door of the pensione opening and finally the bang as it was slammed shut against the other half of the double door.

At first he could not hear anything. Even the music had been switched off. He then heard what sounded like a zip being pulled open, followed by Elvira's voice coming over loud and clear, like a sharp note suddenly soaring above the drone of the brasses. Soneri struggled to hear what sounded like a monologue, but the thick walls of the old house were no help. Pitti must have been totally passive, judging by the absence of replies, or at most would have been mumbling in the same frightened tone he had used when Soneri interrogated him on the steps of the church after meeting him in the darkness of the chapel of Sant'Egidio.

He obviously said something, however, judging by the way Elvira raised her voice yet higher. Soneri was pleased at Elvira's crescendo because it permitted him to make out some of what she was saying. He clearly heard her several times repeat, "So you went to the Abbess". The word "money" came up a few times, thrown in at the end of the sentence. They seemed to be quarrelling, or more probably she was remonstrating with Pitti who, Soneri imagined, would put up with it without reacting. He could see him, head bowed, fearful, incapable of stringing two words together. Then there was a pause and a hush fell over the building, and when Elvira started up again at the same pitch as before, the commissario understood that Pitti must have made an objection. She started castigating him again: "You didn't get there in time . . . Fastlast was in a hurry . . . you wasted time with that . . . he made you put on *what*?"

Pitti had plainly missed an appointment or something important and now Elvira was humiliating him by jeering at his homosexuality. He could not make out the rest, but he picked up enough from her offensive, scurrilous tone. He was a puppet and she the puppeteer. He imagined Pitti running all night from one spot to the next in the city centre, and then late at night turning up to meet that woman whom everyone described as cynical and cold. Silence fell again, but this time a longer silence than previously. Perhaps everything had been said, but why then did Pitti not leave? Soneri listened but there was no sound, until, after an interval, he heard the zip being pulled and then a kind of thud, followed by a whine which sounded like suppressed weeping. It was Pitti and those moans suggested a mixture of fear and apology. This went on for a few moments until the commissario heard Elvira bellow imperiously, "Get out!" in a voice heavy with rage and contempt. The outside door opened delicately and slammed shut loudly, and this too made it clear who was in charge.

8

HE DECIDED TO let things take their course. He was convinced that sooner or later the situation would burst into flames of its own accord, so there was no need to light a fuse himself. With these thoughts in mind, he went quietly back down the stairs and set off home. When he got there, the clock on the *campanile* of the Palazzo del Governatore was striking two. He felt nothing but a deep sense of relief at having reached the shelter of his own den, and to help him relax he lit a cigar and heated some water to prepare a camomile infusion. As he sipped it, he looked out at the silence of the night, one of the things in life which gave him the greatest pleasure, and pondered the mysteries concealed in that mist-interred world: Fernanda's disappearance, Ghitta's murder, Dallacasa's death, Elvira's scary cynicism, and finally Pitti scuttling about all night like a creature on the prowl.

In the last analysis, everything came back to that pensione which seemed to be the well-oiled hinge on which a whole world turned. Before going to bed, he listened to the voicemail which had been blinking all evening. "Have you found your tongue after going back to that bordello?" Angela said, guessing that he had ended his evening there. If truth be told, the Pensione Tagliavini and Fernanda's home were more depressing than any brothel.

He got up late. It was mid-morning by the time he arrived at the questura, which he found in a state of festive torpor. At that time of year, with the holidays approaching, everyone felt they could take it easy. He reflected how right he was to stay at work over the Christmas period and during the summer holidays – all the more so since Juvara attended to all the bureaucracy, leaving him only forms to sign.

"They're still looking for the old girl, are they?" he said to the inspector, hoping to be reassured.

"All the patrols have got a photograph. I had twenty copies printed specially."

With a cigar clamped between his teeth Soneri gave a grunt and went out a few minutes later. In Borgo Angelo Mazza, he hesitated for some time in front of a doorbell alongside a brass plate which read FOTO TROMBI. Once again he was tormented by a feeling of anxiety about wasting time rummaging through matters which had no bearing on the case. Juvara had alerted him to the fact that journalists were hoping to interview him about his investigation. What could he tell them? That every so often he felt compelled to track down photographs from the days of his youth?

Finally he rang the bell. He well remembered the basement premises lined with metal shelves, each one labelled. The criteria adopted for the filing system were plainly very personal. Trombi went by genres: political personalities, demonstrations, sporting events, churches, monuments, and so on. Within each category, the subdivision was chronological, year by year, but the overall principle was highly abstruse. It occurred to Soneri that once its creator was dead, no-one would ever again be able to decipher the code to that strongbox, so packed with history.

"You've not changed much," the photographer remarked as he showed him into his studio.

The commissario could not say the same about him. Trombi had gone to seed, and the skin on his face seemed to flow onto his chin like melting wax. He pointed to a seat while he withdrew into another room, leaving Soneri in an office with small windows which were only a few centimetres above the pavement. He returned with an envelope which he handed him.

"I've been keeping this aside for years. Now at last I can give it to you," Trombi said.

The commissario opened it. When he saw his own face with his boyish smile, and Ada at his side, something deep inside him seemed to crumble.

"When did you take this?"

"In 1975. The date's on the back."

For a moment he thought he was going to collapse. He had been given a glimpse of his life through someone else's eyes, and of an Ada who was not the woman he had known. A forgotten instant from his past was being handed back to him, but it was like being paid in a currency which had been withdrawn from circulation.

"Any more?"

"Perhaps, but you're asking too much of my memory if you think I know where to find them," Trombi said, waving an arm at the shelves.

"What about Ghitta? Do you have any photographs of her?"

Trombi heaved a deep sigh which made his round belly expand before shrinking like a deflated football. His expression became sad and regretful. "She was one of the best-known people in the city, but I read in the paper that there was hardly anyone at her funeral. Don't you find that strange?"

He lifted a small three-step ladder and moved back among his shelves.

"No, I don't find it in the least strange," the commissario said, without taking the trouble to explain why not.

When Trombi noticed Soneri's pained look and saw in his eyes an invitation to let the subject drop he decided not to pursue the matter.

"I don't have all that many pictures of Ghitta," Trombi said, offering him a folder. "She didn't like having her photograph taken. When she was in company, she hid behind somebody else or crept out of the frame. I only managed to get her a couple of times, when she wasn't aware I had my camera out."

There was a close-up taken some years previously, before Ghitta began to show her years and when it was still possible to see that she must once have been a good-looking woman.

"I took that one with a telescopic lens. I'd like to give it to her family, to go on her tombstone."

"There is no family," Soneri said.

The photographer was taken aback, and said nothing more. Meanwhile the commissario continued raking about in the folder. There was one of her in profile, walking along a snow-covered Via Saffi in front of the pensione, others of her at the window waving to passers-by, one waiting at a bus stop, and finally in a publicity shot taken in the pensione's golden years, hands on her hips and surrounded by her lodgers, like a teacher with her class. The caption underneath read PENSIONE TAGLIAVINI, WARM WELCOME AND GOOD FOOD. Soneri studied the row of faces, hoping to come across some old acquaintances.

"They weren't real lodgers, just people picked out because their faces suggested they were good boys and girls," Trombi said. "In those days people still trusted advertising, and some of Ghitta's real students looked like convicts! They needed something better to persuade worried families from country villages."

Soneri put down the advertisement and picked up the last picture in the folder. This time he immediately recognised Ada at the centre of a group of students in front of No. 35 Via Saffi. Ghitta seemed agitated, her overcoat blowing about in the wind.

"There had been a gas leak, and the firemen had evacuated the building," Trombi said.

The commissario looked more closely and identified the mysterious boyfriend standing next to Ada. He had never seen him standing before and he felt a stab of retrospective jealousy over his height.

"Do you know this man?" he asked the photographer, pointing at the young man.

Trombi shook his head.

"Are there any other pictures of him?"

Trombi doubted it, but took the stepladder and went into another room, leaving Soneri staring at the photograph. One moment of life frozen forever. What he liked about photography was its implicit rebellion against time, something we can all identify with. It occurred to him that possibly his obsession with staring out at the night, when the whole city was immobilised in the mist, had something in common with the stillness of a postcard. Right now, all he could hear was the click-clack of heels as they hurried past the little street-level window, the rush of people all a-flutter over their preparations for the festive period, the pressures of life reduced to one vain scurry, everything compressed into one brief dash, or one swift and speedily exhausted flapping of wings, like the flight of a grouse. One click, like Trombi's at the height of the tumult in Parma in the aftermath of the

'68 demonstrations, whether of the killing of Mariano Lupo in front of the Roma cinema, of missiles being thrown, of the occupation of the Duomo, or of marches with chants he could still recall: "*Masacci you pig / You're going to catch it big*", or "*Ricozzi you Fascist / You're first upon the list*". How much time had passed? Hardly any at all, and yet everything had already faded: the faces, the memories and the utopias.

"Maybe I snapped him at some demonstration or other." Trombi was making an effort to remember, and at that moment it occurred to Soneri that he might be one of the last people to be making an effort to recall the recent past of a city afflicted by amnesia. Parma had locked its history away in a dark cellar, and now the whole city was happily trampling over it in its futile, festive madness.

He felt Trombi's hand on his shoulder. His attention had wandered as he listened to the rhythm of the shuffling feet above his head, but when he looked at the table he saw a collage of photographs of faces carefully painted with passion, rage and vitality: beards, moustaches, long hair and heavy rectangular glasses like those worn by Communist Party leader Palmiro Togliatti. He struggled to make out Ada's man behind a banner proclaiming "Student Movement". He seemed somehow to be skilled at concealing himself in the middle of a crowd of protesters, but his height gave him away.

"Look at this one over here and you'll get a better view," Trombi said.

It was the only scene in which he stood out clearly, perhaps because a police charge had thrown the rows of marchers ahead of him into disarray, leaving him with no cover. The camera had caught him in full retreat, and if there was fear in his eyes, he also wore an expression of disdain. At his side, another gangly individual in an anorak was preparing to flee. His face was turned towards the lens at the moment the picture was taken, and that chance pose revealed him to Soneri thirty years later as Selvatici, the restless figure, later a lawyer, who once occupied the room next to Ada's.

"Half these people passed through Ghitta's lodgings," the commissario said.

"Those who weren't from the city, although a lot of them later made a good career here," Trombi said. So saying, he pointed to faces which the commissario struggled to recognise: the future deputy mayor Lusetti with a red scarf round his neck; Councillor Pecorari beside him, fist raised, sporting a Stalin-like moustache.

"A lovely couple, eh?" Trombi said.

"A couple of turncoats," Soneri muttered through his teeth, remembering the sneering looks the pair of them had directed at him during their student days. "Do you know this Selvatici?"

"Not really. All I know is that he's a lawyer, but I've never come across him."

"He was another one of those who lodged with Ghitta. Have you never thought of sorting out all this material?" he said, looking around at the shelves whose depth made the room seem smaller, leaving no more than a narrow corridor between them.

"Where in the city centre would I find the cash to rent a studio big enough? I can only just afford this cellar. The day the sewer bursts, it'll take the whole of old Parma with it."

"We'll all go the same way," Soneri said, as he headed off. "But before the flood comes, keep an eye open for any other pictures of Ghitta and her lodgers. The next time I drop by, I'll take them all to safety."

He was hardly back on the street when his mobile rang. "Have you got your tongue back?"

"Not completely, but I've got a notebook with me. I'll drop you a line."

"You've never written me so much as a postcard. Anyway, I've got something to tell you."

"What?" he said, feeling suddenly under pressure.

"Lesson number two," Angela said.

"Alright, alright. The *Milord.*"

He heard a snort as she hung up.

In the restaurant, she astonished the commissario by ordering tripe *alla parmigiana*. Alceste wrote it down, his silent smile signalling approval. Soneri chose *culatello*, courgette *tortelli* and a bottle of Bonarda.

"Will that be enough for you?" Angela said. "It's going to be a long day."

"I'm not going to be sitting behind a desk. In any case, I see that at long last you've decided to try to make up your calories," he said, alluding to the tripe.

"That may be, but from my desk I can see things you can't."

The commissario abstained from asking what, because that would be playing Angela's game. He hated all these riddles and the theatricality that went with them. He lit a cigar and began puffing slowly.

This time Angela was not playing any game. "You remember the old Battioni factory buildings?"

Soneri nodded.

"Pecorari is at work on a variation of the urban masterplan that will change its use from industrial to residential," she said in the mock singsong voice of a primary school teacher – another habit Soneri disliked.

"So whose paw marks are on that job?"

"You don't really imagine you're dealing with one of those Mickey-Mouse drug pushers whose necks you wring down at the questura?"

"I don't have anything to do with pushers and I don't wring anybody's neck."

"Are you seriously telling me you don't know who was first to seize his big chance?"

"No, but if I had to guess, I'd say Avanzini."

"Well done, commissario!"

Soneri was losing patience, so he turned his attention to the *culatello*. As he chewed his food, he became aware that what was getting under his skin was not so much Angela's mockery as the realisation that he had been caught unawares. Before he had time to descend into one of his black moods, Angela aroused his curiosity once more.

"Want to know something else? The operation wasn't all that easy to pull off, so Avanzini set up a temporary umbrella association which brought in all his rivals, including the cooperatives. Not only that: in the plan brought forward for urban renewal, the agreement with the city council includes a provision that the final balance will include the cost of the construction of the monument to the Barricades."

"Wonderful! So they've even put a price on the old anti-Fascist *Arditi del Popolo*."

"There's a price on someone else," Angela whispered. "And this *is* your business, commissario."

Soneri felt her hand stroke his thigh under the table. "The sooner you get shot of this case, the better for all concerned. It's eating you up," she said softly.

Soneri took her hand and they remained a few moments in that position, their only contact the linking and unlinking of their fingers in time to the rhythm of their feelings. Occasionally they raised their heads, meeting each other's gaze, oddly shy and embarrassed. In this way, without a word being spoken, they communicated everything.

The commissario decided to return to the questura. As he

left the *Milord*, his mobile rang. Juvara was in such a state of excitement that the words stuck in his throat and he did not know where to begin. "Commissario, Amintore Cornetti has killed himself. You know who I mean? One of Avanzini's partners."

"He killed himself or was killed?"

"It seems he took his own life. One shot to the temple with a Smith & Weston. The bullet blew his brains out."

Soneri suspected this was the just beginning, the initial incident that would set off a chain reaction. Now it was just a question of waiting for everything else to unravel.

"But that's not all," Juvara went on. "Cornetti went to the offices of his partner at 14 Borgo Felino to commit suicide."

Soneri recognised that address – Pitti had led him there on two consecutive nights. It was the headquarters of La Maison s.r.l., Avanzini's company, in which it seemed Cornetti was a partner. Cornetti himself was an entrepreneur who had made his fortune in the post-war reconstruction boom. He restored houses damaged by the bombing at a speed which met the needs of an expanding city where the prime objective was to put a roof over the heads of countless homeless families.

The commissario lost no time in getting to Borgo Felino. There were two police cars there already, as well as a small crowd of inquisitive onlookers standing about in the cold. The officers let him into the secretarial offices, where he found a woman and a girl. The girl was holding a handkerchief to her nose and was sobbing. The older woman, who must have been in her fifties, appeared impassive but must have been deeply shaken. The officer pointed Soneri in the direction of a mahogany door which bore the nameplate AVANZINI, SURVEYOR. He pushed it open and the first thing he saw was blood everywhere – on the table, on documents, on the walls and even on the curtains, which were otherwise as grey as the mist outside.

Although elderly, Cornetti was a bull of a man, robust in build. His shoulders slumped over his partner's desk. Presumably, after sitting down in Avanzini's chair, he had taken out his revolver and pulled the trigger. The shot, fired from below, had blown away half his head. The pistol had ended up against the right-hand wall, flung there by Cornetti's final spasm.

Soneri closed the door as the girl started sobbing convulsively once again under the indifferent glance of the older woman. Nanetti turned up at that moment, and Soneri experienced a sense of relief at being able to rely on his colleague's assessment.

"Have you spoken to those two?" Soneri asked the officer in charge.

The officer shook his head. "The two of them seemed paralysed."

Soneri went up to the older woman, who had a vacant expression. Her eyes were open but her face lifeless. "Can you speak?" he said.

She shook herself and nodded.

"When did he get here?"

"We reopen at two thirty. He must have arrived a little before three."

"Was he upset? How did he behave?"

"He seemed perfectly calm, although he wasn't as jokey as he normally is."

"What happened next?"

"He asked if Signor Avanzini was in. We told him he'd be a bit late."

"And then he went in there?"

"First he asked for copies of some documents and contracts.

He sat down here, examined them, and then said he would need to study a licence Avanzini had left on his office desk."

"So then he went into the other room."

"That's right."

"Did he close the door?"

"Straightaway."

"How much time elapsed from that moment until you heard the shot?"

"A few minutes."

"Did you hear anything in the meantime?"

"Not precisely."

"Does that mean you did hear something?"

"We didn't know what he was doing. He seemed to be talking to someone on the telephone."

"You can tell from your desk if the line is engaged."

"It wasn't. He must have been using his mobile."

"Have you informed Signor Avanzini? What did he say?"

The woman shook her head vigorously. "Nothing. He didn't say a word."

"We'll need to find out who he was talking to before he shot himself," Soneri said to Nanetti as he came out of Avanzini's office.

"It really does look like suicide. I've seen so many."

The commissario was about to call Juvara when he appeared in person. "Dig into the background of these two and find out all you can about any connections between them – property, business, work, that sort of thing."

The inspector turned on his heels and disappeared down the stairs. Nanetti looked quizzically at Soneri to work out what he really thought about the whole affair, but before he asked him he took him into a room off the secretarial office. It was furnished luxuriously, and had a glass table in the centre of the room. "It's better in private," Nanetti said.

The commissario lit a cigar. "It seems obvious to me that it was an act of desperate revenge."

"No question about it. Why else would he have gone to his partner's office? He did it to attract attention."

"Maybe Avanzini had ruined him. He's always been a real wheeler-dealer and there's more to him than meets the eye. I've told Juvara to look into the connections between the two of them."

"It won't take us long to establish who Cornetti was talking to before he pulled the trigger," Nanetti said.

"As soon as we've done a preliminary search here, one of my men will have a look at his mobile."

Minutes later, the commissario was handed a sheet of paper. The last number dialled corresponded to Avanzini's mobile. "Just as I expected," he said to Nanetti.

"So it was him he was after. It's a kind of accusation."

"Yes, but accusing him of what?"

"At the end of the day, you'll see it's all to do with money. It's always a question of money or sex," Nanetti asserted with a confidence born of long experience.

With a jerk of his chin, Soneri indicated his agreement before turning away abruptly and leaving Nanetti in charge of the crime scene. He told the secretaries to keep themselves available, then ran down the stairs and out onto Borgo Felino. The mobile started ringing again.

"Commissario, there's no problem, I can search on the internet . . ." Juvara began.

"Alright, alright, you can update me in the office," Soneri said, cutting him off. He had no time for internet searches.

When he got to the questura, Juvara said nothing, but the commissario found on his desk a thick sheaf of papers detailing the history of Amintore Cornetti and his company.

He began reading in the light of the desk lamp given to him by Juvara. Cornetti was a self-made man, an ex-partisan who had started life as a bricklayer before beginning a steady ascent to the position of construction manager. In 1951 he set up a cooperative of housebuilders, which split up a few years later. He then formed the Cornetti firm, with the man the press called "the red builder" as chairman. In the Sixties he employed around sixty construction workers, and fifteen years later, during the first crisis, instead of laying off about half of them to keep the company afloat, he chose not to for idealistic reasons. He remained a communist, and so sank a large part of his own capital into the business until Avanzini came on the scene to offer him commissions for work for the State, the Region and the city councils. No two men could have been less alike. Cornetti was cheery, strong and extrovert, while Avanzini was gaunt, pale and untrustworthy, but it had worked, until now.

"Any relatives?" Soneri asked Juvara, breaking the silence.

"One son. I sent round a patrol car to break the news, then I called him."

"What did he say?"

The inspector shrugged. "He was polite, distant, even stand-offish. It was as if we were talking about the suicide of someone he didn't know."

"Did he have any idea why he might have done it?"

"If he did, he wasn't saying. If you want my opinion, I think he was afraid. He hasn't got his father's backbone. He's afraid they'll make him pay for it."

"In what way?"

"He runs a prefab business. If they take away the public-sector business, he's done for."

Soneri signalled his approval with a wave, and the inspector gave an embarrassed smile.

"I get the impression they were turning the screws on his father as well. I also think that the surveyor, Avanzini, was two-faced and was chewing him up bit by bit," the commissario said.

Juvara put down on Soneri's desk the outcome of the enquiries into Ghitta's lodgers, with the rents and charges each one had to pay. The commissario did no more than glance at them before getting up and going out again, but not before he had moved the lamp to the centre of his desk.

The afternoon light cut feebly into the thick veil of mist which kept the temperature down. He saw no point in going back to Borgo Felino, since he knew that once Nanetti had completed the search of the office and taken possession of all the material which might assist the inquiry, he would have sealed the area off. He headed for Via Petrarca, one of the stops on Pitti's nightly pilgrimage, but Avanzini was not there. A secretary told him he was unlikely to call into the office. "He is devastated," she said, picking out each syllable like a T.V. newsreader.

He continued on his way towards Borgo del Correggio and Via Saffi, pushing past the crowds heading in the direction of the city centre. When he arrived at No. 35 he saw that the shutters on the shisha bar were down, so he moved on to Bettati's barbershop, where an elderly gentleman was ensconced in the chair with lather over his cheeks and his body swathed in a large blue gown tucked in at the neck.

"So they've closed down another one?" Soneri said.

Bettati turned to him with a worried expression. "You mean the Pakistani? They made him shut down for a week because he wasn't keeping to the regulations but that's not the real reason. Nobody in the city centre bothers about regulations."

"I do know they upset some people," Soneri said.

"Yes, sure, but there's no way of knowing if it's because they get in the way of business, or for some other reason."

The commissario gave the barber a questioning look, indicating the man in the chair being shaved.

"You can speak freely. Zoni's from the party's old school. He'd sooner eat a live cat than breathe a word to them," Bettati said.

The man turned laboriously and nodded, shaking some of the lather off his face.

"Did you know that Cornetti killed himself?"

The razor slipped from the barber's hand onto the tray beside him. Zoni spun round once again, but this time more sharply.

"Just before three o'clock, in his partner's office."

The two men continued staring at him with expressions of childlike amazement.

"It means there's something rotten in this city and it's all going to hell more quickly than anyone expected," the barber said. The elderly gentleman turned his face back towards the mirror and did not move again.

"How did he get on with his partner?"

"He despised him. How could a man like Amintore Cornetti get on with a shit like Avanzini? At a certain point he was forced into an alliance with him, because this city has no time for people who actually make things. It's become the land of form-fillers, swindlers, and financiers who jumble up money and debts and then make them rise up like the white of a beaten egg. Cornetti knew how to work, while Avanzini had been to college. Cornetti built houses for people to live in, and his partner built houses to make money. You see the difference?"

Soneri nodded. Bettati was highly agitated and stopped running his razor over the cheeks of the old man in the chair, who now sat motionless, waiting patiently, with shaving foam dripping down his neck.

"When did they go into partnership?"

"In the early Eighties. At first Amintore was O.K. with his own firm because he knew the trade. You could even call him an artist, judging by the way he sculpted stone with his hammer and chisel, but he couldn't get any contracts or make any headway with the tendering system. He set up with that slug only because otherwise he was faced with sacking more than half his workforce."

These were matters Soneri was already familiar with from Juvara's papers, but hearing them directly from someone who had known the victim well made a deeper impact.

"Was Avanzini well connected with the political world?"

"He had contacts everywhere. And now that that right-wing mob is in power . . ."

The old man came back to life and made vigorous signs of approval, but Bettati got in before he could speak. "It's not that certain ex-comrades are any better. They got screwed at the elections and now they run the cooperatives and call themselves managers. They're in it up to their necks, and that's even worse." As he spoke he placed his hand on Zoni's shoulder and with one swift, almost enraged, stroke pulled the razor down his cheek.

"I agree the other guy cheated him," Soneri said.

"Around here nowadays it's only characters like that who get on – the most vile of human beings, hypocrites with no ideals except money, people who couldn't shovel snow in a backyard."

"I really believe the Battioni area has got something to do with it too."

"There's a good example. Cornetti lost a brother there in '44, but to set foot in the place now he has to plead for the good offices of that swine. I wonder if it was worth risking his skin. For what?"

They fell silent and Soneri, who had nothing to add, said goodbye and walked towards Piazzale San Francesco, where an enormous grey gate that slammed shut behind prisoners had once stood. It was the time of day when the streets changed character. The last offices were closing and well-dressed gents were returning to their out-of-town homes, while troops of immigrants were heading in the opposite direction, making for their modest lodgings in the city centre. People were spilling out of Arab shops onto the pavement, and chants from the desert rang out among houses where once the mazurka would have been heard. The shops which offered international telephone services bubbled with a noisy babel of voices as people communicated in their own dialects from one side of the sea to the other. The commissario's mobile struck up with "*La donna è mobile*". At the sound of that unfamiliar music a group of immigrants turned round sharply, as though they had heard the howl of a pack of hyenas.

"Commissario, it's just as we thought," Juvara said. "Cornetti was stitched up. His partner was cutting him out of everything. I've checked on the bids for the Battioni area. Avanzini put himself forward under his own name, with his own company, not with Maison – which included Cornetti."

"Gobbled up and thrown out like a fig skin."

"What did you say?"

"Avanzini treated him like a used tissue."

He heard a murmur of assent. "And another thing: for the Battioni area there was only one bid? Avanzini and his lot."

"What did you expect? They're all in it together."

As he hung up, he heard the creak of Fadiga's trolley in the distance and decided to go to his refuge to see if he had secreted any interesting clippings. As it happened there was one, and a surprising one at that. He found himself looking at the round, jovial face of Amintore Cornetti. Was he another of Ghitta's clients? The fact that he was something of a womaniser fitted in well enough with his exuberant nature, but his use of the facilities in the Tagliavini establishment made less sense. Juvara had told Soneri that Cornetti had been divorced for years, so it seemed absurd that he had to hide away in a pensione and pay by the hour. It was yet another mystery associated with that boarding house where so many young people had once lived. He remembered the immigrant woman telling Mohammed's wife about violent quarrels, and the shouting and bitter reproaches Elvira had directed at Pitti the previous evening, and he had the feeling that some-thing was going to happen that very night. He walked around aimlessly, waiting for the city to empty. He passed in front of a Muslim butcher's where they guaranteed that the meat was slaughtered in accordance with Islamic law, and then a Turkish bar where they served Coca-Cola and kebabs, as well as chips with various sauces whose scent floated into nearby doorways.

He paced around like an animal on the prowl. He had hoped to intercept Pitti or Elvira in that maze of abandoned streets and immigrant dwellings, but after a while he decided it made more sense to stop and wait. He took up his posi-tion in an alleyway which led to an inner courtyard, lit his cigar and kept his eye on the doorway where he had seen Pitti disappear through two nights in a row. Via Petrarca was shaken by successive gusts of wind, while the dark, thick mist floated past.

He stayed there for about half an hour, but saw only a few couples hurrying along. Perhaps the order to lie low had gone out after Cornetti's death. Or possibly Pitti, Elvira and their confederates were meeting somewhere away from their usual haunts. Maybe even in the pensione? As time passed Soneri began to doubt his certainties, which were further eroded by the chill of the mist and the emptiness of a street where nothing seemed to be happening. He was tempted to start walking and leave it to chance to arrange the time and place of an encounter, but he discarded that idea too. The pride of his convictions kept him fixed to the spot. He tried to light his cigar again but only ended up singeing the tips of his moustache. He stamped on the stub and leaned back against the wall. An old woman in the house across the road stretched out to close the shutters and paused a moment to stare at him. About ten minutes later, a squad car drew up alongside him but he waved it away. The driver recognised him, gave a salute and drove on.

Scarcely had the purr of the police car died away when another filled the silence. A Mercedes which Soneri had seen before came to a stop in front of the building which housed the headquarters of the Avanzini Company. Soneri watched Pitti get out, and as the car drove off he saw that he had with him one of those little wheeled suitcases he had seen in Elvira's room. Everything was unfolding as he had expected. All he had to do now was wait.

The visit was brief. Five minutes later Pitti reappeared, but without the case. Instead of turning into Via Saffi he headed for Via Repubblica, walked across Piazza Garibaldi and proceeded under the arcade in Via Mazzini. The commissario kept his distance so as not to be seen, and in this he was aided by the mist. They crossed the Ponte di Mezzo where the bed of the River Parma attracted the wispy mist, water calling to water, water flowing towards an outlet, water drifting aimlessly. At the Rocchetta he saw the monument to Filippo Corridoni depicted as he was struck by a bullet, his back arching in his last living act. Pitti walked round the monument, and then strode out towards Via Bixio. He rang the bell at No. 12 and went in, leaving the commissario wondering about the meaning of this change to the customary routine.

When Pitti re-emerged, he retraced his steps towards the bridge, turned off towards the Mercato della Ghiaia, continued along behind the Teatro Regio, walked diagonally across the Piazzale della Pace and then crossed Via Cavour in the direction of the Duomo. He now seemed to be back on his ordinary circuit. Taking the shortest route, he cut through the narrow streets and came out on Via Saffi. When he arrived at No. 35, he rang once and carried out the same ritual as previously, moving off on the usual diversionary round of the streets. At this point, Soneri made up his mind to give up his waiting game and to take action. He knew the route Pitti would take and followed him in his mind as though he were walking at his side. Viale Mentana, Borgo del Naviglio, Borgo Gazzola with the ladies of the night making eyes at him from the doorways, and at the end of Borgo Gazzola he began to count. He got to thirty-five, the number of the address, and crossed Via Saffi. He pressed the door bell, keeping his eye on the point where Pitti would re emerge, but the click of the lock came first and he went in. He did not switch on the light and climbed the steep stairs as quickly as he could. When he got to the entrance to the pensione, he waited a moment or two before pushing open the door which had been left ajar.

"Wait for me in the kitchen," Elvira shouted from her bedroom, in the peremptory tone of someone confidently in charge.

Soneri waited near the door for the buzzer to be sounded again, as happened a few seconds later. He had calculated the times perfectly. In an investigation, everything is down to timing and rhythm, and what he was experiencing had the beat and throb of a tango. He heard the shuffle of Elvira's slippers as she approached, surprised by that second ring of the bell, and when the woman made him out in the half-darkness her self-assurance dissolved into a grimace of baffled alarm. The commissario said nothing and limited himself to a weary gesture, raising his hand and pointing to the kitchen. He waited until Pitti tapped on the door before he pushed it decisively open. He did not give Pitti the time to utter a word to accompany his look of astonishment. "Come in, and go into the kitchen," he told him.

He waited for Pitti to stumble over the threshold, following immediately behind him. Elvira occupied both the seat and the pose which had been Ghitta's, from where she could check the lobby down to the main door. Pitti, with his bowler hat in his hand, did not know where to go until Elvira angrily pointed to a seat facing her. The commissario took up his position between them, like a priest or a lawyer dealing with a quarrelsome couple. All three remained silent for a while, with the tension building up until Soneri broke the ice with a simple question. "Aren't you going to ask if he found him?" he said to Elvira.

She shot back a cold, furious look. "I'd be wasting my time with a man like him."

"If you're alluding to the fact that he allowed himself to be shadowed, let me tell you that very few people would've been aware of it. You have a very low opinion of the police."

Elvira shrugged angrily.

"In any case," the commissario continued, "he did find him. And he left the case with him."

Pitti trembled as he had done that time in the church when he lit the candles in front of the statue of Sant'Uldarico. It was warm, but he kept his overcoat on and buttoned up, all the while twisting his bowler in his hands.

"What are you talking about?" Elvira said, feigning bewilderment but failing to conceal her fury. Soneri stared hard at her, at first expressing scorn before softening his expression to an ironic, mocking smile. He lit a cigar to calm himself and to help him choose carefully the most appropriate words. "You'd do well not to try to fool me this time," he said.

Pitti stood rooted to the spot, perspiration beginning to break out on his forehead.

"You're running this brothel now," Soneri finally said. After a brief pause, he went on, "And they're not coming here just to get laid. Besides, you were the one who gathered in the cash in Ghitta's name, so what was to stop you carrying on, on all fronts?"

Elvira listened, her cold eyes fixed on him. Her self-possession was astounding. She studied the commissario's every move attentively, looking for some chink that might offer refuge and permit her to escape the trap she found herself in. She was an intelligent woman who knew she was facing an expert adversary, and who judged that her best hope lay in doing nothing and remaining indifferent rather than risk playing a dud card.

"It was a shrewd move to take the blame for one sin so as to conceal another," Soneri said.

He gazed at both of them to see the effect of his words. Pitti looked like a statue. Large drops of sweat resembling blisters had formed on his almost bald skull. Elvira had understood only too well, and her silence was menacing.

"We've got nothing to do with it," she said at last.

"That depends on what you've got nothing to do with."

"Nothing at all. My mistake was not getting out of this place immediately."

"It wasn't easy to get away from Ghitta, was it?"

Elvira shook her head. She appeared deeply shaken,

perhaps feeling that she was the prisoner of too many secrets and too many threats.

"In the early days Ghitta looked after everything, and I was just a lodger."

"That's not quite true," Soneri interrupted her. "You collected the rents, and you did so quite willingly. They describe you as a tough operator."

"She asked me and I was in no position to refuse."

"I know. She lent money to your family and in Rigoso you were all tenants of hers."

Elvira stared at him in surprise. "I wasn't tough. The fact is I despised those women. They hated Ghitta, but they spoke about her as though she was a saint, while letting themselves be robbed of all they had. I've never understood people who praise their executioner."

"But you didn't have the guts to get free of Ghitta yourself – no more than anyone else," Soneri said.

"That's true, but I never liked her and even if I could have . . . Don't you see? She's still persecuting me even now that she's dead. My parents are elderly and I couldn't let her throw them out on the street. If it'd been up to me . . ."

Pitti listened without moving, getting warmer and warmer. It was only then that the commissario noticed that the stove behind him was lit.

"Once Ghitta was pronounced dead, you had every chance to get out, but something kept you tied to this place," Soneri said, drawing on his cigar.

"Exactly!" Elvira gave a nervous snigger. "I received her legacy." She looked at Pitti with calm contempt, her eyes seeming to cut through him. He kept his eyes to the floor, staring at some imprecise point between the table legs. He was a pitiful sight, sweating and awkward, incapable of any reaction.

"And he's the legacy, is he? He was already working for

third parties, so you could've left him to his own devices," Soneri said.

"The perfect servant: silent, devoted and open to blackmail."

"When were you drawn into executing these commissions?" Soneri said, turning to the still motionless Pitti, hat in hand like a peasant confronting his master.

The reply did not come from him. Elvira interrupted again, reminding Soneri of his mother, who had always replied on his behalf to doctors or teachers. "A couple of years ago. Ghitta used him to deliver private messages. She didn't trust the telephone."

"What did she have to tell people?"

"At the beginning, only the times and arrangements of the various couples. He explained this to me," she said, looking at Pitti, who remained obstinately silent. "The business came later."

Soneri bent down to look more closely at Pitti. There were drops of sweat running down his face from his forehead to his chin. His eyes seemed fixed under the table, wide open and staring as though confronted with a terrifying vision.

"Leave him be. It's like talking to a sulky child. Ghitta was smart enough to know how to manoeuvre him any way she wanted. She had a nose for that kind of thing. And then with that vice of his, everything about him made him weak. When the student intake thinned out and the rooms were left empty, Ghitta realised she could branch out into a more profitable, less stressful kind operation. In fact it started with former lodgers asking if she could provide a room for them. She'd remained on good terms with nearly all of them, so they'd drop by quite often to say hello. It seemed natural to allow a couple of hours' intimacy to ex-students who were prepared to pay well for the privilege, and at the same time Ghitta became the keeper of the secrets of some very important people. She felt she was once again at the centre of city life, and she knew how to make the most of the position she found herself in."

"So you landed the job of making appointments on Ghitta's behalf," Soneri said, turning to Pitti and addressing him with what was meant to be a question but which came out like a statement.

Soneri thought he saw Pitti nod ever so slightly. "Take off your coat," the commissario said. Only then did Pitti raise his eyes, revealing the utter terror by which he was gripped.

"Did you hear me? I told you to take off your coat," Soneri repeated peremptorily.

Pitti raised his eyes, but he made no move, until Elvira, with that authoritarian tone she always adopted with him, ordered him, "Take your coat off! Are you deaf?" After a few seconds she went on: "The party's over, Pitti. Everything's bound to come out now."

She spoke as though she had nothing to do with it. Pitti did not dare reply. The commissario wondered if deep down Pitti took pleasure in submitting himself.

At that point he got up slowly, undid the belt and with equal calm unbuttoned the coat, pausing an instant before he pulled it open. There was something feminine and inviting in his movements, although he was trembling. The commissario moved forward, taking hold of the coat at the level of the top button, like a butler assisting a newly arrived guest, and at that moment he saw a package neatly tucked into the deep inside pocket.

He ripped off the wrapping and pulled out a plastic envelope, just like the ones Forensics used to contain their finds. Inside he found several bundles of one-hundred-euro notes. He tossed them onto the table with that mixture of relief and satisfaction a cardsharp finds when he plays an ace in the last round, except that this was not the last hand.

"So this is the pay-off," he said, moving his eyes from the envelope to the couple, and letting his gaze rest on Pitti.

"Certainly, but not for me," Pitti said, finally opening his mouth. As had happened when he first heard him speak at their meeting in the doorway of the Chiesa di Sant'Uldarico, the commissario was taken aback by the low, bass tones of his voice.

"You're not going to tell me again that you owe money to some friend or other."

"No, but she knows what it was for," Pitti said.

"I imagine she does. You've been round to see Avanzini and you left off some documents relating to the bids for what used to be the Battioni industrial area. In exchange, you were given the bribe you were to hand over to some official in the Council. You've both been obliged to play away from home because after the death of Ghitta this boarding house has become a minefield. But explain to me why you didn't just go straight to the person the bribe was meant for? Why did you come here first?"

Pitti looked nervously at Elvira, waiting for guidance. He did not dare reply, even though he gave the impression of wanting to, so as to get the commissario off his back. The seconds went by. Soneri stood completely still, observing the scene, watching Pitti breathe heavily but saying not a word, until the ringing of a mobile cut through the atmosphere. The ringtone was a distorted, music-box jingle of the "Hymn to Joy" – bizarre in that situation.

"Not answering?" Soneri said, noting Elvira's hesitation.

She made no move, allowing Beethoven's music to play on. When it died away, Soneri grabbed her mobile to take a note of the caller's number, but there was no indication of it in the record of calls. He put the mobile down and turned to Elvira. Behind her the long lobby stretched out, with the doors leading off it and, at the far end, the living room which overlooked Via Saffi. The wall-mounted telephone and the shelf beneath it with the device for calculating the cost of calls were a bit further back, next to the main door. At that moment, Soneri understood those mysterious nocturnal calls where he had made out only anxious silences, murmurs and whispers.

"That was the person who was to receive the bribes, wasn't it?" He spoke quietly from behind Elvira, in a tone which might have even seemed gentle.

She nodded, but her expression was serious. Quite suddenly, she appeared bent and cowed. Perhaps she had given in.

"Since the people in question had to stay away from the pensione, they called to let you know where the handover of the money would take place. Is that right?"

Once again a nod of assent, while Pitti now wore a relieved expression, freed from the responsibility of answering.

"Pitti picked up the money, came round here and waited until the call came telling him where to take it?" Soneri went on.

"Originally it was all done here," Elvira said. "They would turn up with their lovers, hand over the cash and do their screwing. Everybody was happy. Ghitta had a tidy income, the city officials got rich and the mistresses received a little something to celebrate all that money."

"But now you two take the share that used to go to Ghitta."

Elvira said nothing, but her expression spoke for her.

"Is the mobile used for the communications registered in your name?" Soneri said.

"No! The S.I.M. card must have been bought in the name of some company. We're talking about smart, powerful people. They're all convinced they're untouchable."

Soneri saw in his mind's eye that shadowy world of dealers, ex-revolutionaries converted to the cult of money, *nouveaux riches*, blackmailers, the undergrowth of a province engulfed by dubious wealth. He recalled too the barricades and the glorious disobedience of a people poor but proud, capable of heroism. The contrast aroused in him a powerful feeling of disgust and made him turn his thoughts away for fear of succumbing to a deep depression.

"Smart, no question they were smart," he repeated as though talking to himself, "but there was a weak link," he added, looking over at Pitti, who had not moved.

"Who would ever have thought that someone like him … All his life he's been parading around the city dressed in that ludicrous style," Elvira said, making no effort to conceal her contempt.

"The only one to understand would be another person who loves walking about at night as much as he does," Soneri said, realising immediately that he had spoken instinctively, without reflecting.

"You mean that you too . . ." Elvira sounded astounded. She stopped in her tracks, her expression half incredulous and half curious.

"There's one other matter to be cleared up," the commissario said, turning back to Pitti. "What were you doing in Via Bixio? The far side of the river is not on your usual round."

Pitti started at Elvira, with the bewilderment of a child looking to his mother for advice. She gave a wave of her hand, granting permission.

"Cornetti's son lives there," he said in his deep voice.

"What did you have to tell him?"

"To keep calm."

"What about? Whose message was that?"

Pitti stretched out his arms to imply that the reply was self-evident. "Avanzini, obviously."

"Why was he being told to keep calm? Was he threatening to reveal something inconvenient?"

Pitti shook his head in denial and as he did so a bead of sweat rolled down behind his ear. "He was to keep calm about the firm – his firm."

It was only then that the commissario grasped the situation. It was a threat disguised as reassurance. "Was he deeply in debt?"

"So it would seem, but they told me to let him know that the banks wouldn't move unless something changed."

"In other words, if he keeps quiet about various shady dealings," the commissario concluded, thinking immediately of a son who betrays his father just to keep afloat. The whole story was marked by acts of betrayal, and perhaps this was the least of them.

There followed a silence which seemed to last an eternity. Soneri was deep in thought and the other two could do no more than wait anxiously. It was, unexpectedly, Pitti who spoke first. "What are you going to do now?"

The commissario shrugged. "You can explain everything to one of my colleagues. I can't make head nor tail of finances and public tenders," he said, while a deep disappointment, as dark as sewage water, threatened to overwhelm him. He had been digging and digging, and had found a path, but he was convinced it was not the one which would enable him to explain Ghitta's death.

9

HE WOKE EVEN later the following morning, when the city was buzzing with cars and with people on the move. As soon as he got up, he felt a strange sense of disorientation, but thinking back to what had taken place the previous night, he realised he was internalising the disappointment and profound bitterness he had felt then and was feeling still. After the half-hearted confessions he had heard, he had lost all interest in the story of bribery and furtive couplings at the Pensione Tagliavini. He remembered Juvara turning up, half asleep and dishevelled, and he recalled handing over the plastic envelope and explaining to him what he had learned. After that, he left without even saying goodbye. He felt let down, primarily by his own intuition.

Standing beside his coffee maker as it bubbled away, unsettled because his routine of rising in the silence of dawn had been disrupted, he reflected that he was back to square one. He saw Ghitta stretched out, already rigid, and was convinced he knew no more now than he did at that moment. He had to begin again, but from where? He had not even had time to think the matter over when his mobile rang just as he was dipping his first biscuit into the coffee.

It was Chillemi. "Soneri, we must meet. You've stirred up a hornet's nest." His tone was confidential, but the acting vice-questore was a hypocrite, always pretending to be everyone's best friend.

"Have you spoken to Juvara?"

"I've seen the report," Chillemi said, lowering his voice to a whisper to underline the gravity of the situation. "We're dealing with powerful people here. Do you realise whose toes we may be treading on? These people are friends of politicians and can get access to the Ministry in three moves, do you understand?"

"You'd be better off entrusting the case to someone else. I've had all I can take of Ghitta's murder."

"I'll see what the magistrate has to say."

Soneri switched off his mobile and turned back to his caffelatte. Was it his fault that the city had become corrupt and appeared more rotten by the day? Was he to blame if the spark and colours dancing over the streets were no more than the polychrome mould that blossoms as an organism decays? Later, as he made his way through the bowels of the city centre, he was almost overcome by the sickly-sweet smell of vomit and fermentation which pursued him all the way to Piazza Duomo. Trombi was waiting for him with photos of Ada's mysterious companion, and when he turned into Borgo Angelo Mazza the spectacle which met him seemed in his eyes similar to the one he had seen in the foyer of the Teatro Regio, even if the fairy lights created the atmosphere of a country dance hall.

From below street level that maddening clatter of feet, like a column on the march, seemed louder than ever. The photographer asked him to wait, and disappeared into his dark room. When he closed the door, a flickering red light went on in the corner above them. Together with the noise of the footsteps, it reinforced the impression of a siege.

"Here we are," Trombi said, as he reappeared. "It's all

I could find. They're images from some years back. I've got nothing more recent. That means he lives a quiet life or else he's left for another city."

Soneri scrutinised the prints. The sight of Ada's face revived in him the collision between police investigation and personal autopsy which was tearing him apart. Perhaps, more than anything else, it was the chance to escape from rummaging about among the detritus of his own past that had made him so keen to follow the trail of the bribes. Chance had dangled before him the prospect of an emergency exit, and he had seized that opportunity.

He thanked Trombi, said his goodbyes and came out from the tomb in which the memory of the city reposed. He found himself once again immersed in that disorderly flood of humanity seeking happiness in shop windows. As he arrived at the sentry post outside the questura, he remembered that he was supposed to call on Chillemi.

The vice-questore was his usual toadying self, standing close to him, speaking in fawning, insinuating tones which reminded him of an elderly parish priest or a street-corner dealer.

"I've heard from Dottor Capuozzo in Amalfi," he informed him, and Soneri imagined the questore with a vast napkin round his neck, licking his lips as he bent over a mountain of *spaghetti allo scoglio*. "He advises caution. He agrees you should be removed from this inquiry."

Knowing Capuozzo, the commissario assumed he was afraid of the problems that might be created for him if Soneri stirred up trouble with politicians, and he gave a little laugh.

Chillemi watched him without understanding. He was not particularly bright – just wily.

"So I sprang into action. I've spent the morning on the telephone," Chillemi said.

Soneri remained silent, watching and waiting for what was to come next.

"In consultation with Dottor Capuozzo, I decided the way forward was to contact the magistrate and suggest uncoupling the murder investigation from the search for the parties involved in the bribery scandal."

He never could reach a conclusion, and the commissario had no patience for his endless preambles. He nodded his head vigorously with the air of a busy man who simply wants to know where it's all going to end.

"There we are. We've decided, Dottor Capuozzo and Dottor Saltapico and I, to entrust the bribery enquiry to Guardia di Finanza, who are experience in these matters. Not least because you yourself told me you were entirely familiar with questions of contracts and balance sheets," Capuozzo added, becoming more self-righteous by the minute.

"Who in the Finanza will be directing the operation?"

"You can contact Maresciallo Maffetoni."

Chillemi wrote a mobile number on a slip of paper and pushed it over the table to Soneri. "But you carry on, eh?" he recommended in the tone he would have used to encourage a child to concentrate on his studies.

Soneri made his way to his office with Chillemi's final words ringing in his ears. He had no idea which direction to take. He was still of the opinion that the bribery network, while centred on the Pensione Tagliavini, had nothing to do with the murder.

"It's not gone well for you," he announced to Juvara a little later.

"What do you mean?"

"The inquiry into the bribery scandal has been entrusted to Maresciallo Maffetone of the Guardia di Finanza. Your career's on hold."

The inspector shrugged. "I've got plenty to do."

"Neither of us is reliable enough for issues involving politics."

"Just as well. That sort of case causes more trouble than it's worth."

The commissario's mobile postponed further conversation.

"Come round to my office," Angela said. "I'll send out for a couple of pizzas."

"Alright." The commissario did not like arranging lunches and dinners, but he said, "At the very least make sure you get them to use real mozzarella – *mozzarella di bufala* – and *prosciutto*."

He was in a grumpy mood as he got up from his desk. This time it was he who felt weighed down by the oppressive banality of meeting as a couple for lunch between one job and the next. Having a meal with Angela would scarcely disrupt his day, but he always looked forward to those strolls with only his own thoughts for company. These at least satisfied his insatiable desire for time alone.

"Would you like to run your eye over the list of Ghitta's tenants?" Juvara asked him.

He peered at it in the flickering light of the lamp on his desk. It had every appearance of a job thoroughly done, everything neatly set out in columns or in boxes in accordance with the iron discipline of some computer programme.

"Do you notice anything?"

The inspector nodded. "In the early Eighties, Ghitta Tagliavini gave Cornetti an apartment rent-free in Borgo delle Colonne."

Soneri stood for a moment in silence, his eyes fixed on

the courtyard where some officers were chatting next to the petrol pump reserved for police cars.

"Cornetti was a house-builder. Why on earth would he have wanted a flat from somebody else? And why should Ghitta have made one available without charging rent?" Juvara said.

"That's the strangest thing of all, considering how attached she was to money," Soneri said.

"And yet according to the records she kept it would appear there was no income from that house in the period Cornetti had it."

"Did you try to find out if he used the place as an office?"

"I went round, but I found only Africans and Arabs there. There's not one of the old tenants left, and the all other apartments have been bought up by some big property firm."

Soneri gave a snort. "This city has been broken apart and no-one can work out where to find the pieces."

Puzzled, Juvara watched him put on his duffel coat and go out, but he was accustomed to the commissario's enigmatic outbursts and knew it was pointless to ask for an explanation.

Soneri walked towards the city centre under a grey sky which hid the Campanile del Duomo and the spires of the Battistero. For some days now, the sun had been bouncing off a buffer of mist which allowed no warmth through, and beneath it the city was putrefying in a choking soup of exhaust fumes.

Angela had cleared her desk and saw that the first thing to do was to calm the commissario down. "My colleague is off sick," she said, locking her studio door.

The office overlooked the Mercato della Ghiaia, and from there the view opened out onto the riverside walk and beyond to the River Parma and the far bank where a wall of houses marked the beginning of the Oltretorrente district. Soneri had always liked Angela's office. It reminded him of the attic of his house in the country from where, as a boy, he had looked down onto the farmyard.

He cut the pizza in two, took his share, folded it to make it a sandwich and bit into it.

"You know how I hate eating from paper," he justified himself.

"You sound like a student from Cambridge."

"Where they eat rubbish wrapped up in paper and drink from plastic cups. I've always eaten off majolica. When you eat badly, there's no real civilisation."

Angela grimaced. "Another of your pronouncements. Not even a *giudice di tribunale* . . ." She concluded with a gesture in which Soneri recognised an advocate addressing a jury.

"What's this story about bribery and corruption?" She said when he failed to take the bait.

"Who told you about that?"

"Have you not read today's paper? It says that the Guardia di Finanza is opening an investigation into corruption in the construction industry," Angela said.

Soneri put down the slice of pizza. Chillemi must have briefed the newspapers the evening before, in time for them to get the news onto the front page. Quite suddenly, the *mozzarella di bufala* turned cold and chewy, the tomato mouldy, the pastry lumpy. A shiver ran up his spine, freezing his thoughts. He understood what lay behind Chillemi's duplicity, but he also knew that he was only the executor: the instigator was Capuozzo. He could just see Capuozzo, with that greasy mouth of his, issuing orders in a noisy restaurant in Amalfi overlooking the sea, surrounded by obsequious waiters bowing and scraping at his every command.

He felt Angela's warm hands massaging his neck before her arms wrapped themselves round him. Feeling like a semi-comatose patient being revived, he let her do as she wished, until finally, slowly, he abandoned himself to her warm body, finding refuge there with infinite gratitude.

Afterwards, the commissario felt the anger inside him cool down and settle into a crust of bitterness, more bearable in itself but more tenacious in its grip. It was yet another wound to be added to so many more.

"You shouldn't have given up. You know perfectly well they detest you and they'll seize any chance to trip you up," his partner chided him affectionately.

"I'd rather have given up on the Ghitta case as well."

"Free spirits like you are always a pain. If you're not a member of the club, you're going to have them all on your back. You should have been a Philip Marlowe, not a regular commissario in a police force."

Soneri snorted impatiently.

"You know that's the truth. You're not a resource, you're a problem."

Confronted with that remark, the commissario fell silent. It had passed over his skin like a razor pulled against the grain, painful but true.

"When all's said and done, we're all bit players, all of us — policemen, murderers, thieves."

Puzzled, Angela looked at him with an expression that suggested she had not really understood. She changed tack. "Why are you so sure that the corruption scandal has nothing to do with it? Ghitta knew, and perhaps they were afraid she'd spill the beans. Or maybe she was blackmailing them. Didn't she do the same to the old women?"

"But then why would they have carried on using the pensione, or using Pitti and Elvira? The night after the murder there were several telephone calls from people in the loop, who obviously didn't know what had happened. If the order to get rid of her had gone out from that circle, they wouldn't have called, because they ran the risk of betraying themselves or falling into a trap."

"It's a funny business," Angela said. "And the deeper you go into it, the more the mysteries pile up – Fernanda disappearing, Ghitta deserted by all and sundry, her man disinherited, her son living like a hermit."

"That's the way it goes. The deeper you dig into someone's life, the more likely you are to come up with something unexpected. We'd find an enigma as well if we were to search too deeply inside ourselves."

"I knew that's what you were getting at. Can you please just get over yourself? All it took was one glimpse of a photograph of your wife for you to end up gazing at your own navel."

"I was desperate to look beyond my navel, but the whole investigation kept bringing me back there. Why do you think I was so keen to give up? I was relieved when I stumbled on this bribery business. At long last there was a twist which would take me away from my nightmares, but I still don't think it's the right track. Unfortunately, I can't stop facing up to my past and everything that was part of it."

"So what's the way out? To go to a psychoanalyst hoping he'll tell you in which corner of your mind the murderer is hiding?" Angela spoke brusquely in a deliberate attempt to shake him out of his mood.

"It's got nothing to do with my brain, but maybe it has got something to do with my life. Anyway, it's in the fertile dung heap of the Pensione Tagliavini that we've got to probe."

Neither of them spoke for a while. Soneri always had the

knack of finding the right word to bring a conversation to an close. Angela was now gazing at him with a half-perplexed, half-convinced expression.

Soneri changed the subject. "Do you know a lawyer called Selvatici?"

"A criminal lawyer, but he's so odd that he doesn't get much work, except from certain circles."

"Which circles?"

"Extremist ones, both right and left, including violent neo-Fascist movements. Anything to do with politics. I know he's always on the move and he'll stay over in other cities for days just to follow a trial."

"He was one of those who took to the streets in the early Sixties and maybe he was mixed up with the Fascists," Soneri said, producing one of Trombi's photographs.

Angela stared hard at it. "It looks like something from centuries ago."

"Everything goes rushing past, and your perspective changes so quickly. You get distracted for a moment and you find the scenery has changed. What was there before? Who remembers? There are people who died for something which ten years later is dismissed as a trifle. If the ones who died had survived, they'd be the first to agree. Now I'm the one with the same job as the police medic who has to cut open corpses that have been exhumed and are putrefying."

The more she listened to the commissario, the more Angela was reluctant to speak. Normally so talkative, she was gradually falling under the spell of the music he was playing, even if, unfortunately, the air was now a "Miserere".

"Where can I find this Selvatici?"

"His office is in Via Collegio dei Nobili, next to the court."

This information seemed suddenly to reanimate the commissario, who jumped from his seat and took out a cigar which he stuck unlit in his mouth. Angela put the remains of the still-wrapped pizza into his hand, and he felt like a husband accepting his packed lunch.

As he walked to Via Collegio dei Nobili, his mobile began to ring. He recognised the number of Chillemi's secretary, a decidedly unpleasant individual. "Can I put you though?" she said, as though there was any choice. Soneri grunted something and heard the on-hold music strike up. Next came, "Commissario, I'm very sorry, but these shit-bags of journalists! They write anything they like, and don't give a damn." The introductory theatrical flourish was one of Chillemi's trademarks. It was his way of assailing the person he was addressing without giving them time to speak. It allowed him to vomit out sufficient apologies to turn anyone's stomach, while hurling abuse at the suppos-edly responsible parties, in this case journalists. Swearing helped to make his speech more colourful, taking it down one step from bureaucratese, thereby making it sound more confidential.

While Soneri was wondering if Chillemi was further up his own arse than anyone else in the questura, the man himself continued to offer apologies and "communicate the regrets of Dottor Capuozzo, who was not at that moment in a position to do so in person". He must have been in Amalfi still, squaring up to the challenge of a sea bass.

"I have to tell you that your name came up at the press conference. If you don't believe me, ask Dottoressa Marinati or Dottor Columbro. It's not the first time. Just a few months ago, it happened to Dottor Naselli."

Chillemi beat out words at the speed of an auctioneer, but Soneri was waiting for the moment when he would exhaust the entire gamut of vulgarities and his voice would fade into a series of low moans. He could measure the seriousness of his own situation from the length of the scene. And he hadn't even read the papers yet!

When the vice-questore finally drew breath, Soneri let a couple of seconds pass before announcing icily, "Doesn't matter."

He had the impression that the receiver at the other end of the line had fallen to the floor. Chillemi must have been disconcerted by the commissario's detachment, because he could not manage to string two words together. Soneri had the satisfaction of ending the conversation without giving him time to start up again. "Goodbye for now," he said, as he hung up.

Arriving at Selvatici's office, Soneri rang the bell, and since there was no reply he pushed open the street door and found himself facing the concierge's booth. "Selvatici? Unlikely to find him at this time of day," the concierge said. He was a squat little man with a big head, making him look like an overgrown mushroom. "Try again this evening, perhaps after dinner."

The commissario turned on his heel and decided to drop in on Marta Bernazzoli. Selvatici was known as the extremists' lawyer, and Dallacasa came into that category. Perhaps she would know something about him.

She offered him a seat, all the while fixing him with her cold, attentive stare. As on the previous occasion, Soneri was struck by the orderliness and cleanliness of the steel and glass surfaces which filled the apartment with light and reflections. They both felt awkward as they sat down, he because he did not know where to begin, she because she feared some further probe into her past.

"Any news?" Bernazzoli said.

"You've heard about Cornetti, haven't you?"

She nodded. "I never thought he'd do it. It's enough to crush all hope."

"He was done for – his company, I mean . . ."

"The company, yes, of course, but he could have soldiered on even without it. Can you really believe he had no money put aside?"

"I've no idea."

"He always had plenty, and he loved life."

"So then, why?"

"Who knows? Why would anyone have killed Mario if the Fascists had nothing to do with it?"

"I've had a look at the file. The investigations got nowhere. There's not the least trace of a possible line of enquiry."

"In these cases, the solution might be the most banal imaginable, or else the least probable."

"His comrades in terrorist cells?"

"That's what some of his colleagues suggested."

"Did you know Cornetti well?"

"I knew him. He was a man of the left, someone who counted in the city. His workers voted Communist. He used to say they were the best, because they had the party discipline in their blood and they applied it in the workplace."

"No-one ever brought to his attention that he was a boss?"

"He thought of the company as a means of financing the class struggle. I understand he gave a lot of money to the party, but from about the mid-Seventies he began to fall out with it. He considered himself a purist and viewed the party leadership in those days as traitors."

Soneri took out a cigar and put it in his mouth, but a dark look from Marta persuaded him to leave it unlit.

"Did he leave the party?"

"Why are you asking me these questions," Marta said, with

a smile of surprise. "Everyone knew he was a sympathiser with the far left."

"Did he finance these groups?"

"How should I know? That was what was being said, but there's so much gossip around nowadays. Cornetti was unique, and highly controversial. His roots were in anarchism, as was the case with many ordinary people from this area. Perhaps that was why – not forgetting his obvious vitality – he couldn't stand being controlled by party rules and regulations. There were always quarrels and disputes, but the executive couldn't expel him because of the money he was donating. He bought their indulgence."

"If he'd been born earlier, he would have joined the anti-Fascist *Arditi*," Soneri said.

"He certainly would. Like them he was a great drinker, a great womaniser, always up to something in the back stalls of the Teatro Regio. Everything he did was over the top. There was something theatrical about his death too. Don't you think the act was a bit melodramatic?"

"He was one of the old guard," the commissario said, making no effort to conceal his admiration. "Is it really possible for a man like him to chicken out and shoot himself?"

Marta smiled and her cold expression changed into one of contempt. "Elephants are not afraid of lions, but they are scared of mice."

Soneri enjoyed the metaphor, although Avanzini was more like a sewer rat than a mouse. "Cornetti would have had to fight on terrain which was far from his natural habitat: shady deals, political friendships, corruption."

"Amintore Cornetti could never have done that, especially with the right in power," Marta said. "But I don't believe that's all there was to it. Shortly before Mario was murdered, Amintore confessed to him that he felt out of things.

He said he no longer understood the world around him."

"Including his son?"

"What a weakling! He spent far too long in his father's shadow, and couldn't find any better way of breaking free than fighting with him about everything. He went so far as to turn himself into a petty right-wing *arriviste*." She jumped to her feet and started walking about the room in the grip of an agitation she struggled to control. She stopped beside the window, looking out anxiously.

"When all's said and done, Cornetti was great right up to the end," she said. "He had the courage to take a decision many of us would like to, but don't have the guts for. Here too he was in a class of his own."

"Everybody's got to play their own part. Just think how useful you could be to other people, with the skills you have." Soneri was fumbling for words in an attempt to console her.

"You can't be useful to other people if you feel you're a burden to yourself. I'm an atheist. What hope can I have? I believe that everything will come to an end, and if even this world rejects the prospect of improvement and becomes the sewer it's turning into, what's the point? Isn't living in these conditions harder than dying?"

The commissario felt as though he was caught in a whirlpool, and that there was only one logical outcome. He was afraid of that conclusion, and as a distraction he took out the photographs Trombi had given him. "Do you recognise any of these people?"

Marta gave a start, and then looked carefully at the images, turning them towards the light. Her eyes lost their cold look and turned softer. "This one is Selvatici, and the other . . ." She hesitated, turning to face Soneri. "He was a student – of engineering, I think. I believe he used to hang out at Ghitta's."

"Can't you tell me his name?"

Marta looked embarrassed, like the time he had asked her about the abortions. "You've already asked me about this person. Why are you so keen to go ferreting about in the lives of someone you used to love? Let it be. It's better for you and for those who can no longer give you an explanation."

"I agree. I wouldn't have done it if this investigation . . . Look, it's not a question of personal curiosity, but of professional duty. Maybe there's a bit of nostalgia for those years mixed up in it all."

Marta seemed once again deeply troubled, and her eyes were veiled with tears.

"I know his name is Andrea, but I don't remember his family name. He was active on the extreme left. Mario mentioned him once or twice. A strange man whose father was a communist, but who grew up in Catholic circles. He took after the priests when it came to discretion. Never seemed to assert himself. He had to introduce himself afresh time and time again because no-one ever remembered him."

The commissario experienced the sting of jealousy. Mystery gave added substance to the figure of a man who revived phantoms which had barely been laid to rest. The deepening shadows outside made the light of the halogen lamps shine out more brightly, dancing on the metallic surfaces. The real blinding light was created inside the commissario by feelings which prevented him from reasoning and which made all lucid thoughts fade into dark regrets. It was better not to probe any more deeply. He said goodbye to Marta, even though he was perfectly aware he was taking flight. From himself and from his past.

"Any news?" he asked Juvara with some anxiety when he returned to the questura.

"Our people are out looking for Avanzini, but he's nowhere to be found. The Guardia di Finanza is after him too."

The commissario groaned and the inspector wondered if it was because he was annoyed at the setback or because he was not interested in the news. "I was talking about the rent-free apartment in Borgo delle Colonne."

"There are only a few more details," Juvara said. "It's not easy making enquiries in a place where there's no memory. Nobody remembers, nobody knows anything."

Quite suddenly, Soneri felt as though he was carrying on his back the weight of too many things which all needed attending to. He turned away quickly and saw the afternoon mail lying on his desk. The envelope on the top of the pile was of the cardboard-pack type, which he opened to find a list of adjectives in the questore's spidery writing. "My very best and heartiest good wishes for a Happy Christmas and a prosperous New Year." In a rage, he tore the card to tiny pieces which he tossed into the basket.

"Why should I bother with people who're trying to make me look like an arsehole?"

"Cornetti had a three-year lease on the apartment in Borgo delle Colonne. I can confirm that no rent was ever paid," Juvara said, in an effort to calm him down.

"So why did they go to the bother of drawing up a contract?"

"There was a sum of money stipulated in the contract, but Ghitta never received it. It doesn't even appear in the balance sheets."

"For appearances only."

"Looks like it. And that's before we come to the oddity of a building contractor who rents an apartment from someone else."

The commissario gestured with the cigar he was clutching

between his index finger and his thumb. "Perhaps it was so he could put someone else there, do someone else a favour," Soneri said.

When the inspector gave him an answering look which implied agreement, Soneri realised he was in all probability not far off the mark.

"What's Maffettone been up to?"

"Who knows? Not so much as a telephone call."

"The famous working relationship between the forces of law and order, eh?"

"I've been looking into the property Cornetti owned," Juvara said, following his usual practice of keeping the really important information to the last. He was one of those who always set the little cherry on the cake to one side in order to savour it at the end.

Again Soneri made a gesture with his cigar, only this time with greater urgency, almost annoyance.

"The company was on its last legs. For some years, Cornetti had not been replacing employees who retired and who were more or less the same age as him. By the end he had a very small staff, three or four journeymen who attended to the subcontractors."

"He went with the flow of the times. Avanzini didn't have many workers either," the commissario said.

"Yes, but he still won the contracts, while Cornetti had to struggle on, clinging to any lifeline they threw him. For the most part he was on his own."

"Alright, we know all this," the commissario said impatiently.

"Personally he was not a rich man," Juvara said, trying to carry on with what he wanted to say. "He had a flat in the Oltretorrente district, a car and a current account which was no different from those of his employees."

The commissario gave a scowl, sticking out his chin. "You'll be telling me next he had money stashed away in Switzerland?"

The inspector shook his head. "The fact is his ex-wife is extremely rich and there's no knowing why."

"The one he divorced?"

"Yes. They met when they were both in the party. She was devoted to him and always forgave him everything he did. They've remained in close contact, and in fact she still did secretarial work for him."

"And she's loaded?"

"She has stacks of cash. Since there was no inherited wealth, it's reasonable to suppose we're talking about money put aside by Cornetti in her name, to prevent it being swallowed up in the event of bankruptcy."

"Were the company's balance sheets clean?" the commissario said, lighting his cigar.

"We're working on that, but at first sight the whole thing looks to me like a total shithouse."

"Who's on the job apart from you? Maffettone?"

"We've got our own external consultants."

"What do you mean by shithouse?"

"The figures don't add up. There's no question there were parallel accounts. A black economy, I mean."

"The same as with every company. With an unofficial black ledger, you can do things you could never put into the official books."

"If it comes to that, you can put anything in the balance sheets. All you need is to know how to dress it up," Juvara said.

"Yes, but it's easier with a secret account, and you pay less in taxes. And then, since you can buy anything you want with money . . . Was that not how it was with Avanzini too?"

Juvara made no reply, his head still bowed over the ledgers. "But what did Cornetti actually buy?"

"How do I know. Perhaps he only paid out," the commissario said.

The inspector looked at him, but could not understand what was going on. Soneri's face had that impenetrable expression he wore when he was he was lost in his own thoughts. Juvara decided to leave the next move to him. The commissario was thinking over what Marta had said about the finances donated to the party and then, after the split, to far-left groups.

"I don't believe he was like the others. For him, business was not totally devoid of ideals. Quite the reverse – business was often captive to his ideals."

Juvara was not sure what Soneri was getting at, but he grasped the underlying concept. "He was born into anarchist and communist circles."

Soneri nodded as he inhaled on his cigar. He was about to change the subject when he remembered that friend of Ada's who appeared from time to time in Trombi's photographs. He was on the point of asking Juvara to look into the matter, but a sense of guilt held him back. He got up and went over to the window, from where he could see that Via Repubblica had finally fallen quiet. The city was calming down and adjusting to the rhythms of the steam which at that moment was rising in spirals from plates of minestrone on tables all over the city.

That thought was all it took to reawaken his appetite. He made his farewell and set off for the *Milord*. But he had no wish to take a seat in the main dining area. He preferred to sit in the kitchen and follow the conversation between the cooks and waiters, or to chat at intervals to Alceste. He was at home there. It was at dinner time that he still felt most urgently the longing to have a wife and children, but as he let his thoughts wander, merely sitting at table recalled so many other pleasing things.

Alceste brought him a plate of minced horsemeat with oil, salt and lemon. "An injection of energy" was the comment that accompanied it.

Soneri needed it. The temperature had dropped further and a freezing mist would soon paint the night white. The steam rising from the pans jolted his memory, and the Bonarda stimulated his imagination, making him think dreamily of that spirit which floated in the darkness like a ghost fluttering in the shadowy wings of some theatre. Later, when he saw the first nocturnal walker emerge from the darkness, he had the impression that he had before him a creature made of the insubstantial stuff of dreams, but he lost him in the labyrinth of lanes that made up the old city. Meanwhile, an insistent creaking sound signalled the approach of the trolley Fadiga was pushing ahead of him. In Via Saffi, he noticed that the shisha bar was still closed, but he carefully avoided passing in front of the pensione, preferring to go instead in the direction of San Giovanni Evangelista. He turned into Via Petrarca, and waited in the same place as before. When someone came out of the main door, he slipped into the entrance hall. Standing in front of the company's entrance, he wondered if Pitti had a prearranged means of announcing his arrival, but after a while he decided he did not care. He knocked, at first gently with his knuckles but then more firmly with his clenched fist. After a while, the door opened a fraction, and a man with a distrustful expression peeped out. The commissario put his hand to the door and pushed, bringing Avanzini bit by bit into full view.

"Who are you?" Avanzini stuttered, terrified.

"Commissario Soneri, police."

Avanzini drew back, now resigned. "I was out of the city

today. I have also received a call from a maresciallo in the Guardia di Finanza."

They went into his studio. "I told him I can't explain the reasons for this suicide, and that I did all I could to head off the bankruptcy of Cornetti's company. I brought him into several deals. There are papers . . ."

"There are so many papers, including those that were passed on to you by officials, and which that ladyboy Pitti stuffed into certain suitcases."

Avanzini checked himself as he was about to speak, so Soneri went on. "Anyway, these are matters for the maresciallo, unless of course the officers in the Finanza ask me to cooperate with them in their inquiry."

Avanzini grasped immediately the element of threat in Soneri's words, and gave a start. Short of stature and slightly overweight, he was as white and soft as a lightly boiled egg. He looked like a newly ordained priest. When they sat down, Soneri's eye was caught by his small, ivory-coloured hands with little tufts of black hair on the knuckles, and could not help comparing them to Cornetti's calloused, thick labourer's hands.

As soon as they were seated facing each other, Avanzini got in first with his reply to what he guessed would be Soneri's first question. "I know what you're all thinking, that it's my fault. You interpret what you think people are imagining – in other words, that it was me that caused his downfall. Cornetti was well liked. He had qualities I lack," he said. Soneri detected in him that bitterness common in self-conscious people.

"You can hardly say they're in the wrong, as regards the misfortunes of his firm."

"Cornetti was too pig-headed to realise that times have changed. He went about with a notebook writing down income and expenditure. He did his sums with a pencil," Avanzini said.

"That's as may be," Soneri silenced him brusquely. "The difference is that you had the politicians on your side and he did not. Is that what you mean when you talk about keeping up with the times?"

Avanzini fixed him with a fearful, malevolent stare. "What I'm saying is that he would've gone out of business in any case, whether I was involved or not, but I do realise that people like me are destined to arouse hostility, while men like Cornetti are not."

The commissario saw what he was getting at. He was an introvert, the other a showman. He was a weasel, the other a red-blooded male. He had women only out of need, the other out of passion. He had grown up in the school of accountants, the other in the tougher school of life.

"I deal only in facts, and these tell me that Cornetti killed himself in your office. There must have been some reason for that, don't you think? Perhaps you believe that the buying and selling of public officials has nothing to do with it?"

"It was they who kept on tormenting us with one demand after another. Otherwise they wouldn't have given us any work."

Soneri sniggered. "I'd say it was all home-made, like baking. It takes two to tango, as they say. By the way, did you not party together in the Pensione Tagliavini?"

Avanzini raised his eyes towards the commissario, as though afraid of some punishment. "You're making me out to be some kind of monster, but you're wrong. I'm no plaster-cast saint but nor am I . . ." His words trailed off with a vague gesture which was meant to indicate an unspecified someone.

"Cornetti?"

Avanzini made no reply. He seemed unsure whether or not he really wanted to take a step which might cost him dearly. He clasped his hands to his chest, and gave a scowl of sheer malice.

"He was no saint either. He paid the party as well. Have you any idea of how much money he tossed their way?"

"He does not appear to have asked for anything in return. At the end of the day, they threw him out."

"You're a bit on the naïve side for a police officer. Do you really believe that with the party in charge he didn't receive some little favours?"

"I wouldn't rule it out, but I couldn't prove it either." The commissario was beginning to lose patience with this ugly little man whom he disliked more and more by the minute.

"If you want to know the truth, Cornetti went to rack and ruin by a different route. It was because of the company he kept, not because we cut him out of deals."

"What does that mean?" Soneri said, drawing deeply on his cigar.

"Have you any idea how happy he was to work with us? Our systems and the contracts we won didn't upset him in the very least. I can't stand the way he's made out to be someone morally incorruptible while I . . ."

"So he did go with the times," the commissario said.

"No!" Avanzini bellowed, his wavering treble voice rising to a sharp crescendo. "He dealt with us because he still held on to the dream of revolution."

For a moment Soneri remained silent, smoking and wondering how to fit that piece of information into a framework he could still not fully grasp. It then occurred to him there must be a link with the extremists.

"Even if he did finance certain extreme left groups, it was

definitely not because there was anything in it for him. It only caused him trouble," Soneri said.

"Those were corrupt circles as well, commissario. These are individuals who would not hesitate to issue threats, and at times follow them up. You know what I think? In the final analysis, he was their hostage, and that's why he killed himself. To divert attention from all that, he committed suicide in my office. A great piece of theatre, typical of the man."

"How can you be so sure that's how it went?" Soneri said with a touch of irony.

Avanzini made a gesture, while his face was a mixture of scowl and smile. "I am sure, that's all there is to it. He'd become a milch cow for that lot, the communists."

"Do you know who?"

"How could I know? I do know that he was under pressure and was receiving demands by telephone. Cornetti's secretary confessed everything to me – that he'd been living in fear."

Silence fell between them. The two men did not even look at each other for a moment as each fixed on some vague point in the room. Soneri heard Avanzini's voice start up again, but it seemed more distant, as though he were speaking through a loudspeaker attached to the ceiling.

"It was them that bankrupted him," he stated with certainty, before adding in a more confidential tone laced with malicious delight, "You didn't expect that, did you? But you'll have to get used to the idea that even the great Cornetti was not the purest of men."

10

WALKING ALONG VIA Saffi ten minutes later, Soneri felt somehow dirty. He ran into Dirce, that dumpy parcel of a woman, who greeted him with her usual piercing, brazen stare. His route took him to Piazzale dei Servi but as there was no trace of Fadiga, he continued at a brisk pace to Selvatici's chambers.

He pressed the buzzer and waited until he heard the click of the lock. In the entry hall, he saw to his right and left staircases leading to the upper floors, and straight ahead an inner courtyard with trees and parked cars. In the gloom a door opened.

"This way," the lawyer said.

Soneri was ushered into a large, low-ceilinged office, furnished in the style of the Vittoriale, the former residence of Gabriele D'Annunzio. Crimson was the prevailing shade of the velvets and damasks. There were carpets on the floor and everywhere there were weapons. Sabres and rifles, pistols, and ancient muzzle-loaders were hanging on the walls, alongside bayonets, hand grenades, Fascist and revolutionary symbols. Skulls were arrayed prominently on the desk at which Soneri took a seat, and for a moment he had the impression of facing a satanic altar. Lower down, a collection of daggers lined the walls. The commissario searched in vain for the double-edged blade of a *corador*.

"I am a collector and I have all the necessary licences," Selvatici told him.

The commissario studied him for a few moments. His hair was now white, but apart from that he looked as he had always done – low forehead, deep voice and a nervous twitch that caused the muscles between his chin and neck to contract.

"I never doubted it. I remember you as being punctilious," Soneri said.

"Do we know each other?" Selvatici asked hesitantly.

"Pensione Tagliavini."

Selvatici stared at him. It was impossible to say if his expression was alarmed or merely thoughtful.

"The room opposite hers – Ada Loreti, I mean."

"Ah! Of course. It was so long ago. Anyway, I've lost touch with so many people. I'm out of town a lot."

"I know. You do a lot of work in political trials."

"That's fairly obvious, isn't it?" he said, gesturing with a circular sweep of his arm around his studio. He gave every appearance of being naively pleased with having earned that level of attention.

"You were involved with the Dallacasa murder case, were you not?"

Selvatici struggled for a moment to find the words, and then began to wag his index finger from side to side as a sign of denial. "I was still doing my apprenticeship. It was a big trial, but it got nowhere."

"You must have had your own ideas."

"It was an execution."

"That we know. A bullet in the back of the neck."

"The means employed in a crime tell us a lot. You ought to know that."

"It's at the forefront of my mind."

"Then you must have reached the conclusion that everything is explained by that fact alone."

"It would seem not to have been the Fascists."

"Indeed. They wouldn't have killed him that way. They'd have shot him down in the street, in an ambush."

Selvatici was on his feet, pacing up and down as he used to do in his room at the pensione when rehearsing an address to the jury in an imaginary court. As Soneri watched him walk to and fro in his office, it occurred to him that Selvatici could very well match the description of the supposed murderer provided by Mohammed. He picked up a hand grenade which had been defused and gazed attentively at its rough shell.

"So you too are of the opinion that it was his ex-comrades?" Soneri said.

"I wouldn't rule it out. Or a woman. The means employed point in that direction. It wouldn't be the first time," Selvatici said, glancing at his bookshelves lined with criminology manuals and annual crime registers. "Dallacasa was a ladies' man. Maybe he overreached himself."

Soneri shrugged sceptically. "Women don't kill for that sort of thing. They have other ways of making you suffer." While the lawyer went on pacing up and down without replying, he pulled out one of the photographs. "Do you happen to know where I can find Andrea?" he said as casually as he could.

"Which Andrea?"

"This one," Soneri said, pointing to the man in Trombi's photograph.

Selvatici came over, bending his long body over the image Soneri held under the table lamp. "He was often photographed with you."

The lawyer straightened up solemnly. "I've no idea what became of him. I haven't seen him in years."

"What's his surname?"

"Fornari."

"Were you friends?"

"No, he wasn't really friendly with anyone. I doubt if he had any close friends at all. He didn't talk about himself much. How come you didn't know him?" Selvatici stopped short, in obvious embarrassment.

The commissario understood what he was getting at and felt it like a stab in the chest. Selvatici knew that Ada had become his wife, and he also knew about her and Fornari. Plainly ill at ease, he did not know how to get out of this awkward situation.

"Relax," Soneri said to minimise any embarrassment. "It might seem a delicate matter, but I assure you it interests me from a different point of view. Personal issues don't come into it."

This was not true and perhaps that was obvious, because Selvatici gave him a perplexed look. "Be that as it may, I haven't seen Fornari since those days, and I have no reason to believe he's kept up with his other ex-comrades either. Maybe he's moved to another city."

"Was he from Parma?"

"From the mountains, Monchio di Corti, but he came to town ages ago."

"He made the same journey as Ghitta," the commissario said.

"His father knew her well. He sent him to the city as a student because she was there to look after him. Fornari was a very introverted boy and needed to be looked after."

"He doesn't appear to have been one of Ghitta's lodgers."

"He had a room in Fernanda Schianchi's apartment, next door. He was so shy that you didn't even notice him when he was there. That was his father's fault. He crushed him with his over-exuberant personality. The boy tried to emulate him, but he never managed to go his own way."

Selvatici had taken once again to walking up and down, and was once more speaking as though addressing a jury.

"Who was his father?"

"In Monchio, he was known to everyone as 'the vet'. As far as I know he was once an officer in the Communist Party in the Lunigiana district, and moved to this side of the Apennines in the Sixties. It might have been because of his job, or maybe he wanted to make a new life for himself. I came across his name a couple of years ago while I was looking through papers relating to an old case in Florence against some communist activists from Massa who were accused of killing a Catholic trade unionist during a strike. He was convicted of manslaughter, but got a light sentence because there were extenuating circumstances. From that time on, he distanced himself from the party. He didn't even attend partisan reunions, although he'd been a member of the Garibaldi Brigade under the name 'Rosso'. They say he had real guts and that the sight of him terrified people – ruddy complexion, imposing physique, fire in his belly."

Soneri said nothing, trying not to give away how significant this information was. Even though everything was still confused, he sensed he was close to a solution. He now knew who Rosso was, the man who so terrified Ghitta, and he also knew who his son was. He wondered how Ghitta had managed to unearth that nickname, which no-one at Monchio or Rigoso could have known since it was so deeply buried in the affairs of years long gone. He had hoped that the investigation would take a turn away from his private life, but unfortunately he was once again forced to recognise that it was charging at him full on. This awareness was so crushing as to discourage him from probing any further, but that had been the situation from the beginning.

He pulled himself back together and noticed that Selvatici had sat down at his desk, and was observing him curiously.

"I was thinking of this Rosso," the commissario said, to excuse himself.

"A remarkable man," Selvatici said, plainly pleased with himself.

"And his son? You were telling me he's not made of the same stuff."

"Not the same at all. Introverted, with a complex about not being like his father, while the father, knowing what his son was like, went to all lengths to protect him, which only made matters worse."

"Was he active on the far left?"

"Yes, he was involved with many groups. He was a somewhat woolly theorist who tried hard to move into the limelight. What really interested him was to be 'someone'. I don't think he cared much for ideals."

"He wasn't the only one," Soneri said sarcastically.

"He was searching for something which would make him feel part of some grand project. Maybe he had never in all his life had to shoulder responsibilities."

"The ones who really believed in it all are the ones who came to a bad end," Soneri said, thinking of Fadiga and others now buried in unmarked tombs or scattered in various corners of the world.

A gleam of interest passed over Selvatici's face, but his tone was resigned. "Or else they're reduced to living out their passions by keeping them artificially alive," he said, in a clear allusion to himself.

Soneri ran his eyes over the weapons on the walls. "Is this all your past has left you?"

"I am a criminal lawyer, and crime is my business."

"Mine too, but I see things differently."

With these words, he took his leave of the lawyer, but he was troubled as he left that quasi-shrine. A delicate chapter of the investigation was opening up, and something within him was protesting. He looked up at the clock on the Campanile del Duomo. It was not too late to telephone Juvara. He imagined him at home in front of his computer, surfing the internet. He had developed ideas of his own about his colleague's solitary vice, which he threw in his face every so often as a joke.

"Are you working or do you have company?"

"No, I was looking at . . ." Juvara replied vaguely.

"You remember Ghitta's houses in Rigoso?"

"Of course. I showed you the list of them."

"Yes, yes, but did it turn out that that some were let out on a virtually rent-free lease? In the village as well as elsewhere"

"Yes, there was one in Monchio."

"With a nominal rent, like the one in Borgo delle Colonne?"

"It was officially in usufruct – to an elderly woman, Desolina Galloni. She's in her eighties and a bit soft the head."

"You're my living archive," Soneri said, satisfied with the answer even if it left confused thoughts whirring about in his head like tombola numbers in a bag. He felt he should at least have the patience to fix them one by one into the correct slots, starting with "Rosso", the only man capable of frightening an iron lady like Ghitta. Why had he scared her so much? And why only in the last months, overturning an equilibrium of silences, complicities and compromises which had held good for years?

Soneri decided to go back to the pensione. He stood in front of No. 35 and took out his keys, but there was no need of them because the outside door was kept ajar by a wad of cloth jammed between the two panels. He climbed the stairs, lighting his way with a pocket torch to the apartment door, where he stopped to listen.

He could hear nothing. He put his key in the lock and turned it, but was assailed by a waft of gas which prevented him from breathing and forced him back out onto the landing. He went back to the door and pulled both panels wide open to allow the gas to escape. With a handkerchief pressed against his mouth he went in, holding his breath. He threw open the windows before proceeding to the kitchen, where he remembered having seen the gas tap.

A few moments passed before the cold air blew through the room, and only then did the commissario switch on the light. He checked the cooker plates and noticed that the switches were off, as was the main gas cock at the wall. He did not understand. He looked at the heaters in the bedrooms, but they too were all at the off position. Had there been a gas leak which someone had come along to attend to, even though they had then left the house filled with an explosive mixture? Or perhaps the apartment was not quite sufficiently saturated? Did someone intend to blow up the house to eliminate Ghitta's world once and for all? Or was he dealing with an aborted suicide? Only when this thought occurred to him did he realise the danger he had been in. All it needed was the ring of the door bell. Nevertheless, he was not convinced it was a trap, nor that he was the target. And yet, suppose that his cigar had been lit . . .

He searched the empty rooms. In Ghitta's room, everything was as it had been when he was last in it. Even the overturned drawer was exactly where it had been left by the forensic squad. Elvira's room was empty. It looked as if she had gone for good. It gave the same impression as looking at the camp beds of soldiers the night before demob. Ghitta's world was now finally fading away. The building was ready for the workmen who would transform it into an estate agent or the branch of an insurance company. The city devoured its provisional symbols with the voracity of vermin, and thousands of people of Soneri's age would soon be speaking in the past tense of that corner of old Parma: "There, in Via Saffi, where there used to be ..."

For him it had been a close shave. The explosion which Soneri had only just avoided would have done the demolition workers' job for them. He began to wonder where Elvira might be. Perhaps she too had vanished like Fernanda. The list of missing persons was growing too long, and in a murder case they could be counted as dead, even if officially only "presumed dead". When he closed the windows, he was aware of a lingering smell of gas, so he left the shutters in the small drawing room beside the entrance open, and sat down for a smoke. As he looked out on the deserted Via Saffi, sprinkled with hoar frost, he reflected that this would likely be the last time he entered the pensione. He did not know where his certainty came from, but he was sure of it. Very rarely is it possible to have an awareness of the last time you will meet a person or find yourself in a particular place, but at that moment Soneri was convinced he would never come back there, and for that reason he lived those minutes with great intensity, conscious of the intolerable weight of a past which was coming to an end for him.

He sat a long time on the couch where he had spoken to Elvira on the night after the murder, but now imagining he was there with Ada. He loved the night as it was seen through that window, almost making him believe that he had somehow come home, but that feeling was replaced by foreboding – someone was on their way. He surmised that the gas been prepared for one specific person. As he looked along the street, which was growing whiter and whiter, he was surprised not to see Pitti approaching. Perhaps he too had vanished? The main players in the story seemed like fugitives from the stage, a further sign that something was about to happen. At around four o'clock sleep overcame him and when he awoke, although the dark and the mist were almost as impenetrable as before, he knew the city was reawakening. He listened intently, and from outside a sort of subdued rumble could be heard.

It was followed by footsteps. Soneri looked out cautiously and on the pavement, undecided and hesitant, he saw Chiastra wrapped in a heavy overcoat and wearing a dark felt hat with a little feather stuck in the band. He watched him push open the outside door and disappear inside. He heard his feet land with heavy thuds on each step. When the old man reached the landing, he dragged his feet as though unsure which bell to ring. Finally, the bell rang out loudly, breaking the prevailing silence. Soneri stared at the door, thinking that the bell would have made the perfect detonator for the gas-filled apartment.

He pulled open the door and for a few seconds before the light went off, he saw the figure of the old man standing before him. Chiastra stood impassively in the dark, undecided, until the commissario took him by the sleeve and pulled him inside.

"Are you always an early riser?" Soneri said.

"I don't sleep very well and there are a lot of shift workers in the village. I take advantage of that."

"Did you have an appointment with Elvira?"

Chiastra nodded.

"She's gone, like Fernanda, but she was planning a great send-off for you. One almighty bang."

The old man stared at him, not understanding what Soneri was driving at. He took off his hat, which made him appear even more awkward.

"Did she tell you to come at this time?"

Once again Chiastra nodded.

"What was so urgent that she had to tell you now?"

Chiastra looked up with the expression of a frightened child. "I don't know."

The commissario took out a cigar to calm himself. "She told you to be here at five in the morning and that there was no urgency?"

"Elvira knows I get up early so for me it was no great sacrifice."

Soneri moved his face close to Chiastra's. "The place was filled with gas. If I hadn't let it out, you'd have been blown sky-high the moment you pressed the buzzer. It would seem that Elvira did have something urgent on her mind – getting rid of you. So the question is, why?"

The colour drained from Chiastra's face, and a tremor ran through his body, causing even his lips to tremble. They seemed to want to open, if only he could find the words. The commissario looked hard at him and repeated, "Why? You're not even the heir."

Chiastra seemed petrified, his face fixed in an expression of fear and his eyes gazing into the darkness of the room. He reminded Soneri of Pitti as he stood next to the now-cold heater under Elvira's menacing gaze, and the comparison made him realise how much women were in charge of this whole story. He blew out his cigar smoke and a neat little cloud drifted towards Chiastra's face, but he did not move an inch.

"When did she call you?" the commissario asked, in an attempt to proceed systematically.

Chiastra shook himself and seemed happy to get back to basics. "Last night, but it wasn't Elvira who called. It was a man. He introduced himself as her father."

"What did he say?"

"To come this morning, when I would find something Ghitta had left for me."

The commissario was about to ask more about this man when he noticed a tear in Chiastra's eyes, although there was no sign of pain in his expression. The tear had been shed with seeming indifference, as though from the branch of a freshly cut vine.

Soneri changed tack. "Do you really not know who Rosso is?"

The old man shook his head.

Soneri prompted him. "Fornari, known as Rosso in Lunigiana, and 'the vet' in Monchio."

Chiastra seemed genuinely surprised, but the commissario had observed too much play-acting to willingly abandon his suspicions.

"Why had he taken to threatening Ghitta?"

"If it really is Fornari . . ." Chiastra seemed to lose his way. "With him, there was a conflict of interests."

"What kind of interests?"

"Houses, land. He wanted to buy a farm which had once belonged to the Landi, a noble family, the most powerful in Monchio, but Ghitta got in ahead of him and 'the vet' was beside himself. He wanted it at any price, and by any means."

"But Ghitta wouldn't sell? But what did it matter to her?"

Chiastra heaved a sigh which might have been a sign of impatience. He was struggling to dig up old histories and retell tales that seemed to him obvious. "You really had to know her. I've told you she was desperate to be thought better of in the town than she was. That farm had once been the property of nobility, do you understand? It wasn't a matter of a house and a bit of land. What interested her was that at long last she would appear to be on top. They could carry on thinking of her as a worthless woman if they liked, but they also knew she was in command."

In the silence which followed, it occurred to Soneri that no man has a more efficient jailer than himself. He tried to imagine Ghitta's fixed and vain idea, rooted in her brain like a cyst, of refashioning a reputation for herself.

"I don't understand why that farm mattered to Rosso."

Chiastra gave a bitter smile. "A party membership card doesn't change a person. He said he was a communist, but those who've got an education mix more easily with their own kind than with people like Ghitta or me. He was the veterinary surgeon. He always spoke approvingly of the common people, but he never had to live like them." Chiastra gave another deep sigh, and continued, still with the same bitter smile on his lips. "When you get to my age, commissario, you begin to tally up what you've achieved, and if there's something missing, you find some self-justification or you'll never have peace of mind. I understand the vet. Everything had gone wrong for him – his ideals, his career on the mountains and even that wretched son of his. After all that, he must have been thinking of at least constructing a tomb worthy of spending his final years in. All that was left of what he had dreamed of being and doing were wealth and reputation, and he held tightly on to those. And anyway, the rich always remain rich, at least in their minds."

"But from that to making her afraid of him – Ghitta was used to battling over questions of self-interest."

"Oh, she could have eaten fire, but this time she had too many people lined up against her. Fornari must have known what was going on around here, and maybe he had even threatened to make it all public."

"Bribes, wife-swapping . . ."

"Ah yes, I don't know if he had spies or if that other one . . ."

"Who?" Soneri asked.

Chiastra shook his head in a sort of tacit accusation. "Elvira Cadoppi. She lived with Rosso's son. Ghitta thought she could keep her under control with the threat of evicting her family, the ones in the village, but it was not enough. Perhaps the vet had already found another place for them to stay."

"Do you know Desolina Galloni in Monchio?"

"Of course. She's a tenant of Ghitta's, but . . ." he interrupted himself, waving his hand about, palms upwards.

"I know, but quite often groups of young people, including Rosso's son, used to go there. Why was that?"

Chiastra seemed uncertain. "It seems they could have a wild time. They came from as far afield as Tuscany. They all met up, and would hang out in Desolina's for a bit."

"Was this during the holidays?"

"No, mainly at the dead times of the year. It seems they'd no work to go to."

"Was Andrea Fornari there too?

"He was the only one who was always there, trotting about like a servant, but maybe he was only trying to be hospitable."

"Do you think they tried to get rid of you because you knew about all these goings-on?"

Chiastra stretched out his arms. "How would I know? Obviously my time hadn't come."

"But you do know a lot, and you didn't tell me everything the first time we met."

"I didn't think it was important. I still don't believe the vet had anything to do with it. He can fly off the handle, but there's no real harm in him. He and Ghitta were good friends for a long time."

Chiastra was gazing around as though trying to find his way. Soneri got to his feet and suddenly felt the accumulated exhaustion of a night without sleep.

"Did Ghitta really not leave me *anything*?" Chiastra said in a faint voice.

Once more the commissario saw a tear appear in those eyes, which remained impassive, and the thought occurred to him that the promise which attracted the old man to that place was even more cruel than any havoc the gas might have wrought. Having nothing more to ask him, he let Chiastra go and watched him from the window as he made his way towards the bus station. He tried to imagine what it must be like to be nearing the end of your days and find yourself betrayed by the one person who had given your life some meaning. Perhaps Ghitta had endured too much pain to be able to concern herself with other people, or perhaps she was no better than those she was surrounded by.

When Soneri went out, the frost had put a layer of white over everything, and a wind was blowing which made his ears freeze. He turned into Borgo del Naviglio, glancing as he passed at Bettati's lighted window, on the other side of which the barber was sitting on the revolving chair reading his paper. When he heard the door open, he turned round but nonchalantly carried on reading.

"You're up early," he said without looking at him.

"I haven't even been to bed."

"They've caught three terrorists in Tuscany," Bettati said, holding out an article in the paper. "They're searching for others. They're citing the Dallacasa case. Seems someone's started talking about the past. Maybe it was a sympathiser with the old guard, but they're not releasing his name because he's a turncoat who's decided to cooperate with the magistrates. Anyway, it seems more and more likely that we're talking about a settling of scores among extremists."

Soneri moved nearer to read the article, but he was too confused to be able to concentrate on the words.

"Did you know about an apartment in Borgo delle Colonne that Cornetti was renting from Ghitta?"

"I thought he had a lover there."

"Did you see him go in and out very often?"

"Not me personally, but others did."

"On his own?"

"Come on! There was no end to the toing and froing, young folk mainly, maybe students, because nobody round here recognised them."

"There's a suspicion that Cornetti was being blackmailed ever since he gave up financing the far-left groups, and that the shot that killed him had its roots in some political fracas or other."

The barber pulled off his reading glasses, and went over to the heater to put his hand on it. "Anyone who speaks like that didn't know Cornetti. He was full of contradictions, but he managed them well enough. He got by on pure instinct. He was a communist and a businessman, he was a member of a party of moralists, but he had many affairs. He financed extremist groups because he saw in them the passions he'd felt in his twenties, but then he would trot along to the Teatro Regio and sit in the boxes hired by industrialists. You had to take him as he was."

The mobile interrupted their conversation. It was Juvara. "Commissario, there's been a call from the office of a lawyer, Zurlini, in connection with the will."

"What has that got to do with us?"

"He wants to know what to do and he asked if Fernanda Schianchi has been traced."

"You know what to tell him? If she hasn't turned up within ten years, he can apply to have her declared dead."

"I know, but there is one outstanding question, and he wanted to know how to proceed without interfering with the investigation."

"What outstanding question?" Soneri asked in growing irritation. In the meantime, he had left the shop and was crossing Piazzale San Francesco where the statue of Padre Lino, the Friar of the Poor, stood.

"The one relating to the Landi farm."

The question stopped Soneri in his tracks. "Outstanding in what sense?"

"Three months ago, Aristide Fornari raised an action to have the sale to Ghitta declared null and void. There was a dispute between the two. Now that she's dead, the lawyer wants to know if he can proceed with the business of the will, which includes the farm, or if he should drop everything."

"Tell him to ask the magistrate," Soneri said, his thoughts already on other matters. He instantly reconsidered what he had just said. "When was the action raised?"

"Mid-September. Is that important?"

The commissario winked, as if Juvara could see him. "Everything fell apart at that moment, that's the truth," Soneri muttered as he wandered around the Piazzale in front of the Old Prisons, without knowing which street to take. He was about to switch off when Juvara spoke again.

"Commissario, have you forgotten there's a glass of wine this evening at the questura?"

"What for?"

"Like every other year, the day before Christmas Eve."

"I've nothing to drink to."

"Everybody'll be there, to exchange festive wishes."

"That's exactly my point. Can you see me raising a glass to Chillemi? Anyway, it's not true. The only ones who'll be there are the unlucky ones who couldn't get the time off."

"Commissario, I can take your place in here for anything else, but when your presence is needed, I can't . . ."

"Alright. Let's say it's a moral obligation."

"We'll have a glass of spumante, grab a canapé or two, and afterwards perhaps we'll exchange genuine good wishes between ourselves in the office."

"We're going to need all the good wishes we can get," Soneri said, thinking of Ghitta and Rosso. Everything started from there, from the disturbance of a balance which had held for years, concealing under a surface of apparent provincial banality a world of corruption, ferocity, vendettas and failures. But what was really wearing him down was the realisation that that dark zone was his too. He was compelled to walk in it, perhaps coming up against the certainty of having confused appearance with reality.

The feud had originated in September with Rosso's threats and Ghitta's counter-threats, and with the blackmail in which she found the satisfaction of revenge and the legitimisation of her new dignity as superior. Was that the motive? If so, what had Ghitta threatened to do? Once she was out of the way, another had feud started over the clumsy attempts to re-establish the traffic of backhanders and furtive couples in a pensione which had lost its mainstay, all unfolding in a world festering like a corpse being eaten by worms in a grave. Had the malaise occasioned by living in that state of putrefaction been more fearful than the spectre of bankruptcy, and had that factor driven Cornetti to shoot himself? Or perhaps the bankruptcy had been total, both of the company and of ideas?

He walked about, not even feeling hungry. A cloud of depression descended on him, adding to his exhaustion. He crossed the Ponte di Mezzo, came within sight of the monument to Filippo Corridoni near the Rocchetta and then proceeded down Via Massimo D'Azeglio as far as the Chiesa della Santissima Annunziata. He turned into Via Imbriani, and from there into Borgo Marodolo, which was so narrow that not even the mist could get into it. He looked closely at the name plates on the doors and had no trouble in picking out the house belonging to Pitti's mother, Gina Montali. He stood back for a few moments to examine the façade marked by deep wrinkles on which the straw-yellow shades typical of the houses in Oltretorrente could still be made out. At that point he heard a soft, timid voice behind him. "Don't ring the bell. My mother would start asking questions."

"She might ask you why you stay at home in the evenings nowadays."

Pitti looked nervously over his shoulder, and then said, "Could we go somewhere else?"

"You afraid I might be taken for your lover?" Soneri said ironically.

Pitti blushed before moving off without a word.

"Would you like to arrange a meeting in a quarter of an hour in the chapel of Sant'Egidio?" Soneri said, still speaking in a tone of mockery.

Pitti accepted the jibe with indifference. In company he was accustomed to receiving slights and being given orders, but as he walked at the commissario's side dressed in that absurd garb, as though he were a baronet fallen on hard times, Soneri felt a surge of pity. Everyone had their part to play, and Pitti's was a caricature. They went into a café in Pizzale Picelli, another place which recalled the libertarian past of revolts and great figures who were now forgotten spectres looking out from marble plaques at the entrances to streets in a city without memory.

"This will be the first Christmas without Ghitta," Pitti said, his eyes fixed on a decorated Christmas tree next to the bar. He sounded like a widow.

"Did you use to spend Christmas with her?"

"The afternoon, every year without fail."

"And who else came along?"

"Oh, so many people! Her close friends, and when there used to be students around, some of them would stay on for Christmas."

"Was Cornetti there? Signora Bernazzoli? Chiastra? Fernanda Schianchi? Elvira? What about Andrea Fornari? You know Fornari well, don't you?"

Pitti looked at him, intimidated by his almost threatening tone of voice.

"You should know him," he murmured quietly.

"Of course," Soneri said, but in a different tone. "What kind of relationship did he have with Ghitta?"

"He lodged with Fernanda, and you didn't see much of him. At Christmas he greeted everyone, but then he went off with Elvira to Monchio."

"Where is she now?"

"Probably somewhere in the mountains. She goes back to see her family in the festive period," he said, with a tremor in his voice.

"And what about you?" The commissario poked his chest with the two fingers which held his cigar. "Where will you be going? I should warn you that there's a smell of gas in Ghitta's pensione."

Pitti turned pale and began to tremble. The commissario noted how his fingers struggled with the coffee cup the waiter had put down in front of him. He was an easy victim. All it took was for someone to raise their voice to terrify him. Nevertheless, he attempted an improbable diversion. "Gas?" he said, in a very poor imitation of surprise.

"Don't pretend you didn't know. It doesn't suit you." Soneri's peremptory tone caused Pitti's resistance to crumble entirely. He saw Pitti's cheeks swell out as he made an effort not to vomit. He put his hands over his eyes as they filled with tears. The commissario kept his eyes on him as he relit his cigar, aware that he still felt some sympathy for him.

He put an arm round his shoulders. "Now tell me everything," he said calmly. Pitti shook himself and looked at him gratefully. "It was my fault. I lost my head," he began in his low, sorrowful voice. "I wanted to disappear, but at the same time, I was outraged with Elvira. Ghitta was the only person who didn't treat me like a servant, so when they killed her, they killed my dignity as well. You saw what I had to put up from Elvira, didn't you? And I'm certain that treacherous bitch had something to do with the murder," he said bitterly.

Soneri considered these words briefly, then returned to the central facts. "What did you want to do? Why switch on the gas, and then switch it off again?"

"And that allowed you to understand everything? That one strange fact?"

The commissario nodded, but then he added. "I still don't understand why you brought Chiastra into it. Hasn't he been through enough already?"

"Poor man, but it might have been the best solution for him too. It was what he wanted, after all the other things he'd put up with. That was why I had no scruples. I wanted to use him to get my revenge on that woman. They'd all have blamed her since Chiastra went about sticking his nose in everywhere, and knew all about those bizarre meetings organised by Fornari up in Monchio. The old man blabbed too much in the village, as Elvira well knew because she'd heard him a couple of times on the telephone expressing his concern about them. She was so sure of her power over me that she threw caution to the wind."

The commissario looked at him gravely. "There was an easier way for you to take revenge. You had only to tell me the whole story."

Pitti seemed to shrink nervously, his face painted with pale anxiety. "You see what I'm like. Elvira took advantage of my weakness. She threatened and humiliated me. I always swallowed everything, but over time resentment built up inside me and at the end it erupted."

"You should never attempt things you're not cut out for," Soneri told him. "You've realised now that I understood everything from your indecisiveness. Elvira would have left the gas turned on, but she's too smart not to know that suspicion would inevitably have fallen on her."

Pitti had by now surrendered and was gazing at Soneri in admiration. He gave the impression of a poor, unremarkable, outraged soul in search of protection, about to throw himself into the commissario's arms, like a girl.

"I was out to get it over and done with. I was in despair," Pitti said, his voice distorted by a lump in his throat. Soneri imagined him stripped of his circus costume, dressed in the insignificant clothes of a very ordinary man in the street. "I began to cough and I was scared. So, stupidly believing I could undo what I'd done, I turned off the gas switch and fled."

"And when did the idea of telephoning Chiastra occur to you?"

"Almost at once. As I was coming down the stairs, I thought of that despairing old man and it seemed to me I was almost doing him a favour. He would have died believing that Ghitta had not forgotten him. Don't you agree that was generous of me? And at the same time, I'd have got Elvira into trouble. Lastly, the pensione would have been blown sky high. Better make it disappear than letting the memories linger."

"And then you had the brilliant idea of stuffing a rag in the door so that it would stay open and Chiastra could walk right in. After that, you pretended to be Elvira's father and arranged an appointment, except that I spoiled the plan and faced the risk of . . ." The commissario stopped. Only at that moment did he really think of the possibility of being blown to pieces, and only then did he feel the fear he should have felt earlier.

Pitti's hands were shaking, and he nodded weakly. "And what's going to happen now?"

The commissario's thoughts were still on the explosion he had narrowly escaped, and the rage that welled up inside him made him want to beat Pitti about the face. He was sure he would not even try to ward off the blows. "You know perfectly well what should happen," he said.

Pitti said nothing, his hands still trembling. The commissario let him take a sip of coffee before continuing. "However, seeing that you and I are the only ones who know about the gas . . ."

Pitti looked at him tentatively. He was obviously well practised in dealing with innuendo and the more sinister undertones. A split second later a little smile lit up his face. He was already prepared to undertake acts of treachery out of cowardice, and Soneri found himself once again tempted to slap him across the face, but instead, he did something worse. He shook Pitti to his very core by arousing in him what must have been the most unbearable of all nightmares. "What would your mother say if she were to find out about all this?"

Pitti began shaking once again, and then turned imploring eyes on him.

"You could help me," the commissario said, in a tone which brooked no argument.

Pitti nodded vigorously, anxious to ward off more fearsome spectres.

"Do you know if Ghitta was receiving threats?"

"She gave the appearance of being well liked, but in fact she had many enemies. She could never form any kind of relationships except those based on give and take. She was confident only with people when she had the upper hand."

"So obviously they hated her."

"She was keen to act as the one in charge, maybe because she had previously been held in such contempt."

"But then, with this Rosso, she couldn't manage to win any advantage over him, and so she feared him."

"Do you know the full story? Ghitta kept it under wraps. That man must have been a monster," Pitti said, scarcely managing to conceal his admiration. "There had been real tension between the two of them."

"Because of the farm on Monchio," Soneri said.

"Exactly. A bit of nonsense. She should have let him have it. It was only a symbol, but she was keen on symbols, to show off, to let them see how far she'd come, because they still thought of her as a whore. Whenever she bought something, they'd say in the village, 'There's money in whoredom'. In other words, she had to start from scratch every time, buy something more, something bigger, to really flummox them."

"Like the Landi farm?"

"I've already told you. It was a symbol."

"Look, status symbols matter to communists too," Soneri said, seemingly annoyed at having to listen to things he already knew. "The point is Ghitta was issuing threats as well."

"Did you imagine anything different?"

"How long had they been quarrelling?"

"For a year, to the best of my knowledge. From the time she acquired the farm."

"The threats were flying about, but only for three months."

"I understand that Fornari raised a case in an attempt to have the deal declared invalid. The idea was to have old Landi declared mentally incapable when he signed over the farm. Fornari was trying to persuade the eldest son to reopen discussions about the whole thing on the basis that the price was too low."

The commissario went back to the point that mattered most to him. "She was afraid of him. She was aware that Rosso knew all about what was going on at the pensione, probably because he was using Elvira. Or perhaps he had the sense to know that he could get the farm from her, since she'd tricked an elderly man suffering from dementia, but what I'd like to know is how she defended herself. She was threatening him, but with what?"

Pitti stared at him first with discomfort and then with mild bewilderment. Soneri understood he was afraid of disappointing him, and perhaps cause him to break their agreement.

"I didn't hear everything. Sometimes Ghitta would talk freely because she trusted me and knew I depended on her, but latterly when she was in conversation with Rosso, she wouldn't allow anyone else to be there. Sometimes, when the telephone rang, she would answer and ask the person at the other end to call back later. From her apprehension, I knew it had to be him. I knew her well and could tell from her expression."

"So you didn't grasp everything?"

Pitti got agitated and stopped to think before launching

into an explanation of matters which could not have been totally clear even to him. "Only once did I think I'd got to the bottom of it all. They seemed to be talking about somebody else. She said, 'I know what he's up to.' She repeated those words twice before hanging up."

Soneri carried on smoking without saying a word. He was deep in thought, but not coming to any firm conclusion. "Nothing else?"

"No, after that I didn't hear a thing."

The commissario glanced at the clock and saw that it was now twenty to twelve. He thought of the reception at the questura, and felt his stomach turn over. Apart from anything else, the spumante was invariably very poor quality, served from one of those bottles with a plastic top.

"Don't you disappear as well," he told Pitti before going out.

"You'll find me around, or you can always come in here and leave word. The barman will get in touch with me."

II

THE SPUMANTE WAS exactly as he had feared, a fizzy drink rather than a wine, an insipid propellant for corks which popped out in a gush of foam. The party was like a bureaucratic liturgy with a grotesque finale. Chillemi, standing in for the questore and the prefect, who were both on holiday, was charged with opening the bottles. Once he had raised his glass, Soneri took just enough of a sip to confirm his suspicions of the wine. He found a quiet corner where he emptied the rest into Chillemi's fig tree and put the glass down on the table, declining a refill. When he made to leave, the vice-questore stopped him and took him aside. "Have you heard about the operation carried out by the Digos team?"

"Against the terrorists?"

"Exactly, the reds. Digos has a constitutional duty to keep me informed because we're involved in a secondary branch of the investigation. You remember the Dallacasa case?"

Soneri nodded.

"It was them, the Tuscan column, who got rid of him. He knew too much and they were afraid he'd start talking. It's an old case, as you know, but there have been suspicions flying about for years. It seems Dallacasa wasn't in agreement over the armed struggle."

The information Chillemi gave him was the only useful

thing to come out of that evening. The commissario tried to think it over, but there was too much confusion in his mind. He heard Chillemi start up again. "I wanted to let you know myself, because they told me you got them to bring out the files on the case," he said, with a touch of malice. Was he really alluding to the fact that Soneri was getting nowhere with this case, as with the Ghitta business?

"Thank goodness the Digos people are making the effort to solve cases," Soneri said, with a fake sigh.

"I was only meaning to pass on some information," Chillemi said, pretending in his turn to be offended. "In part, I was hoping to make up for the involuntary injustice over the bribery business. You know what the press are like."

Soneri shrugged, feigning resignation, and turned to go, almost bumping into Juvara, who was standing behind him. Chillemi stared at him without knowing what to say or do.

Back in his office, Soneri flopped onto the chair behind his desk. He felt worn out. Juvara looked at him and came up with a malicious diagnosis. "You're doing too much overtime. Working too many nights."

"How else am I to pay the mortgage," the commissario joked. Juvara looked almost convinced.

Soneri grabbed the telephone and pulled it towards him, but paused for a moment. "I've never been any good at communicating bad news," he said to Juvara. "I'm going to call Marta Bernazzoli to tell her about another death." Noticing Juvara's puzzled expression, he added, "Dallacasa's been killed a second time."

Marta Bernazzoli replied after two rings of the phone. "It's Soneri," was all he could say. He heard a sigh and a kind of sob. "Perhaps I've got nothing new to tell you," he went on, hesitantly.

"There are some things you know, but which you would rather not hear said aloud. Many patients prefer to avoid hearing in words what they already know only too well."

"You remember that conversation we had some time ago? Then it was you who did not want to confirm what I'd heard about Ada."

"Lies are often therapeutic. The important thing is to avoid pain, isn't it? If you hadn't wanted to get to grips with your past, you'd be a more balanced and happier man, wouldn't you?"

"I've never been balanced. Happy yes, some of the time. Unfortunately, I can't tell you any lies. You already understand everything, don't you?"

"When I heard about the arrest of some members of the armed movement in Tuscany, my last doubts vanished. To be honest, I always knew. If they've got the man who killed him, it won't give me any great satisfaction. It couldn't. Am I wrong in thinking that you and I resemble each other in some ways?"

The question resonated in the commissario's mind. For a few seconds he felt it vibrate inside his head like the tolling of a bell.

"Perhaps, but you're not obliged to wade through all the sins and sorrows of the world every day."

"I'd like you to come and see patients doubled up with pain, their mouths wide open in a scream, their faces deformed by a mask of suffering. Don't you think that's worse? Each and every time I step out of an operating theatre, I can't help but tell myself that it's all so senseless, futile. When I'm faced with such misery every day, how do you imagine I see this clown show?"

Holding the receiver in his hand, Soneri stood there searching for something appropriate to say, but he could not find it. He felt the vibrations continue to resonate inside his body, without realising that it was because his heart was beating faster. Marta continued talking, her voice no longer sobbing but as precise and sharp as a blade.

"It's time to stop deceiving ourselves and others. When I enter the operating theatre, I see what we're made of: stinking innards, chimeras and spectres, all making up a briefly attractive whole which old age then destroys. Nothing else. Any hopes of constructing a more comfortable world have long since deserted me. Neither we nor the priests have managed it. Can I ask you one thing? Give up rummaging in your past? None of it is going to last in any case."

Soneri heard a short sigh and immediately afterwards she hung up, leaving the commissario with the receiver in his hand, staring into the middle distance where he met Juvara's eyes. "She already knew. She's always known," Soneri said.

"If you ask me, that woman knows the whole story, but we'll never get anything out of her. Maybe she's afraid, or maybe she doesn't want any more pain to add to what she's already suffered."

"I understand her. She's lucky she can avoid it," the commissario said.

He was already on his feet when his mobile rang. "Do you think we could manage to spend a quiet day together at Christmas, or are you off to a reception with your squad?" Angela said.

"I've already had one glass of spumante and that's quite enough for me."

"Alright, you can have the panettone."

"I'd rather have Christmas cake."

"Listen, commissario, are you going to give me a straight

answer? Are you going to spend Boxing Day as well as Christmas in the sanctuary of your own home?"

"There's still some time to go. I can't make up my mind right now."

"It's Christmas Eve tomorrow! Are you trying to tell me Santa Claus is going to bring you some exciting presents and you have to be there for him?"

"I wrote him a long letter and I do believe I've almost persuaded him."

"After the arrest of the terrorists, you mean? Have they anything to do with Ghitta's murder?"

"I've got half an idea on that subject. Anyway, doesn't everybody go back home for Christmas?"

"Except you. But let's get one thing clear. I'm not going to be standing over a hot stove preparing your *anolini*, waiting for you to turn up." She hung up.

Soneri turned towards the cloisters, where he saw a group of officers from the Guardia di Finanza walking in the direction of the stairs leading to the questore's office. He made out the figure of Maresciallo Maffetone, solemn and upright, with his cap pulled almost over his eyes.

"They're going for afternoon tea with Chillemi," he thought aloud, as Juvara called him to the telephone. "Friar Fiorenzo for you."

It seemed as though everything had suddenly sprung to life, in keeping with the frenetic pace of the Christmas shopping. For a quarter of an hour, he had been trying unsuccessfully to get away.

"Commissario, the woman who left the knife has come back," the friar began, in a state of agitation.

"When?"

"Two days ago, at dawn, more or less the same time as before."

"Why didn't you let me know sooner?"

"I had many doubts about it. Even now I'm not sure whether I'm doing the right thing."

"What did she say to you?"

"Oh, nothing particularly new, but my intuition told me that she had a heavy weight on her conscience."

Soneri muttered something in agreement, but it did not amount to much. Matters of conscience did not come within his professional competence – although he was no longer entirely convinced of that certainty.

"Do you have any idea why she came back? She's not a regular churchgoer."

"No, and she's not one of my parishioners. I don't know why. Perhaps because every so often she drops by here. She told me the last time that she took great comfort from my words, so it may be . . ."

"Did you at least get a look at her as she was leaving?"

"I saw something of her, but she was wearing a heavy over-coat and had a scarf over her head. In any case, I only saw her from behind. A woman of medium height."

"She might have had the decency at least to be very tall or very short," the commissario snapped.

"I realise . . ." Friar Fiorenzo apologised. "However, I did ask her to come back and make her confession before the Christmas period, or even on Christmas Day itself."

"And what did she say?"

"That she might come, but she couldn't promise."

Soneri sighed, thanked the friar and put the phone down. He turned to look at Juvara. "You're not a very good Christian, are you?" he said, pointing a finger at him.

The inspector gave him a perplexed look and shrugged.

"So to make up, you're going to have to do some penance," Soneri said. Juvara was already uneasy, and now he began to go red with a blush which started at his neck and worked its way up to his face. He leaned back to listen.

"Tomorrow morning you're going to go to the Chiesa di Sant'Uldarico to wait for the good friars to open up. You'll go inside, kneel down and start saying your prayers like a good Christian preparing for Christmas. Since it's Christmas Eve, you won't arouse any suspicion. The number of believers swells at Christmas time."

Juvara was about to ask for more detail, but Soneri got in first. "While you're there, keep your eye on the confessional and the moment you see a youngish woman of medium height, dressed in an overcoat and headscarf, stop her and call me."

"Do you have a more precise description?"

"At that time in the morning, the only people who'll be there are elderly women. A young woman will stand out. Oh, I nearly forgot. The church opens at five o'clock."

The colour drained from Juvara's face, but he said nothing.

"Anyway, I'll be close by as well," Soneri said.

At last he was able to get up and take his duffel coat down from the peg. He felt something sharp in his right pocket and when he stuck his hand in to see what it was, he remembered it was a present he had bought for Juvara. "What are we going to do? Put it under the Christmas tree? Or do you want to open it right away?" he said, holding it out.

The inspector could not wait, and in his smile Soneri caught a residue of childhood. The present was an anti-virus device for his computer, updated for the New Year. "A protection against your solitary vice," he said.

A few minutes later, he was striding across the smoky dining room of the *Milord*, past diners already tucking into dessert. "Are we not supposed to be fasting at the moment?" he asked Alceste.

"Ah, the old ways! The only ones who remember are people of our age."

"At least you keep to the old ways in the kitchen," Soneri said.

"That's getting harder and harder all the time," Alceste snorted, showing Soneri a plate on which someone had cut off the fat from their *prosciutto* and pushed it to the side. "Have you ever seen the leg of a Parma pig with no fat? And then they happily guzzle a hamburger in some fast food joint."

"I'd like to tell them where to stuff their hamburgers," the commissario said.

"Would you like some chicken and chips?" Alceste said with heavy irony.

Soneri looked at him askance. "Isn't this the season for *baccalà*? Maybe with a helping of polenta."

"Sweetcorn pâté served with fish from the Baltic, as they used to write on the menus at the Communist Party functions in the Sixties."

The commissario was plunged back into the reflections that had been tormenting him since he made his first steps in this investigation. Alceste watched his expression darken and made no further comment. He went into the kitchen and sent out a waiter to serve him.

It was after three o'clock when Soneri left the establishment. The streets in the city centre were jammed with people scurrying about on the pavements, their mackintoshes and fur coats brushing against each other in a casino-like frenzy. The illuminations reinforced this impression. A clown show, as Marta Bernazzoli had said. Soneri turned into the lanes in a district which was uncrowded and had no shops, and reached Via Saffi. A group of immigrants stood chatting in front of the shisha bar, which was still closed, while an improvised African market was displaying its highly coloured wares under the colonnade in Borgo delle Colonne.

At precisely that moment, he heard brass instruments ring out nearby as a band struck up with a partisan song. Cornetti, carried shoulder high to the accompaniment of music he had always loved, was bidding his last farewell to what had been his home district. The scene seemed somehow grotesque. The cortège was followed by a small crowd among whom Soneri recognised his former workmen by their strong, calloused hands. Behind them came an improbable mixture of anarchist black banners and communist red flags, followed by Friar Fiorenzo in his robes and various partisan societies carrying their placards aloft, a procession of elderly men, some with fists raised and others with shoulders hunched under the weight of too many misadventures.

With the band at its head, the crowd moved forward. It passed alongside the walls of San Francesco, down Borgo delle Colonne where the band played *Bandiera Rossa* in homage to what had once been the street with the greatest number of communists in the city, attracting the astonished looks of the immigrants, the only people giving their full attention to what must have seemed to them an event organised by a hospice. In a thickening mist descending on the streets, the funeral procession proceeded towards Borgo del Naviglio and the places associated with the 1922 barricades, before coming out on the ring road where a hearse was waiting. Cornetti had bid goodbye to his own haunts and to much else besides. What Soneri saw was a small army of the faithful in sad retreat, some exhausted and limping, and others leaning on their walking sticks. He watched the banners being folded up and put away, and witnessed the last, haphazard salutes given under the curious eyes of the first prostitutes as they prepared for another long night.

Standing by the roadside, he observed people slipping away one by one until the last participant was swallowed up by the fog.

"It brings a lump to my throat," he heard a voice behind him say.

Soneri turned round and saw Bettati. "We meet rather too often at funerals these days."

"It looks as though destiny has put them in a queue, one after the other," Bettati said.

"I'd like to think there's nobody else in the queue."

Bettati made a face suggesting helplessness. "Anyway, it is true that Cornetti had run out of patience even with those extremist groups."

"Who told you that?"

"His foreman. He'd seen him in a state of exasperation just a few days before he shot himself. He said there was no humility left, and that young people today came over as arrogant know-alls who'd never done a hard day's work with a spade in their hands."

"It's hard to disagree with him."

"Yes, but these people had even been threatening him. The problem was that everyone else in politics was worse, a bunch of scoundrels on the make, like Pecorari and Avanzini."

"Now they'll draw a veil over Cornetti and all this," the commissario said.

"They may well do so," Bettati said, taking his bicycle by the handlebars and pushing it along the pavement. The two men walked a while in silence. "However, one of these young folk must have taken a liking to him. There was one tall, thin guy paying his respects in the mortuary. I don't think I've seen him before."

Instinctively the commissario thought of Andrea Fornari.

"It could have been one of the far-left gang who used to hang out in that flat."

Bettati stopped and stared at him, then continued on his way without saying a word.

"When did you see him?"

"Early this morning. I went to the mortuary as soon as it was open. I like to get as close as possible to people, even when they're dead. There's no-one else around at that time."

"When did the other guy turn up?"

"Just as I was leaving. I got the impression he'd been waiting for me to go. I turned round for one last look and I saw him going in."

"Maybe he was a member of one of those groups. He might have had something on his conscience," Soneri said, thinking of the woman who had gone twice to make her confession to Friar Fiorenzo.

"I think they should all have a weight on their conscience, now that there's no political consciousness and everything's gone to the dogs, but I wouldn't be too sure," the barber said bitterly.

It was getting dark and at that time of day the frenzy on the city streets was even greater. An invisible mixer was tossing the crowd about beneath an immobile blanket of mist as thick as béchamel sauce. Soneri cut through the throngs towards the questura and went in by a side door and along a vaulted corridor where a sentry stood guard. Angela had been right. Everybody goes home for Christmas, including Fornari. But where would he be now? Perhaps up at Monchio assisting in the slaughter of a pig? Who would plunge in the knife on this occasion?

Juvara arrived just in time to ward off further gloomy thoughts. "Mayhem," he announced, waving his arms about. "They're rushing here and there, and don't know where they're heading. Christmas must have infected even the arseholes."

"Over at the Digos offices they're in a meeting which has been going on for more than two hours, with admin people running up and down with bundles of paper in their hands. They've even called the Florentine magistrate who's in charge of the terrorism case back from his holidays."

"So that's his escort waiting down in the courtyard."

"Even Maffetone's at it, running up to Chillemi's office and back again."

"So we're the only ones at peace, as though we were in the eye of the cyclone, with absolute chaos all around," Soneri said, with a touch of resignation.

"I had to hand back the Dallacasa file. They wanted it in the Digos office," Juvara said.

Soneri looked down at the cloisters, as he often did when he was lost in thought, but on this occasion instead of the usual stillness he saw a flurry of officials, officers and drivers rushing about in the kind of hysteria seen at Grand Prix races. The blue cars of civic dignitaries were pulling up at the foot of the stairs leading to the offices of the vice-questore, while unmarked police cars were parked one beside the other under fir trees whose tops were lost in the mist. "Does anybody know what the fuck is going on?" he asked, slapping his hand down on the desk so firmly that he knocked over the lamp stand.

Juvara looked on helplessly.

"Go and see if you can find anything out," Soneri told him, his tone almost imploring.

The inspector went out without a word, leaving Soneri in a rage. Hoping for a call from the floor above, he stared at the telephone, but it stubbornly refused to ring. No-one was looking for him now, nor had they been earlier. He watched a car from the Guardia di Finanza arrive, its lights flashing. A couple of officers got out and made for the same staircase as the others. The whole landing occupied by the questore and his deputy was ablaze with light, a sign they were working flat out. If that was unusual at any time of the year, it was a hundred times more so on the day before Christmas Eve.

Juvara came back in and his expression was enough to tell Soneri he had got nowhere. "Commissario, I haven't got much to say. They treated me like a criminal."

"Do you at least know if they're dealing with terrorism or bribery?"

"Both. Chillemi's leaping from one meeting to another."

"Are they talking about issuing arrest warrants?"

"I think so. A friend in the central office told me that some arrests have already been made and that other warrants will be executed either today or tomorrow."

"I hope they at least let them enjoy their Christmas dinner," Soneri said, with deeply felt bitterness.

Juvara gave a nervous laugh. He too was plainly put out by the whole business. "We've still got the old woman's murder," he said, in an attempt to console him.

"Wait and see if they don't try and take that away from us too," Soneri said, attempting to sound nonchalant. "Anyway, we'll find out tomorrow."

"Why tomorrow?"

"Because all this mucking about will be over by then. We've just got to wait for the big show."

Juvara stared at him without understanding, but he was long accustomed to cryptic replies from his superior.

"Fancy a meal together?" Soneri suggested to Angela. Fortunately, he had remembered his promise to call her as soon as he left his office.

"Alright. As it's Christmas why don't you come to my place, but don't expect some sort of family feast." She then said, "We'll follow tradition and have a light meal."

The commissario was at the corner and could hardly object. "You're right. We must respect the old customs."

Angela lived quite near the questura, and once in her house Soneri jumped up every time he heard a squad car pass, or saw the reflection of a flashing light in the window. On each occasion, he got up from table and ran to the window like a child on the lookout for Father Christmas.

"Maybe if I'd done you some *anolini* or one of those dishes overflowing with fat that you're so keen to devour at Alceste's, you'd have been able to stay sitting at the table," Angela said.

"This is not exactly the kind of meal that's makes you struggle to get to your feet," he said, toying with two pieces of mozzarella no bigger than a prune, garnished with lettuce with no dressing. His eye was drawn immediately afterwards to the bottle of natural mineral water.

Just then the wail of a siren rang out, and he leapt to his feet yet again. "Carabinieri," he said, returning to his seat.

"I've never seen you so restless. You're like a bird battering its wings against the bars of its cage."

"I think we're at the endgame, but I'm not throwing in my hand yet."

"If it's because they're cutting you out, forget it. It's always been the same. You're not like the rest of them, and if you were, you wouldn't be here."

The commissario looked at her gratefully, but could not help noting the signs of tension on her face.

"Even if I do try not to bother about it," he began, but could not find the words to finish his sentence.

"I know, but in part it's your own fault. You always work on your own and you never leave space for anyone else.

Obviously, they're not going to make space for you either. Add to that the fact that you're impossible to control, and politically you're . . . In the questura, they're all near-Fascists. Some of them might make out they're moderates, but others have Il Duce's face as a screensaver on their mobiles."

Another flashing light sped past like a tidal wave on the street below. Soneri thought he was facing a sleepless night, or at best a night disturbed by bad dreams. Angela was sitting beside him on the couch when his mobile rang. She moved aside, but held up her hand with four curved fingers and sharp nails.

It was Juvara, struggling to control his breathing. "Commissario, they've arrested Avanzini."

"Who have? The Guardia di Finanza?"

"Maresciallo Maffetone in person. The whole thing was set up so as not to attract too much attention. Avanzini turned up in his car with his lawyer at his side, low-key, but the journalists had been tipped off and they descended on him. He said he was there of his own accord to clear the issue up with the magistrate."

"That old hypocrite could wriggle out of a locked safe."

"It seems he's ready to sing, so they might let him out right away. The official reason for the arrest was to avoid any possible degradation of the evidence."

"Of course! After waiting three whole days! So much for degrading the evidence."

"That's not all. Since the offence is bribery and corruption, they're not going to be able to leave Pecorari at liberty."

"Anything's possible." Soneri sounded sceptical. "They'll come up with some excuse to make as little fuss as possible. Anyway, what about the other inquiry?"

"I've learned there's some activity here, but the main action is in Tuscany."

"What do they want from us?"

"If only I knew! Maybe some details. I arrange to meet my friend in the central office every so often, and he keeps me posted."

"You can go home. It's late."

"I'd rather stay here. It's like watching an anthill!"

"In that case, don't bother going to Sant'Uldarico tomorrow morning. I'll see to it myself."

"But why? If I don't get to bed, it'd do me good to go for a walk at about five in the morning. Should I or should I not become a good Christian?"

"Some day you might be one. Meantime, you're a good devil."

"Change that dreadful ringtone," Angela ordered him as he hung up.

"Don't you like Verdi?"

"That music is offensive. A lot of my colleagues have it and they always make me listen to it just to annoy me."

"I'll do my best. Juvara's always promising to change it for me, but he's never got round to it."

After a final snort, she relaxed and embraced him warmly. For some time afterwards, the commissario was oblivious to sirens, flashing lights or the roar of squad cars.

"Addicts who shoot up must feel the same way," he said as he came back to himself.

"I'm more effective than any drug," Angela informed him severely. After a few minutes, Soneri began to get agitated again. She looked at him in resignation. "You need either a blow to the head or a sleeping pill."

The commissario made no reply, but he looked increasingly worried when cars began to race by at top speed, pursued by others with flashing lights.

"Do you want to tell me what's wrong with you?" she said.

It was only then that he managed to identify clearly the cause of the unease he had previously attributed to the shock of being shut out of the investigation. "I'm worried about tomorrow," he said.

"Why? What's going to happen tomorrow?"

"It's Christmas Eve and I always go and give my good wishes to Ada's father."

Angela nodded and murmured, "I understand."

"It's not that simple. It's not going to be the same this year as other years."

"Ah, then I don't understand."

"Look, I don't want to talk about it, partly because it's only a suspicion."

"These suspicions of yours . . ." She was about to complete the sentence, but broke off. She decided that there was no point in imagining too much, as it only served to create anxieties in advance.

The commissario made to get up and put on his duffel coat when his mobile started ringing again, much to Angela's irritation.

"You were right. Avanzini's getting out," Juvara said. "It might be house arrest. He's telling them everything."

"Just as I thought. He's got no balls. All you have to do is stop him weaving his own web. Maybe he's got himself all tangled up in it over the last three days."

"Now it's Pecorari's turn. He came on foot from the city chambers. He brought his lawyer with him."

"What about the journalists?"

"Chillemi pretended to come down hard on them. He dispatched two officers to chase them out of the cloisters, but then he leaked the information that Councillor Pecorari would be coming in through the back entrance on Borgo della Posta. As a result the journalists took up various positions, some at the door and others on Via Repubblica. When Pecorari got there, he found them all hovering around him like vultures."

"Chillemi will never change. He's keen to preserve appearances, but he's too fond of being on the front pages."

"Commissario, it's absolute chaos here."

"Has anyone been looking for me?" Soneri said, feeling as he spoke that he had put his finger on an open wound.

"No, nobody," was the embarrassed reply.

"Just as well," Soneri said, cutting him off before he could go any further. And it was true – none of it mattered to him anymore.

12

HE COULD HAVE sworn he was woken by a police siren. He got out of bed while Angela was still asleep and felt overcome by an unpleasant feeling of exile, the same sensation he had experienced as a boy when waking up on the first morning of his holidays with his parents in a claustrophobic seaside boarding house in Liguria. That first thought was enough to arouse in him the regret and guilt of matrimonial infidelity. He groped his way to the bathroom, feeling lost as he always did when he stayed overnight. As he washed, he heard a police siren. It had not been a dream.

He left just in time to savour those final moments when the city was still sunk in its nocturnal peace. It appeared that the duty of arousing the city had been entrusted to the Franciscans of Sant'Uldarico, become from the moment the church doors swung open, the silence was broken by vans and trucks from newspaper offices or bakeries, followed a few minutes later by the footsteps of the old women moving as fast as they were able to keep their morning appointments. He waited for Juvara, but saw no sign of him. He moved silently towards the chapel of Sant'Egidio from where he could keep an eye on the central nave and the confessional, into which Friar Fiorenza let himself shortly afterwards.

He waited for about thirty minutes in the sepulchral

silence, watching the old women come and go. He would have liked to say a prayer, but felt unable to do so. The epicentre of his emotions was too deep to manifest itself even with a sign of the cross. After waiting in vain, he left the church just as the city was coming fully to life. The mysterious woman had not arrived. He called Juvara, but his telephone rang for some time before a sleepy, childlike voice answered.

"If you behave this way with your dates, you'll never get a girlfriend," Soneri reproached him cheerfully.

"I fell asleep on the couch," he mumbled, still half-asleep, before being startled into life. "Bloody hell! It's nearly seven!"

"It's alright. You were better off staying in bed. She didn't turn up."

"I stayed awake until four, but then . . ."

"It's a sign you're still young," Soneri said, with a touch of envy in his voice. "O.K., give me a brief report on what's been going on during the night."

"They released both Avanzini and Pecorari after an interrogation lasting a couple of hours. House arrest for the pair of them. Chillemi went off at about three, but I doubt if he will have got much sleep. He's on a high. This is his big moment."

"What's on the agenda for this morning?"

"They've announced that another magistrate is on his way from Florence in connection with the part of the inquiry relating to the terrorists."

The commissario's mood darkened.

"As far as I can gather, they've got hold of the address of some terrorist base around here, and perhaps they're actively looking for someone," Juvara said.

"Now that you've had a rest, keep an eye on the situation and let me know immediately if there are any developments."

His father-in-law was expecting him, and Soneri knew he would have to make an effort to keep in check the emotions

the visit would re-awaken in him. He tried to put on a professional air.

Pino stretched out his great calloused peasant hand. "It's
good of you to remember every year," he said, ushering him
into the kitchen.

Soneri took a quick look around, enough to verify that
everything was still in its place. He would rather it had not
been so. The two men stood in awkward silence, frozen by an
embarrassment which hovered over their every gesture. Ada's
absence created an emptiness which deprived them of words
and drained away their thoughts.

"Give me your coat," Pino said at last. "Will we smoke a
cigar together?"

The smoking became an accomplice to their silence. With
a cigar between their fingers, the absence of words became
more tolerable.

"So how are things?" Soneri said at last.

Pino stretched out his arms and replied with an ironic
smile: "For me it's the last waltz before the music stops."

Soneri tried to offer encouraging words, but his voice was
tired. "There's still time. The bandsmen have only just learned
the rhythm."

Pino gave another smile, but this time the irony was tinged
with bitterness. "You know when you really feel old? When
you know more people on the other side than on this, more
friends dead than alive."

"I'm old too, then. In my line of business, I get to know
people only when they're dead."

As soon as the words were out, he realised that that notion
applied to Ada too. But the old man could not know it and
he smiled again, still in the same manner. Irony was perhaps

his dominant cast of mind, or perhaps the indispensable drug which might make the last waltz bearable.

Smoke wrapped itself round their silence. "I've brought you something," Soneri said, as he planted a Christmas hamper of dried fruit and salami on the table.

"You shouldn't have," Pino said. "I eat very little now." He said no more for fear of putting into words what Soneri believed he could read in his eyes. He was sure he had been on the point of saying something about Ada, before drawing back out of delicacy, or perhaps out of fear of the pain his words would cause both of them.

"There's no sense in not talking about it," Soneri said, gently.

From behind the veil of smoke, Pino nodded. "It's like toothache. When you have it, you can cope to some extent, but you avoid biting on the bad tooth."

It crossed the commissario's mind that he would have been more than happy to act that way, but the time had come for action. He had to assume once more the role of the policeman. He was ashamed, but knew he was being truthful in both parts, as husband and investigating officer.

"Do you mind if I go up to Ada's room? I would just like to spend a little time there."

Before he had completed the sentence the old man agreed, without looking him in the face, as though his thoughts were elsewhere. Perhaps he was thinking of his daughter, or of the uselessness of those grey days. Christmas must be a misery for him.

Everything in his wife's bedroom had been frozen at the time of their youth – the photographs on the walls, the fashionable modern furniture of the moment, the curtains and the duvet. A sense of the vanity of things overwhelmed him and all of a sudden everything appeared senseless. A hard lump of contracted emotions, made of material resistant to all solvents, stuck in his throat like a mouthful that had gone down the wrong way, and the mirror in front of him reflected back an unwelcome image of himself. Were those tears glistening in the eyes of his reddened face? He had no wish to pay heed to them, and threw himself into searching feverishly in the drawers.

The first thing he came across was a photograph of Ada taken when she was a baby, in a dress trimmed with lace. He found other photos which amounted to a narrative of her life: Ada in a park, Ada on her first day at school, Ada at her first Holy Communion, Ada on an outing with her secondary school, Ada in the white uniform of the nursing college, then many class pictures and some close-ups of her with her friends, the thoughtful look which mark the end of adolescence. There was nothing else. That was not what Soneri was looking for. There must be somewhere in those drawers an undiscovered artefact which corresponded to the thick shadow which concealed a part of her existence.

He knew the techniques of the house search and employed them to the full, but he felt like a thief when his hand gripped a bundle of letters which seemed as if still warm from being carried in a pocket. There in the middle was a photograph of a very young Andrea Fornari, his face bearing traces of a long and tormented youth. In the faint light of the lamp on the bedside table, Soneri sat down on the bed which had cradled Ada's dreams, including that of a love which had faded, perhaps her only genuine love. He gazed avidly at the letters, confused in his own mind, staring at Fornari's neat handwriting. His eyes wandered down the lines, searching for confirmation, which he quickly and unequivocally found.

I find myself unable to sacrifice what appears to me now like a sacred duty for a life wholly dedicated to the fulfilment of a purpose which, however attractive, is purely private. Of course I love you, but if any sense is to be given to our times it is necessary to serve another purpose. You have no wish to follow me, and so, when all is said and done, you do not fully understand me. If you really wanted to share everything with me, you would abandon your plans to be a nurse and dedicate yourself to other people in a different way. Helping one's neighbours means above all changing the conditions in which they live, and doing so involves using methods which seem to you reprehensible and violent. The refusal expressed in your last letter indicates a deep gulf between us. I have never felt you to be so distant. Perhaps that is natural if we are discussing a goodbye, but perhaps this distance is nothing other than the emergence of two visions of the world which are too divergent. If now I speak in the language of emotions, I feel distraught, but if reason prevails in me, I believe that this is a natural conclusion.

I embrace you with deepest love,
Andrea

He read every word of the letter in one go, and failed to notice Pino standing at the entrance to the bedroom. From where he was seated, Pino seemed to occupy the whole space of the doorway. He could not make out his features, only his dark outline against the grey light of the morning. He expected Pino to be angry, but when he began speaking Soneri heard a calm, even gentle voice, as though he were addressing Ada when she was still a girl lying in that bed where he used to wake her for school.

"Now you know why she kept those years hidden from you."

In the dim light Soneri nodded, but his father-in-law could not see that reaction and stood waiting for some response.

Sensations crowded in on him pell-mell, like disconnected stills in a poorly edited film. Everything appeared to him impalpable, mere appearance, non-being. Marta's words about life as a "clown show" still rang in his ears. A sad inebriation assailed him for a few moments, before with an effort of will he made the attempt to anchor himself again to the living moment, even if that too was merely appearance.

"I do understand now," he whispered.

The old man drew deeply on his cigar. The thick clouds of smoke made his outline even more opaque. "She had made a pact and had no wish to betray him. I think you will understand that. She was in love with him and wanted to redeem him. She didn't succeed, but she was desperate to keep her promise," Pino said, wounding Soneri to the quick with his words.

"Nor did I know . . ."

"About the abortion? That was another consequence of the regrettable choice of Andrea Fornari. What were they to do? She was still a student, and he had virtually gone underground as a terrorist. What future would they have had? Ada had an abortion courtesy of Ghitta Tagliavini, and I think that from then on neither one of them could stand her. Something in the unconscious. I believe they transferred their sense of guilt onto Ghitta."

Soneri would have liked to understand what his role was, or might have been. He felt he was stranded somewhere, almost an outsider, but he did not dare ask for fear of what his father-in-law might reply. He preferred to listen and imagine the intentions behind the words, and meantime focused on the trauma of the abortion and the scar left on Ada's stomach like a ticking bomb set to go off at some point. "That affair condemned her," he said in a neutral tone, as though talking to himself, but his thoughts went also to Ghitta and to how she too had been destroyed by an error of her youth from which she never recovered.

"Was that the reason?" the old man said.

"That was what the doctors suggested. A prior wound. Ghitta had no medical training."

He saw Pino lean all the weight of his tired body against the frame of the door. He drew deeply on his cigar, making the tip glow.

"Are you saying that this might explain what has taken place? An act of revenge on Ghitta?"

Soneri shook his head. "Perhaps deep down, but I don't believe that was the principal motive." After reading Ada's letters, an idea was taking shape in his mind but he could not yet formulate it with precision.

"He got his life together in Milan, a normal life, as Ada would have wished. In the final analysis, he saw things the way she did, but by the time he made up his mind to abandon the armed struggle, you were already on the scene," Pino said.

Pino's words left him distraught. He felt like a plug used to stop a leak, but which had then become part of the furniture of someone else's life. He could not put into words the question he needed to ask. He found himself debating in a hall of mirrors in an attempt to escape the self-image reflected in what he was hearing.

Meanwhile Pino went on speaking. "Ada begged me to make a promise in case she passed away." He paused to draw again on the cigar. "I told her not to be so stupid as to think of an agreement like that, that it was against nature for children to die before their parents. Anyway, the promise was that once it was all over, I would tell you everything she couldn't bring herself to tell you herself. And that seems to be what has just happened."

Soneri still wondered if the story was really closed. Ada

was dead and Andrea had managed to get his own life together, but what about Ghitta? Could he have murdered her for revenge? Or because she knew too much? Once again he had the feeling that he had in his grasp the logical connections binding the whole story, but that once again they were slipping away from him. He was continually opening doors which gave on to antechambers but never really took him anywhere, as happened with those long-drawn-out dreams which last a whole night.

"Now you know everything," Pino said with a sigh. "I hope you're not angry with me, but I couldn't break the promise I had made to Ada."

"She should have told me herself," the commissario said, in a tone which failed to conceal his resentment

"She couldn't."

Soneri gave a bitter smile. "Because Andrea was her passion and I was no more than a rebound."

Pino shook his head in a way that indicated understanding. "Don't think that you counted any less for her. For my wife, I too was a rebound, to use your expression. Then Ada came along. Passions are spent, the rest remains."

"The rest might not be spent, but perhaps it festers instead."

Soneri jumped to his feet, oppressed by the smoke-filled gloom, and held out his hand to his father-in-law, who looked back at him in the hope of finding in his eyes some trace of forgiveness. "I know I've upset you, but do not think too badly of me," he said. "It was perhaps the last thing of any importance I had to do in this world," he stammered.

Soneri moved close to him, put his hand on Pino's arm and squeezed it gently in a gesture which, given his shyness, was as near as he could come to an embrace.

*

He wandered around the city trying to calm down, but the throng of people which prevented him from walking at a normal pace caused his temperature to rise even higher. And then his mobile rang.

"Have you seen the papers?" Angela said without preamble.

"No, I haven't been to the office yet."

"So this gloomy tone of voice has nothing to do with the articles celebrating the success of Maffetone?"

"Nothing at all. It's to do with things that are much more serious. I've been to see Ada's father."

Angela's groan made it clear to him that she understood.

"I'll explain everything when we meet," he said.

"This evening," she specified.

"Alright," Soneri agreed, somewhat reluctantly. "Are we still going to be fasting?"

"Of course! It's Christmas Eve."

He put his mobile away, and looked up to see a newspaper hoarding with the headlines shrieking out: "MAXI-OPERATION BY THE GUARDIA DI FINANZA. POLITICIANS AND BUSINESS LEADERS UNDER ARREST." And underneath: "CITY IN TURMOIL."

He looked around at the bustle of ostentatious elegance, at the streets filled with people busy with last-minute shopping for food and presents, and chuckled to himself. None of them gave a damn about questions of bribery. Each was intent on their private affairs, and fully focused on the narrow horizon of their own narrow interests. He chose not to buy a copy of the paper. It was not the larceny operated by Chillemi and Maffetone that was his principal concern, but the conversation with Ada's father. The investigation had been from the very beginning an inquiry into himself, conducted relentlessly, allowing for neither concessions nor omissions, but now weighing on him like a life sentence.

In the streets of the city centre he kept an eye open for Pitti, but it would have been impossible to pick him out in that never-ending flow. He thought obsessively of Ada and Andrea and of their union, as well as of Andrea and his father, Rosso, up there in Monchio, obsessed by the quarrel with Ghitta. The more he thought about it, the more convinced he became that his wife's great love had some connection with the murder of the landlady.

A little later, when the day was dying, the tidal wave which had swept him along dumped him like a dead fish in an unexpectedly quiet lane. Once there, he had to answer the mobile which had been ringing for a while. Juvara informed him that there was even more commotion and that more arrests were expected, this time by the Digos squad. When he hung up, he felt himself happily removed from all that upheaval. He heard a soft bell announcing vespers, and when he looked up over a wall of ancient stones he could just make out in the mist the campanile of Sant'Uldarico.

He arrived there after tramping through two narrow streets jammed with cars. He went in through a side entrance and found a seat in the chapel of Sant'Egidio. It seemed a good idea to say prayers – like the elderly ladies kneeling on arthritic knees, but he found himself unable to perform or act out rites he knew well but no longer practised. His religious feeling, if it could be so called, was more an attitude of the spirit than of overt behaviour.

He heard the bell for vespers ring out again as the women hurried to their seats. It was at that moment that he saw Elvira, dressed entirely in black with a dark scarf over her head. She hesitated at the church door, looked around and made the sign of the cross before advancing slowly in the yellowish light of the candles. She moved towards the pews and tentatively stretched out her hand to touch the end of the second row, as though afraid it might burn her. She sat down, causing the bench to creak. Friar Fiorenzo must have already been in the sacristy, because no-one was going into the confessional anymore. Another priest came out in his vestments and started to celebrate Mass. Elvira took part in the service together with the other women.

Friar Fiorenzo returned before the homily, crossed the nave, genuflected and made for the confessional. The Mass was as brief as the last Mass on a Sunday and was soon over. The priest told the congregation to go forth in peace and left the altar. Soneri remained in the darkness of the chapel. When the other women had left, Elvira got up and walked to the confessional. The commissario came out of the chapel to wait for her. Her confession lasted longer than he expected. He saw her kneeling, but all he could see clearly were her ankles and feet, which moved about from time to time in seeming discomfort. She got up but stopped to say something, bending towards the grate before emerging, adjusting the black scarf over her head as she did so.

As soon as she was out of the church she took off her scarf and tucked it into her handbag. Soneri followed her, worried that she might head for the crowds on Via Repubblica, but instead her route took her through the side streets. Soneri could not make up his mind about stopping her, but hoped to find a quiet spot in the misty silence of Christmas Eve. They walked from the Borgo del Correggio towards Via Saffi. She turned left and strode in the direction of the pensione, reaching No.35 soon afterwards. Soneri had been tailing her and at that point he had no further doubts. "Elvira!" he called out.

She turned, a little surprised, but not unduly, as though she had guessed what was going on.

"We started here and now we're back here," he said.

"That's how it goes. So it's written."

Soneri assented in silence. She looked at him challeng-
ingly, in keeping with her usual habit of defending herself
by attacking others. The commissario could not stand such
behaviour and all the accumulated tensions of that day were
united into one direct, angry question, "Where is Andrea
Fornari?"

She turned pale and pretended not to understand. Before
she could open her mouth, the commissario said, "There's no
point in trying to make a fool me. If I don't get to him first,
he'll end up in the hands of the Digos, and perhaps that'll be
the worse for him."

Elvira realised the game was up. She took time to think,
raising her eyes towards the dripping gutters. A few seconds
were sufficient to convince her of the uselessness of flight or
self-justification.

"He must be in Milan. He'll be back in Monchio tomorrow
to see his family."

"Are you supposed to join him?"

"Yes, I was going to set off very soon."

"But you wanted to pop back here one last time."

"I know. Stupid sentimentalism, but I have spent many
years here."

"And then there's the remorse you tried to dispel by
enlisting Friar Fiorenzo's help."

"I knew nothing about it, believe me, and even now I can't
work out what was going on in Andrea's mind. Ghitta would
never have spoken, I'm sure of that. She was issuing threats
only to persuade Rosso to let go of the Landi property. You'll
never understand. In the world of the mountain folk, the old
mentality and even some almost barbaric customs are still
alive. I am certain she would never have spoken out about
Andrea's past, but he went off like a self-propelled robot. He
seemed to hate her for some other reason."

"I too think there were other motives."

Elvira stared hard at him, but the commissario said nothing more. "If there was anything else," Elvira said quietly, "I know nothing about it." There was a pause during which snatches of conversation in languages unknown to them were carried through the mist.

"You might know more about this story than I do," she said.

Soneri had no idea if she was acting a part or was sincere in what she was saying. "The more I think about it, the more absurd it seems to become. Ghitta would never have said a thing, of that I am sure," she said again.

"My job is to bring in the murderer, and the fear that Ghitta might talk is motive enough," Soneri said, with a certain resignation.

"Perhaps not the main one."

"Every action of ours is the child of many motivations, but only one is baptised."

Elvira understood that Soneri could not be moved. "There was nothing I could do to stop him, and he did everything possible to get me involved. Andrea is very insecure. It was always up to me to comfort him and explain the right thing to do. When he confessed to me that he had killed Ghitta, he was already desperate, distraught. He had acted on impulse, moved by hatred for all the threats his father had told him about. His father reproached him bitterly for having been involved with the armed struggle. He failed to realise that Andrea joined the terrorists in a desperate effort to be like his father. Andrea wanted his father's approval, and all he got was his affectionate contempt. That's why he was keen on some exemplary action. Because he made him feel a weakling, 'the vet' – Rosso, that is – drove Andrea to carry out an act of violence."

"And then he regretted it and came running to you?"

"Like a child. He couldn't string two words together, he was stuttering, he was distraught. He told me he'd picked up a pork butcher's knife at home and set off for the pensione to talk to Ghitta. I've no idea what he had in mind, but at some point Ghitta began reproaching him in exactly the way his father did. They're made of the same unyielding material, forged in the mountains. And so he killed her."

"So what did you tell him to do?"

"To disappear. It was the only way to avoid worse problems. Once he was away from here, he might have recovered some clarity of mind. I took care of the knife, but when I saw Ghitta dead, I was overcome by panic myself. At that moment, I realised I'd become an accomplice to murder. I should have forced Andrea to turn himself in. He'd thought long and hard about it, but a decision like that was going to bring in other people he didn't want to involve. How could he conceal his past? He was on police files as an extremist, and he'd been suspected for ages of having been in contact with underground groups. They were just waiting for the right time to nail him, and he knew he wouldn't have been able to hold out for long. And he would have compromised comrades with whom he'd shared a common passion and years of struggle."

"It would only have been a matter of time in any case."

"Perhaps. Meanwhile the issue of bribery and corruption emerged. I hoped that would have changed the course of the inquiry and perhaps muddied the waters."

"But you did not take the power of remorse into consideration."

"No, I thought I was immune to that, but there are some things you have to experience in the cold light of day."

"Why did you go to Friar Fiorenzo? Weren't you all

anti-clericals?" Soneri said, chewing the cigar which had gone out.

"When you're on your own and there's a weight like that crushing you, you feel you can't stand it and then you look around. I was in that position, and the only one I could find was him."

"Scratch, scratch, and all that's left are the priests."

"With all we set out to achieve with our banners flying . . . When I wanted to haul myself out of the shit, the only support I could find was Friar Fiorenzo." Elvira laughed bitterly.

"Alright, let's go," Soneri said to her gently, relighting his cigar. She nodded and followed him without giving him any trouble. Only when they were at the door of the questura did he turn to her to ask, "Don't you agree it was a useless crime?"

"In my view, Ghitta would never have spoken out, but we'll never know for sure."

13

COFFEE CUPS, SACHETS of sugar and a couple of pages of notes scribbled by Juvara lay on Soneri's desk. "We've reached the end of the road," the inspector said, resting both hands on the desk to pull himself laboriously to his feet.

Drawing on the cigar, which was almost out, the commissario observed him in silence. It had been dark outside for almost an hour, but beyond the gate of the questura, people were still scurrying about on Via Repubblica.

"We'll have to inform Saltapico. He'll need to interrogate Elvira and sign an arrest warrant for Fornari."

"We'll also need to go and see Chillemi," Juvara said.

"I can't tell you how pleased I am at the thought of ruining his Christmas dinner. Anyway, you see to it."

Juvara picked up the papers with Elvira's typed statement and went out. Soneri watched him cross the courtyard wrapped in a raincoat which resembled a cloak. The vicequestore would probably see him as a cross between a jinx and one of the Three Magi.

The enquiry into Ghitta's murder was complete, but in no sense did Soneri feel victorious. He knew that for the rest of his life he would carry the scars of the case, as also that sense of emptiness and aimlessness he experienced many times during his walks in the mist.

The mobile made him jump. "Well then? When are you coming over?" Angela's voice was full of enthusiasm.

"Soon. I've got to attend to the last formalities before I can close the case."

"At long last we'll have a quiet Christmas. Has there been a final twist you've kept hidden from me?"

"I've just finished interrogating Elvira. Fortunately, there's still such a thing as conscience, and sometimes it weighs down too heavily on people. Fornari's a weakling, a lout. She says he had no motive for killing Ghitta because she'd never have spoken, but he felt he was under attack. On top of that, his father thought he had no balls, so he wanted to make the grand gesture."

There might also have been an element of lingering rancour over Ada's abortion, but Soneri made no reference to it.

"Stupid people do more harm than villains," Angela said.

The commissario did not consider Fornari stupid, but rather a weak man in search of some cause which would make sense of his life. Did not life, after all, have a tragic resemblance to homicide? Did it not always end with a death? Did not time kill us by wearing us out day by day with one small slight after another, leading to the final surrender? Time has no more need of an excuse than does an executioner. It simply does its job. It is the victim who must give himself a motivation strong enough to endure the daily grind. Perhaps Fornari was seeking exactly that. Soneri understood him perfectly because he himself, having reached middle age, was still in search of his own cause.

Soneri changed tack. "How about asking Alceste to provide dinner?"

"Don't even think about it," came the reply. "I've been in the kitchen all afternoon and you know what that costs me. I lack the housewifely vocation."

"What have you prepared?"

"Roasted vegetables, *erbazzone* and a selection of soft cheeses."

"A menu fit for someone recuperating from an operation to remove an ulcer."

"Can you not make a sacrifice for Christmas Eve?"

"I've already made my sacrifice. I've had no lunch."

The very thought of another meal of fasting and abstinence tightened his stomach, but every sign of hunger vanished when he heard Juvara approach, his arrival announced by heavy footsteps and the swish of his thighs rubbing together.

"Chillemi wants to see you," he said.

Soneri gave a long-suffering sigh. "I'd have been as well going myself."

Juvara threw out his arms. It seemed he wanted to add something, but Soneri jumped to his feet so abruptly that he had no time to get the words out. "At least this new irritation has got him hot and bothered?"

"I don't think so," Juvara said, with the expression of someone apologising for delivering disappointing news.

In his superior's office, Soneri was faced with the usual scenario. On this occasion, he was met by the secretary with the freshly permed hair, clearly displeased with the amount of overtime she was compelled to put in. Chillemi, on the other hand, seemed in an unexpectedly jolly mood. He launched straightaway into renewed apologies for the newspaper articles which had appeared on the bribery and corruption scandal. "Is there a more shitty class of people than journalists?" he began, choosing one of his classic opening gambits. "Both Saltapico and I went out of our way to tell them that the investigation was initiated by Commissario Soneri on behalf of the crime squad." He spelled out every word as though he were dictating to his freshly permed secretary, but before he got to the second act, Soneri interrupted him. "I've already said it doesn't matter," he said, speaking in the coolest and most indifferent tone he could muster.

Chillemi flopped down quite suddenly, like a boxer after an uppercut, and it took him a few moments before he could pull himself together and start up again. "Well anyway, let's move on. You have concluded that Fornari was the murderer of Ghitta Tagliavini?"

"In view of the statements made by Elvira Cadoppi, I don't think there's any room for doubt."

"Everything's falling into place. We'll add this new charge," he said with studied nonchalance.

"Add it to what?"

"A few hours ago, Fornari was arrested in Milan by the Digos squad for being part of an armed gang."

Now he understood why Chillemi was in such a good mood. He was happy to be able to minimise the significance of Soneri's enquiries by announcing that they had already picked up Fornari without his assistance, and on more serious charges than some provincial crime.

"That was the motive for Ghitta's murder. He was afraid she'd talk," Soneri said.

"People of greater importance than a landlady have been singing, like those repentant ex-terrorists who have been cultivated for some time by Digos. A major breakthrough. Everyone will be talking about it."

Now Chillemi was staring defiantly at Soneri. It was clear he had been rehearsing his part meticulously.

Soneri was forced to admit that Chillemi had succeeded in wounding him yet again, but there was nothing he could do about it. He made an effort to feign indifference and not let his rage show. "In any case, I need to get the magistrate to sign the warrant to have him detained pending his appearance in court. The way things are, he'll be notified in prison."

"Indeed," Chillemi said, unable to conceal his delight. "No problem. We'll add this squalid little incident of provincial life to the charges arising from the main enquiries. And anyway," he added, twisting the knife in the wound, "it would seem that this Fornari was only small fry." Fixing a gaze of haughty superiority on him, Chillemi went on, "It's no more than a sideshow. All you have to do is hand the papers over to the magistrate. There's no need for you to trouble yourself over it any more."

"I'm very grateful. I have so much to do," Soneri said coldly. Pushing back the heavy chair, he got to his feet. Chillemi accompanied him to the door, and tried to shake hands, but Soneri was moving so quickly that he did not even see the outstretched hand.

"Happy Christmas," Chillemi shouted after him, in a tone which sounded to Soneri like a sneer.

Soneri raised his right hand without turning. "All the best!" He almost ran into the secretary with the freshly permed hair, who gave him the kind of look that a mother-in-law might give. He said nothing and went out.

"Perfect timing!" Juvara said when Soneri walked in. "It's half-past seven on Christmas Eve, the time the shops shut and everyone sets off home for the festivities."

"Never seen a case like it. All we need is a confession and Fornari too will be all set for midnight Mass."

"Fit for bureaucrats, like the ones in the admin offices."

"We've done a small job of marginal importance, nothing more than a bit of embroidery," the commissario commented bitterly.

Juvara grasped his meaning. "Chillemi?"

"I could only feign indifference. For the time being it's the only weapon I have, but one day they'll push me too far and I'll smash in one of their faces."

"So he actually managed to downplay the fact that we'd solved a murder case?"

"Fornari is in a cell thanks to the Digos squad. Terrorism charges. In comparison, our case is a mere trifle, a little provincial tale, in Chillemi's own words, and besides, Fornari is small fry. Our investigation was no more than an insignificant add-on to a line of enquiry carried out by others. Understand? Alright then, let's enjoy the festivities."

He pulled out a fresh cigar and lit it. He held out his hand to Juvara and almost embraced him, this being as far as his character would allow him to go. He made to leave the office.

The inspector detained him one moment more. "Commissario, I must tell you one final thing, even if it's not very important."

Soneri gestured to him to go on.

"Elvira had no weight on her conscience. All she wanted was to get out of the whole business and land Fornari right in it."

The commissario saw the final flicker of light in the case extinguished.

"How do you know?"

"I phoned Friar Fiorenzo and he confided it to me. Not officially, but I picked it up from his tone and allusions. You know what priests are like."

Soneri drew a deep breath intimating understanding, and went on his way. At last the streets appeared empty, and there wafted from the grocery stores a scent of salami that mingled with the mist. He had never felt so alone as he did that Christmas, not even on the one which fell immediately after Ada's death. He felt as though he had undergone an amputation. He had an image of himself as a malformed man, a warped, unrecognisable being like a war veteran who feels pain from a phantom limb.

"You look as though you're thoroughly annoyed with someone or other," Angela said to him later, looking at his sombre face.

He made no reply. He chose to speak only a few moments later, when Angela had disappeared into the kitchen.

"I wish I knew who to get annoyed with," he said, feeling the same powerlessness as someone swatting away a swarm of mosquitoes in the dark. Too many things had slipped away from him in those years, including an important part of Ada's life. This was no small matter for a commissario.

"I know what you're thinking," Angela said, breaking into his thoughts, "but it's water under the bridge now. We all have a duty to move on."

The problem was that everything appeared to Soneri to have already moved on, well past him. He observed other people with the detachment of a person observing an army of ants. The world seemed to him framed in unbearable futility: Ghitta with her pig-headed determination to triumph over the contempt of her townspeople, Fornari oppressed by life under his father's shadow to the point of joining a bunch of hapless criminals, Elvira permeated by proletarian pettiness, Cornetti lacerated by irrepressible passions, and Chiastra dying slowly of an excessive fidelity which age had not tempered. They all seemed to him like circus clowns, as Marta Bernazzoli had described them, and they all lived in the dimension of the absurd, murderers and victims alike, with nothing to distinguish one from the other.

As he ruminated in this vein, Soneri started smiling again, but with a distant expression that frightened Angela. "I've never seen you like this," she said.

"You're quite right. I've never felt this way before."

At that moment, the grotesque looked to him like the

symbol of the world and even of himself. He was no longer moored to that Cartesian rock of self-knowledge to which he had always clung, from which the Ghitta case had definitively severed him.

"Every crime I have ever had to investigate has slapped me in the face with the futility of our existence. Until now, I have always tried to make light of it, but this Ghitta business . . . You know what's behind it, don't you?"

Angela looked hard at him without making any reply. She had no idea what to say. She would have liked to offer him consolation, but she risked making herself look ridiculous. There were moments when silence seemed more appropriate than any words. He understood how close Angela was to him, and the looks they exchanged were pregnant with meaning and with genuine intimacy. Soneri felt her firm, reassuring body, and he clasped her gratefully to him as though he had finally found the rock he had been searching for all those days spent wandering about in the greyness of the city and in the dark anxieties of the investigation. He experienced the same feeling later, seated at table, dining on what his woman had prepared for him.

"The only one missing from the roll-call is Fernanda," Angela said.

He had forgotten all about her and had not even discussed her with Chillemi. Nor had Saltapico asked about the old woman.

"If you ask me, he's killed her as well," Angela said.

It came to Soneri that regrettably he was not altogether done with that troublesome case. "Now that the waters are calmer, maybe she'll turn up again. If she was afraid before, she has no reason to be so now."

"The rest of them are still around."

"You mean the politicians and the businessmen? They'd

never dirty their hands. They've too much to lose."

"Shall we go to the Duomo at midnight?"

"I can't bring myself to mingle with that bunch of hypocrites. Let's go and find Fadiga. He's got as much right to a happy Christmas as them."

They walked along the white pavements. The frost was a substitute for the snow, which seemed unable to decide whether to fall or not. The mist hovered as still as water in a well over the deserted space around the Mercato della Ghiaia. Soneri stopped and looked around. They were in the centre of the piazza and in the greyness they could make out only the solid, dark outlines of the closed kiosks, nothing more.

"That's our condition," he declared, with a theatrical twirl which took Angela by surprise.

She gave a feeble smile, and to prevent them tumbling back into some mental cul de sac, she took him by the arm. "Come on, let's find the way."

He refused to sleep in Angela's house. He did not want to get into the habit of fleeing, but wanted instead to familiarise himself once more with the house where he was going to have to start living again. Christmas morning, finally free of frenzy, had a proper holiday feel. The day crept in slowly, and the only change from the night lay in the altered colour of the mist. He went down and walked around the still sleeping city, passing close to the lighted shop windows. In one he saw a large Christmas tree hung with red lace knickers instead of the standard decorations, which made him think that to stare at shop windows it was necessary to have a policeman's stomach.

The questura was still asleep when he arrived. The gate at Via Repubblica was closed so Soneri went round the back to Borgo della Posta, where a guard was on duty. The corridors were deserted, the offices locked, and only from the operations centre were any voices to be heard, and even there in subdued tones. When he got to his desk, he telephoned Juvara. "Happy Christmas," he said, in a high-pitched voice.

The inspector sounded drowsy. "I'm trying to catch up on sleep. I haven't had much time in bed recently."

"We forgot all about Fernanda."

"Do you think Fornari eliminated her as well?"

"Who knows? When the gentlemen in the Digos squad in Milan deign to send us a message, we might even be able to find out from the protagonist himself."

"It's the festive season now, commissario. Put your mind at rest and take it easy. It was us who solved the case, wasn't it?"

"You're right. We should take it easy. In a minute or two I'm going to shut up shop and head off."

"O.K. then, and good wishes."

"I'm going to need them," Soneri said.

He started clearing up his desk and allowed himself to savour the peace of Christmas. He glanced over at the piles of foodstuffs gifted to the police, and thought he should pass them on to the Caritas food bank before it all went bad. He switched on his desk lamp and collapsed into his armchair. A quarter of an hour later, the main gate swung open to admit some official cars bringing dignitaries to offer seasonal greetings to the Prefect, who had come in specially for the occasion. It was at that moment that Soneri saw a figure appear and walk slowly in the direction of the fir trees. He stared closely at her, and as she passed among the trees he had the impression of reliving the scene from some days before, when everything started off.

Fernanda was wearing the same long overcoat, had the same weary gait and even the same floppy bag over her arm. The commissario waited for everything to unfold as though in a well-rehearsed script. His telephone rang and the guard told him an elderly lady wanted to speak to him.

"Send her up," he said.

Shortly afterwards, Fernanda appeared before him with a face drained of all colour. "I threw the die, and it ended up in the square which sends you back to Go!" he said to her.

Fernanda looked at him with the expression of a deaf person who cannot quite grasp the words spoken. "Well, these days I've done the rounds, I can tell you," she said.

She propped her walking stick against the desk as she had done on the previous occasion. The commissario noted that she was going through the same rigmarole.

"This morning I did agree to see you," he said.

"If only you had done so a few days ago."

"We wouldn't have been able to save Ghitta in any case," he said decisively.

"No, we couldn't have saved her," she agreed.

"Where have you been all this time?"

"Where do you think? Have a guess, Soneri."

She used his name in a tone intended to emphasise their long-standing acquaintanceship. The commissario peered at her, and in the midst of the wrinkles on her face he saw a pair of deep-set, malicious eyes staring back at him.

"We've been searching for you everywhere. You might have explained to us . . ."

"You weren't the only ones looking for me."

"Who else?"

"Pitti, for one. Elvira sent him to find Ghitta's various female ex-boarders because she thought I might have sought refuge with one of them."

"Who else?"

"That young man, I think."

"Andrea Fornari?"

"I knew as well as everyone else that some time ago he'd fallen into bad company. Was I supposed to hang about waiting for him? That's exactly why I came to you, but all I found was that Juvara. He didn't exactly inspire confidence. Could I trust myself to tell him everything? It would have been different with you. I knew you when you were a student. I think I can tell what people are made of."

"Well, anyway, I came along. All you had to do was tell me."

"You didn't seem very interested. At my age, you need to be sure."

Soneri thought that he really must have given the impression of not caring much about an old lady's statement, only remembering later that he had known her. His curiosity had been aroused too late to get the situation back under control.

"Where did you go?" he asked.

She looked intensely at him. There were a few hairs on her chin which trembled as she breathed. "Up there, to Ghitta's son's place. Chiastra gave me a lift in a friend's car. Do you think I was chosen as sole heir for no good reason?"

"I didn't suppose so," Soneri said.

"I cannot dispose of the legacy in any way I like. There are terms and conditions. Perhaps you know only one part of the will."

"It's not my business. I'm not a lawyer."

"Ghitta made some additions to her will, and these have been lodged in the offices of her lawyer, Zurlini. They were added as a codicil to the will, and they mean that I'm no more than the executor. I will inherit, but I've got to oversee a grand work which will bear her name. All the detailed work will be carried out by the lawyer. I'm nothing more than the guarantor. I was the only person close to Ghitta in her last years. We lived like sisters."

"What will this grand work be?"

"A hospice sited between Rigoso and Monchio, where there are only old people left."

"Did she want to be reconciled with the people in the towns?"

Soneri saw the wrinkles distend, but rather than a smile, it was a smirk that appeared. "It might seem that way, but the truth is quite different. She wanted them to remember her, or rather she wanted them to be obliged to remember her. The hospice will be very large and will supply accommodation for a lot of old folk from the nearby villages, where Ghitta was known because she did the rounds as faith healer. It will be built in the upper part of Rigoso, from where it can be seen day and night by everyone, even by tourists coming off from the main road for the Lagastrello Pass. The sign on the façade will read CASA DI RIPOSO GHITTA TAGLIAVINA, the same as for war heroes or saints."

"Do you think all this had anything to do with the murder?"

"Yes and no. Everything is connected, commissario. It's true that Fornari was afraid she'd talk, but do you really think the spite that surrounded her counted for nothing? Do you think the judgment his father and the townspeople passed on Ghitta made no impact on the enfeebled mind of that boy? And then, from the time she got moving on the hospice project and started lobbying politicians for a contribution from public funds, everybody knew about it and that gave them an additional reason for resentment. That woman was the very Devil," Fernanda said, in tones of admiration.

Without saying a word the commissario signalled his agreement, but Fernanda was no longer looking in his direction. She gave the impression of sifting through thoughts dug up from some time in the past.

"Maybe that's the truth," she started up again. "Maybe Devil is the right word. The hospice will seem to the world a work of charity, but the townspeople will see it as a monument to their defeat. They would rather have erased Ghitta from their memory, and instead they will now have no option but to read her name every day. Many of them will have to undergo the added humiliation of passing their last years in those rooms, and it is hard to imagine a more terrible affront to their pride. We're talking about people of Ghitta's age, the very ones who despised her most. And yet, for everyone else, for those of you who live in the city, Giuditta Tagliavini will be a great benefactor. In a few years when we're all dead and gone, she'll seem the same to people who live up there. History can be deceptive, wouldn't you say?"

"I find it vacuous," Soneri said, all the while feeling a hard lump inside him growing more and more solid. "It's made up of illusions which soon fade. Would you believe me if I said I've reached the point where I don't make much of a distinction between killers and victims?"

Fernanda bowed her head forward slightly and rested her elbows on the desk. Soneri waited for her to come back at him, to add something more to help clear up an affair which was not altogether rationally comprehensible, but perhaps she was of the same mind as him. Soneri understood she had chosen silence. All things considered, it seemed the best approach to him too.

"We are nothing, Fernanda," he said with a sigh, "and nothing is what we leave behind. Ideas, politics, memories, love affairs – all vanished, mist, like the mist that has been hanging over us for months."

It was indeed a misty Christmas, like a protracted November.

"Best wishes, commissario," she said, and she went out.

"Merry Christmas, Fernanda."

VALERIO VARESI is a journalist with *La Repubblica*. *A Woman Much Missed* is the fourth in a series of crime novels featuring Commissario Soneri, now the protagonist of one of Italy's most popular television dramas. *River of Shadows* and *The Dark Valley* were both shortlisted for the Crime Writers' Association International Dagger.

JOSEPH FARRELL is professor of Italian at the University of Strathclyde. He is the distinguished translator of novels by Leonardo Sciascia and Vincenzo Consolo, and plays by the Nobel Laureate Dario Fo. He is writing a book about R.L. Stevenson in Samoa, to be published by MacLehose Press in 2016.

ALSO AVAILABLE

Valerio Varesi

RIVER OF SHADOWS

Translated from the Italian by Joseph Farrell

A relentless deluge lashes the Po Valley, and the river itself swells beyond its limits. A barge breaks free of its moorings and drifts erratically downstream; when it finally runs aground its seasoned pilot is nowhere to be found. The following day, an elderly man of the same surname falls from the window of a nearby hospital.

Commissario Soneri, scornful of his superiors' scepticism, is convinced the two incidents are linked. Stonewalled by the bargemen who make their living along the riverbank, he scours the floodplain for clues. As the waters begin to ebb, the river yields up its secrets: tales of past brutality, bitter rivalry and revenge.

MACLEHOSE PRESS

www.maclehosepress.com

Subscribe to our quarterly newsletter

Valerio Varesi

THE DARK VALLEY

Translated from the Italian by Joseph Farrell

Commissario Soneri returns to his roots for a hard-earned holiday, a few days mushrooming on the slopes of Montelupo. The isolated village of his birth relies on a salame factory founded by Palmiro Rodolfi, and now run by his son, Paride.

On arrival, Soneri is greeted by anxious rumours about the factory's solvency and the younger Rodolfi's whereabouts. Soon afterwards, a body is found in the woods. In the shadow of Montelupo, the carabinieri prepare to apprehend their chief suspect – an ageing woodsman who defended the same mountains from the S.S. during the war.

MACLEHOSE PRESS

www.maclehosepress.com

Subscribe to our quarterly newsletter

Valerio Varesi

GOLD, FRANKINCENSE AND DUST

Translated from the Italian by Joseph Farrell

Parma. A multi-vehicle pile-up on the autostrada. In the chaos, the burned body of a young woman is found at the side of the road. But she didn't die in a car crash.

Commissario Soneri takes on the case, a welcome distraction from his troubled love life. The dead woman is identified as Nina Iliescu, a beautiful, enigmatic Romanian, whose life in Italy has left little trace, aside from a string of wealthy lovers from Italian high society.

Even Soneri is irresistibly drawn to Nina: a victim whose charms could not protect her from the perils of immigrant life. But her worshippers are an unappetising congregation – was Nina a sacrificial lamb, or a devilish temptress?

MACLEHOSE PRESS

www.maclehosepress.com

Subscribe to our quarterly newsletter